Other Books by AJ Adaire

One Day Longer Than Forever

Friend Series
Sunset Island - Book 1
The Interim (a novelette)
Awaiting My Assignment - Book 2
Anything Your Heart Desires - Book 3

It's Complicated

by

AJ Adaire

Desert Palm Press

It's Complicated

By **AJ Adaire**

© 2014 AJ Adaire

ISBN-13 9781501031793
ISBN-10 1501031791

Desert Palm Press
1961 Main Street, Suite 220
Watsonville, California 95076
www.desertpalmpress.com

Editor: CK King
Editor: Sue Hilliker
Cover Design: AJ Adaire (http://www.ajadaire.com)
Cover Art: ©Gordon Swanson
(http://www.dreamstime.com/capturednuance_info);
©Kriangsak Hongsuwanwattana
(http://www.dreamstime.com/fomengto_info)

Printed in the United States of America
First Edition October 2014

ACKNOWLEDGMENTS

To those of you in the medical and counseling fields, please forgive the liberties I have taken in telling my story.

DEDICATION

As always, to my partner, who puts up with me...thank you for the first thirty years.

To my readers, who continue to support my work by buying my books and writing reviews or letters to me to tell me how much they've enjoyed them.

To my cheerleaders and support team: thank you for all the hours you've invested in encouraging me, as well as reading, improving, and publishing my work. I'm glad that you have (at least so far) enjoyed reading it. Thank you OQI, Sue H, CK, MEB, Lee, Pat, CJH, Bee, Sally T, MCH, MK, FDC, Susie, Theresa, and Betty.

It's Complicated

Chapter One

VICTORIA BRANNINGHAM HAD A guilty pleasure. Every day she would take a detour, sit on the boardwalk, and wait for the runner to show up. That's where the guilt came in, knowing she should be elsewhere. Despite Tori having no idea why she was drawn to the stranger, it just felt to her as though her day was incomplete if she didn't see the white-haired woman run by.

Tori sat on a bench opposite the curly fry stand and looked north toward Seventh Street where the stranger always stretched before she began her run. Behind Tori, the cadence of the ocean waves hitting the shore, marking the passing of time, made her even more aware of the closing of the narrow window she had remaining before she had to leave her position. She checked her watch for the third time, her disappointment mounting. The woman was behind schedule today. Tori couldn't delay much longer. She was at the limit of the time she allowed herself.

The wooden walkway, lined on one border by mostly closed stores, was sparsely populated now. Once the season opened, the whole town would blossom into a bustling community of vacationers and visitors. For now, it was still too early in the year for anyone, other than the stalwart locals, to be out braving the chilly weather. Willing the warmer weather to hurry, Tori preferred to optimistically think of the time as 'early spring' rather than 'late winter.' She pulled her collar higher around her neck and stuffed her hands deeper into her pockets as she hunched her shoulders against the penetrating wind.

Finally! From her vantage point Tori saw the runner start her stretching routine. She would wait till the woman started to move before she began walking north in her direction. By doing that she could watch as the runner approached her. If everything worked out perfectly, they would cross paths near Mooreline and Tori could exit the boards near the water slide on Eighth, where she'd parked her car earlier.

Tori started to walk, eyes focused on the compact body and easy stride of the runner coming toward her. Her body in motion was something to behold...beautiful, just beautiful. If not for the red sneakers that made her progress easy to follow, her dark glasses and navy form-fitting jogging outfit would have allowed her to blend in. Her luminous white hair was tucked under the pink breast cancer awareness cap, and on really cold days, she generally wore a fleece jacket and gloves of medium blue.

A wry thought crossed Tori's mind. *If I were directing a movie of my life, I would probably film this scene in slow motion as she runs toward me, the only soundtrack the ever-increasing tempo of my beating heart instead of "Bolero" like in that movie with Bo Derek.*

As was their habit, because they saw each other several times a week, as they passed each gave a nod to the other. Tori's timing was perfect today. She arrived at Eighth Street, veered left and turned to watch, unobserved, the fleeing form of the runner who left her crisp, fresh scent on the wind in her wake.

Tori sighed before she turned to make the short walk to her car. With the engine now running, she cranked the temperature knob onto full heat and switched on the fan to high before blowing warm air into her hands. *This is insane.* She dropped her head into her hands and allowed herself a quick cry before she blew her nose and checked her appearance in the rear view mirror. Tear-brightened green eyes rimmed with dark lashes stared back at her with reproach.

All right, I know...I'm going. It's not like she'll know that I'm ten minutes late. Maybe I'll catch all the lights green. Eight green-lighted minutes later, she exhaled a sigh of relief, allowed herself a quick smile, parked in her usual spot at the nursing home and rehab center, waved at Ernie, the guard at the door, and took the elevator to the third floor. She walked the familiar path to the nurses' desk, where she waved to MJ.

"How is she today?" She already knew the response.

"She's resting quietly." MJ came closer so she could talk more quietly. "I gave her a nice bath today, and a good massage with some moisturizer. I plan to file her nails tomorrow."

"I can do that while I'm here tonight."

"You're running late today."

"Just a little. I, uh, went to the boardwalk and just lost track of time."

"Really. That's not like you. Everything okay?"

Tori made brief eye contact, nodded, and looked away. "I'd better get in there. See you later." She made the short journey to Liz's room. The hallways were bright and freshly painted. Decorations hung everywhere, made by the rehab clients in occupational therapy classes housed in a different wing. Liz was in the wing dedicated to long-term care.

Tori paused in front of the door to gather her courage. At first she'd held out hope, watched Liz's every move, searched her face for any sign of recognition. Initially, she thought there were glimmers of recognition in Liz's eyes. Now, after nearly three long years, she'd given up on Liz's recovery, finally coming to a closer acceptance of the doctor's declaration. Liz was in a permanent vegetative state. She'd watched her once beautiful lover wither to someone she hardly even recognized.

After the accident, Liz's mother and father couldn't accept that their daughter was gone and insisted she receive life support. In her heart, Tori knew that Liz would have hated living that way. Unfortunately, the relationship Liz and Tori shared had no legal standing. Frank and Claudia had the final decision and they refused to have life support removed.

A deep breath fortified Tori enough to put a broad smile on her face and push the partially closed door open to enter Liz's room. "Hello, sweetheart. It's a gorgeous day today. It feels like spring is finally preparing to make an appearance."

Liz's eyes were closed. Machines surrounded her, monitoring her vital signs. Tubes ran from and to various parts of her body to supply nutrients and carry away waste. In the very beginning, it sometimes seemed that Liz actually was responsive to questions or comments. As time passed and Liz's brain continued to swell, she'd become unresponsive, slipped into a deeper coma, and eventually into a vegetative state. Tori grieved for the loss of her partner's laughter and the love they shared.

As Liz's condition deteriorated, her parents, Frank and Claudia still wouldn't let their daughter go naturally. Liz's mother was the most vehement in her belief. "Tori, we know that Liz will wake up one day. We won't let her go. The doctors are wrong. She'll get better." Efforts to explain reality gained no traction with Claudia. Despite Frank seeing the situation more realistically, it was his habit to acquiesce to his wife's wishes, so she got her way and Liz received life-sustaining treatment. As half of a lesbian couple in Pennsylvania, Tori's opinion carried no legal weight, so the decision was out of her hands.

Frank and Claudia announced their decision to bring their daughter back to their hometown at the Jersey shore and place her in a facility near their home. Tori's mother and father tried to convince them to wait, but they remained firm in their conviction.

Tori kissed Liz's forehead before settling into the chair she drew nearer to the side of the bed. Despite the fact that she got no response, Tori continued a dialogue with her partner. "I went to the boardwalk again today. I told you before how much I enjoy watching the ocean and the other scenery." She sighed. *I'm such a shit. How can I lie to her like that?*

"I promised MJ I'd do your nails today. No polish, just the way you like them." Liz's mother always applied bright pink polish to her daughter's nails. She didn't believe Tori that Liz wouldn't like them that way. Half an hour later, her task was completed. "There we go. All done." Tori tucked Liz's hand under the covers, folded the sheet over the top, and settled back in the chair.

"Guess what? I have a surprise." She leaned over and whispered conspiratorially. "I got us a new lesbian novel. It's by one of your favorite authors." Tori reached into her bag, took out the book, and read the title. "I thought we'd both enjoy this one. It's a romance with a little mystery mixed in. The love story is for you and the mystery for me. Okay, here we go. Chapter One." Tori began to read.

Chapter Two

IT WAS IN THE market, while standing in front of the melons trying to decide if they were ripe enough to purchase, that she noticed her. Something drew Tori's attention and when she looked up, there she was. The faded denim jeans that rode low on her hips looked inviting to the touch and incited a forbidden desire to run her hands over them, to feel their softness, and to appreciate the toned skin and muscles Tori suspected were hidden beneath. Even though casually dressed, the woman exuded style and sensuality. The term 'well put together' flashed through Tori's mind. Tucked into the jeans, a navy blue and white striped cotton shirt, starched and wrinkle free with the collar and cuffs turned up, completed the outfit. Her prematurely white hair was just collar length and stylishly feathered. The familiar aroma of a clean, light scent tickled Tori's senses, daring her to bury her nose in the soft hollow of the woman's neck and trace with her hand the blue lined pattern on her shirt downward over the swell of her breast.

The woman, perhaps subconsciously aware of Tori's scrutiny, reached up to run her fingers through her thick, shiny hair as she raised her eyes. Catching Tori's gaze as she glanced up, she flashed a quick smile, revealing even white teeth, a single dimple on the right side of her face, and the most gorgeous shade of blue eyes Tori had ever seen. Tori, hoping she hadn't been caught admiring, grabbed what seemed to be the ripest melon from the pile at the same time the fabulous woman plucked an apple from the precariously stacked array.

A shriek caused Tori to look up in time to witness the woman's attempt to keep the apples from tumbling from the case. She'd managed to prevent them from falling on the floor but was trapped in position, unable to move for fear of dropping all the fruit onto the floor.

"Hang on. Let me help you." Tori circled the counter and began rearranging the apples, neatly stacking and reorganizing them into a more secure display. One by one, she carefully removed the last few apples that were resting against the woman's breasts, enabling her to stand up. "Nice save."

"Thanks, quick reflexes. I appreciate you coming to my rescue. No telling how long I'd be stuck like that at this time of night." She looked around at the store that was nearly devoid of shoppers at a little after eleven o'clock on a Friday night.

"My pleasure."

"You look very familiar, do I know you?"

"Not technically. I think we may have seen each other on the boardwalk. You run, I walk."

"Oh right. I thought I recognized you."

Tori didn't say any more and the woman gave a quick wave, turned her cart and prepared to head up the vegetable aisle. "Well, I'd best get a move on, or I'll never get done, nor will you. Thanks again for saving me."

Before Tori could respond, the woman rounded the corner and disappeared from view. *Why didn't you take the opportunity to introduce yourself you idiot? 'My pleasure.' Brilliant repartee. Oh well. She's right, might as well get a move on.* With only one register open, Tori found herself in line behind the same woman just as she was finishing up with her order.

The cashier totaled the bill. "That'll be nineteen eighty-four, please," she said extending her hand to the attractive woman who was frantically searching her pockets for her money.

"Crap! I left my wallet in the car. Can I just leave the bag here while I run out to my vehicle to get my money?"

The cashier shrugged, her mouth occupied by chewing and cracking the wad of gum in her mouth. "I'm here all night, so I personally don't care…" She tilted her head in Tori's direction. "I can't ring her up until I close out your transaction, so it's up to her."

Fixing Tori with a warm, dimple-punctuated smile the woman asked, "If you can wait, I'll be quick, I promise. It might save you time in the end."

It was at that moment that Tori realized all eyes were focused on her. Quickly calculating the time it would take and considering the status of her melting ice cream, Tori offered an alternate solution. "Look, here's twenty bucks. Wait for me while she rings up my items.

We can walk out to the parking lot together and you can pay me back. It'll be faster."

Tori paid for her own groceries when the cashier finished totaling her order and joined the waiting woman. As they carried their bags to the parking lot, she pointed. "That's mine." The car's lights blinked and the horn tooted as she directed the remote in the direction of her vehicle and depressed the button. "You've rescued me twice already, and I don't even know your name. I'm Bev...Beverly McMannis."

"Tori Branningham. Pleased to meet you."

"I'd like to thank you properly, Tori. I know it's too late for dinner. Umm...I could buy you a drink instead? Look, it's the least I can do."

Tori could feel her pulse pounding in her temple as she flashed a quick grin. "I'd love to get together with someone who shops at odd hours like I do. However, I don't expect you to treat. Anyway, I can't tonight, my ice cream is melting."

"How about lunch or dinner tomorrow? I'm relatively new here and I could use a friend." Bev produced a card from her wallet and handed it to Tori along with a crisp twenty-dollar bill.

A laugh bubbled out of Tori as she read the card. "This is too weird. You live right down the street from me."

"No. Really? Great! Call me in the morning and we'll make plans." Bev's smile lit up her face.

"Okay, it's a date." It was too late to call back her hasty response as Tori realized the implication of her words. "Uh, I mean, uh, I'll..."

"Really, it's okay." Bev reached out to clasp Tori's hand, giving it a gentle squeeze. Her soft, full lips curved into a warm smile. "I'd like it if you would consider it a date. I've lived here for over two months and you're the first friend I've made. And dating...well, that's a long story." Her attempted smile came up short of sincere.

Tori wondered what caused the woman's sadness. She noted, with relief, the fine wrinkles that appeared at the corners of Bev's eyes when she smiled. *Maybe she's closer to my age than I thought, maybe mid-thirties at the most.* Reluctantly, she released her grip on the slightly shorter woman's hand. "Let's keep it a plan. I know it's cool out here, but I'd better get going before my ice cream melts."

"Right, sorry. Will you really call?"

Tori mustered her most sincere look. "Sure. I'm looking forward to it." They stood, each slow to turn away. Tori grinned. "Threshold paralysis."

"What's that?"

"You know when people start to say goodbye, then remain on the doorstep for another fifteen minutes like we're doing. I really do have to go...ice cream, remember?"

"Oh right. Okay, go! I'll wait for your call."

They followed each other from the store parking lot to their condo buildings where they parked on Dwayne Street in adjacent spots. They were the only sign of life on the deserted street. As they slammed their car doors, Tori pointed to her building. "I'm there."

"That's mine, there," Bev responded, adding a smile. "Talk to you tomorrow?" Tori nodded and Bev turned and gave a quick wave before heading into her building.

Tori's unit was in a raised condo building with parking underneath, a necessity in the beach town in-season. Her parking spot at the end of the row was farther from the door to her building than the spot on the street where she parked off-season when the entire town was nearly deserted. In-season, she'd be grateful for her assigned parking space under her building despite its distance from the door. Until the tourists arrived she enjoyed the luxury of hauling her groceries only a few steps to the entrance of her building.

Chapter Three

EXACTLY TWELVE MINUTES LATER, at precisely one minute past twelve, Bev's phone rang. Puzzled, she picked up the phone and tentatively said, "Hello?"

"You said to call tomorrow, and I promised I would. Technically it's tomorrow." Tori smiled when she heard a laugh on the other end of the phone.

"No. Actually, it's today." Bev switched the phone to her other ear and settled into a chair.

"I guess. Regardless, I figured you'd still be up. I know you invited me to lunch but uh...I was wondering if you might be interested in some ice cream now? I'll understand if you are about to go to bed..."

"Stop right there! I'll be over in a few minutes. Do I get a cherry and whipped cream?" Bev's eyes twinkled with mischief.

"Have you been a good girl?"

"You have no idea how good I've been, Tori. I can be there in a couple of minutes if you'll give me your address."

"I'm in number twenty."

"Good, got it. I'll be right over. Start scooping."

Tori smiled as the phone went dead. She glanced around her orderly apartment. Her nearly compulsive neatness did have its benefits. At least she could spontaneously invite someone over and not have to race around and clean up. She headed for the kitchen to prepare the ice cream. Just as she began to scoop she heard a quiet rap on her door, so she reversed direction and tugged the door open. "Welcome. Come on in."

Bev entered, leaving a trail of her now familiar light scent behind. Her eyes swept the room registering details. "Nice place. Lived here long?"

Nodding, Tori answered, "Thanks. Um, a little over two years give or take." Tori could hardly take her eyes off her guest as she glided around the living room, stopping here and there to examine the room. The motion of her body was a thing of beauty to behold. *What is it about this woman? She completely undoes me.*

Bev leaned over to examine a photo of a bird in a frame resting on the coffee table, the only decoration in the stark room. She stood, casually brushing her fingers through her hair, pushing it away from her face. "You're very tidy."

"Thank you?" When Bev didn't comment further she added, "Is that a good thing?"

"Oh definitely. I'm not a slob by any stretch. If pressed, I'd have to admit I'm more relaxed in my housekeeping practices than you. I wouldn't object to living this way if someone kept it like this for me, I just can't invest this much time in doing it myself."

"It's really not that hard, you just have to keep after it, pick up after yourself, and put everything back in its proper place when you're finished with it. It's easier, too, if you don't have a lot of stuff."

"I don't have a lot of personal stuff." Bev allowed her eyes to travel the perimeters of the room before adding, "I certainly have more than you. You live like a monk. Don't get me wrong...your place is lovely. What I find interesting is that I can't get a read on you from your surroundings. Like that photo there, for example. It's a picture of a seagull on a streetlight. It could be anywhere. Is it significant?"

"Not to anyone but me. I like a particular bench on the boardwalk. The gull likes to sit there. Looking at the photo reminds me of the enjoyment I get from sitting there too. That's all." Tori glanced around and shrugged. "Come on, I promised you some ice cream. Come into the kitchen with me while I dish it up."

Bev followed behind Tori and took a seat at the kitchen counter while her host prepared the ice cream. Pointing to a beautifully framed photo resting on the counter, the only personal object in the immaculate kitchen, Bev asked, "Is this you when you were younger?"

"Yes."

"Cute. Your hair was darker here, almost black."

Tori self-consciously touched her hair. "I let it grow out. I got tired of dying it...didn't really have the time anyway. I kind of like the grey mixed in now."

"It suits you. I like it. My hair began to turn white twenty years ago, when I was eighteen. By the time I was twenty, I was completely white, like I am now."

"I like your hair, it's very attractive and suits you somehow. It's positively luminous...gorgeous."

"Thank you. Over the years, I've vacillated about how I feel about it."

"Did you ever dye it?"

"Oh, sure, although I've finally come to a peace with it and it's just part of who I am now." Bev turned her attention back to the photo. "You look happy in this picture. Who's the woman...girlfriend?"

Tori, unsure how much she wanted to reveal, quickly ran through her options. "Yes. Girlfriend, partner, love of my life."

Bev leaned forward to hear what Tori said. "And..."

"I'm sorry. I don't like to talk about it." After a brief pause she added, "However, if we're to be friends, you should know." Still, she held back. Tori added a swirl of whipped cream to each bowl, fished a cherry out of the jar, and held the spoon out, offering the sweet treat as a conciliatory gesture.

Bev accepted the offering and plucked the cherry from its resting place. The spoon dipped into the jar again emerging with two more cherries. Tori placed one on each serving of ice cream and pushed Bev's portion toward her.

Before Bev dug into her treat, she sought Tori's eyes. "I'll still be your friend, you know. You don't owe me any explanations."

"No, I want to tell you. You see I find you very attractive, not to mention sexy. I need to say it and you need to know, in advance, that despite those facts, I'm not available. My situation is...complicated."

"Okay, look. Let's eat our ice cream and talk about brighter things. You think about what, if anything, you want to tell me. If we're going to be friends, there's plenty of time for deep discussions. Tonight, let's just talk about lighter topics."

Tori, who had earlier appeared to shrink like a balloon in a freezer as she anguished over what and how much to reveal, seemed to regain her footing. A quick smile appeared as she sampled her ice cream. "Umm, good. Okay, let's start with you. Tell me about yourself. You said you're new here. What prompted your move to this area?"

"I was looking for something different, I guess. Last year, I sold a computer program I'd developed to a large company near Atlantic City. It was..." Bev hesitated, reflecting on how to phrase the rest of the thought. "It was, uh, shall we say...lucrative. After I sold them the program, I signed on with the company to provide training for their staff and to monitor functioning until they are comfortable using it. They seem to want me to stay on part time to assure it keeps functioning properly and to provide impartial oversight to its use."

Bev paused to eat some of her ice cream before continuing. "Umm, you're right, this is good. Thank you. Anyway, the job requires that I be available overnight. At first, I thought that I'd hate working at night. After doing it for a while, the work hours are growing on me, except for the fact that I find it's lonely. I only work days if I do training. Most of the time I just have to stop in for a couple of hours at night to problem solve their issues. I stay as long as I'm needed, after that I'm free to go on my way. There is a guy there, Victor, whom I'm starting to train in deeper aspects of the program. I usually call in about midnight to see if he needs me. If all is well, I don't even have to show up. I can actually log in from home to take care of most issues although I prefer to go in. It gives me a chance to talk with the people using my program and allows me to see what adjustments I need to make as I rewrite and update it. I'm negotiating with two other companies in Chicago now to buy my updated program. They're waiting for the next version I tailored for each of them, which I should finish later this summer. If they buy it, they'll probably want me to do some additional customization for them."

"Well, today really is a lucky day. Guess who also works night shift. We've each found a playmate."

Bev flashed her dimple.

"A computer geek, eh? I'm impressed. I hate the computer-based record keeping system we use for keeping track of the drug inventory at my job. It's so cumbersome. I'm sure I'm inept. Although it just seems that the database program we use seems more difficult than it needs to be. In order to make an entry, I have to access two, sometimes three different screens. Compared to using the program, I can keep the records easier on one sheet of paper. I know using the software makes it easier to sort and track things, I just wish the entry process were easier." Tori scraped the bottom of her bowl. "I enjoyed that. I enjoyed the company more."

"Yes, me too. I guess night work explains why we're both wide awake and eating ice cream at this hour." Bev handed her empty bowl over as Tori extended her hand for it. "So tell me what you do."

"I'm a hospital pharmacist. It's really more of a managerial position than what you probably think of as a pharmacist's typical duties...I do a little bit of everything. Most of the time I work nights unless I'm training or doing a workshop with the medical staff on a new medication. Technically I supervise the pharmacy department and the staff."

"So have you always been a night owl?"

Glancing over at the picture of her partner, Tori hesitated. "For a while now, since I moved here."

Bev waited for Tori to continue but when it seemed to be the end of that conversation she said, "I appreciate the treat and the company, as well as your rescuing me earlier at the food store." She flashed a sincere smile. "I'm going for a bike ride on the boardwalk in the morning. Want to join me?"

"That sounds like fun. How early?"

Bev checked her watch. "Well, it's a little after one o'clock. Being that it's off-season we can ride any time. How about nine? I'll meet you in the parking lot downstairs."

Tori smiled. "I'm looking forward to it." She walked her guest to the lobby door and stood watching as she made her way across the parking lot to her own building. Once there, Bev turned and waved before entering her apartment. Tori went inside and headed straight for the phone, dialing the number from memory. Upon hearing the familiar voice she asked, "How is she this evening?"

AJ Adaire

Chapter Four

THE NEXT MORNING DAWNED cool and blustery. Tori arose early, made a quick trip to see Liz and returned home to meet Bev. Already dressed in layers, she added a lightweight jacket as she got out of her car and discovered Bev already waiting in the parking lot. She gave a quick wave in greeting before pointing to the metal rack at the end of the building where she kept her bike chained. A few seconds later, she pulled to a stop next to Bev and greeted her with a smile. "Good morning. Bit on the chilly side today."

"A bit. Still, not bad for this time of year. Want to do the boardwalk or the bike path?"

"Let's try the boards, it's a better view. If it's too cold we can regroup."

They pedaled single file along Seventh Street and waved to the officer parked in the police car at the base of the ramp to the boardwalk. Once up the steep ramp, they turned right and headed south passing the closed shops and stores that lined the route at that end. The boardwalk was nearly two and a half miles from end to end, and an easy ride this time of year. Riding abreast of each other at a leisurely pace, it wasn't long before they came to the end of the business section and began passing the huge houses that faced the beach. They rode in a comfortable silence until Bev asked, "Would you like to live in one of those places?"

With a shake of her helmet-clad head, Tori denied her desire to do so. "Too close to the water and too much risk of flooding."

"Your place is just as close."

"I know. Since I'm on the top level, flooding isn't a concern for me, other than for my car, which is on the ground floor. Wind might be an issue in a bad hurricane. Still, my place is pretty protected by the building in front of mine, on the boardwalk. Although it obstructs the ocean view a bit, on a positive note, it also serves as a wind break when those nor'easters hit." As they passed Twenty-first Street, Tori called, "Hey, want to cut up here and get some pancakes for breakfast?"

"Absolutely. Let's go."

Bev took the lead, with Tori enjoying the view of Bev's tight body from behind. Riding downwind, she could smell the faint aroma of Bev's perfume as it floated on and mixed with the crisp ocean air, an intoxicating combination. She realized the level of her arousal as the bicycle seat created a pleasant pressure and friction between her legs and an unwelcome, mounting sense of guilt in her mind. Arriving at their destination, they parked their bikes against the building and upon entering the restaurant the hostess seated them without a wait.

The waitress approached with coffee, but they waved her off. "Hot tea for me please."

"Me too," Bev said, giving the waitress a friendly smile.

The waitress returned with the beverages and took Bev's order first. "I'll have the buttermilk pancakes and a large orange juice, please."

"Make that two orders, please. That sounds good."

As the waitress hurried away toward the kitchen, Bev asked, "So, do you have to work tonight?"

"No, usually only Sunday to Thursday. If I have trouble sleeping later, I might go back to visit my, uh...my partner. She's in the long-term care unit that is part of the medical facility where I work. It's right across the bridge on the mainland, down by the bay."

The returning waitress interrupted the conversation to deliver their tea. When she left Tori changed the topic. "I'm glad we have a nice day."

"Yeah. I thought about catching a movie later, although I hate to waste a nice sunny day. Tomorrow is supposed to be warmer still."

"Have you ever been to the point, to the bird observatory?"

"No, I haven't. I've been to the town and the mall area. However, so far it's been too cold for the bird sanctuary. Is it worth the trip?"

Tori paused as the waitress served their food order. They prepared their pancakes, lathering them with butter, followed by a generous amount of syrup. "Umm, good. Yes, to answer your question, the observatory is less than an hour from here. They do some interesting demos, butterfly banding, have nice hiking trails, and there are usually guides to point out different birds. It's a major migration route so you can see a large variety of birds, especially waterfowl. Lots of hawks too."

"It sounds wonderful. Maybe we can go together sometime?"

"I'd love to share that with you. They have some great trails meant for easy hiking."

"How about another bike ride tomorrow?"

Tori hesitated, torn between her desire to accept and her sense of responsibility. "I'm sorry that I can't do it tomorrow. I like to spend the afternoon with Liz on Sundays. Maybe we could do it again later in the week if the weather holds."

"That's great, anytime you're available. I heard there's a zoo nearby as well."

"Yes. I haven't been in years. Last time I went it was nice. Well maintained."

"I'm glad we met. Winter here was pretty lonely. I'm glad I finally met a friend to do things with. I guess during the summer the place really hops."

"For sure." Tori finished up the last of her breakfast. "Those who stay year round spend all summer complaining about the lack of parking and all the crowds. Yet there are some of us who probably miss the tourists when the season ends, some more than others."

"I'd imagine the businesses miss them the most."

"Undoubtedly."

The waitress brought the check and Bev snatched it up. "My treat. I still owe you that lunch or dinner I promised you. Just consider this a down payment."

"It's really not necessary. Thank you. Consider your debt paid in full."

They walked to their bikes. Before they got on them, Bev said, "I am so full. Glad we have to ride home and work off some of those calories."

The ride back was pleasant. They stopped in front of Tori's building where Bev dismounted and took off her helmet. "If you have no plans for dinner tomorrow night, how about coming for pasta?"

"I generally spend Sundays reading with my partner, Liz, after which I have dinner with my friend, MJ. Then I hang out until I have to sign in for work. Before I return to my condo on Monday morning, I visit with her again, come home and catch some sleep."

"Okay. I understand." She toed her kickstand up and threw her leg over her bike.

"No, wait...don't misunderstand. I'd love to accept your dinner invitation...I just can't do it tomorrow. How about Monday? Sauce, or gravy as my Italian friends call it, is always better the second day anyway."

"Okay, that'll work. I'll expect you on Monday evening. Is around six okay?"

"I'll bring the wine and I'll tell you about Liz. Standing in a parking lot isn't the most appropriate place to do that."

"Deal."

Tori thoroughly enjoyed their time together and gave Bev a genuine smile as she pedaled away. She chained her bike to the rack before heading upstairs for a shower. Dressed in jeans and a long sleeved, navy blue turtleneck, boat shoes, and a fleece jacket she felt good. She'd enjoyed the exercise and the light conversation she'd shared with Bev. She glanced at her watch, suspecting she was too late for lunch. *If I hurry, I might make it in time.*

.

Chapter Five

FIFTEEN MINUTES LATER, TORI signed in, waved to the nurse on desk duty, and strode down the hallway to Liz's room. "Hi honey. I know I'm late. I hope you'll forgive me when I tell you that I had fun. I had a nice bike ride today and breakfast with a new friend." She told Liz about her meeting with Bev, keeping her telling of the encounter 'G-rated' and innocent of any prurient thoughts she'd harbored. *I feel guilty enough without confessing to my lover that I'm attracted to another woman. It's just that I'm so lonely.*

"That's all my news." Tori glanced at the book on the bedside table and grimaced. "How about I read some more from the romance we started yesterday? Your mom can read to you from the book she chose when she comes back." She opened her messenger bag to retrieve the lesbian romance novel and opened it to the bookmarked page. The books helped her maintain her spirits.

Holding a one sided conversation was always difficult. Reading allowed her to spend time with Liz and do something they'd always both enjoyed doing together. Listening to the sound of her own voice and becoming immersed in the story sometimes enabled her to forget that her lover would never wake to discuss the story she was reading nor be able, ever again, to hold a normal conversation with her, or exchange physical and emotional intimacies. Still, they had committed to each other. In the eyes of the law their relationship had no legal standing. However, more importantly, they'd made their promises to each other...to love one another through good times and bad, in sickness and in health. She wouldn't break her word to Liz. She'd stay the course as long as her partner was still in this world. To remain faithful was a commitment they'd made to each other years ago, and she vowed to herself again, with renewed conviction, that she'd continue to honor that oath.

MJ knocked at the door and walked over to stand behind Tori, placing her hands on her shoulders and giving her a brief massage.

"Umm, that's nice. Thank you."

MJ gave Tori's shoulders a final squeeze. "Come with me. I figured you'd be in this afternoon when you didn't show up this morning. I brought dinner and there's extra...definitely enough to share with you.

"Thanks. I'd be glad to join you. You're doing a double again?" Tori stood, placing the book in her bag after carefully reinserting the bookmark. "I'm ready for a break anyway. Been here since one and it's now what...five thirty? Lead on Macduff."

Settled in a nearly empty corner of the pleasantly decorated break room, they opened the containers MJ pulled from her bag. "Here, can you heat this soup? I'll get us something to drink. Water?"

"Yes, thanks. I'll meet you back here. You know it'll be a while. That microwave takes forever."

"Stop whining and get to it. I don't have all day."

Tori knew from the smile on MJ's face that the criticism was good-natured and not serious. She wished they were somewhere she could pull the giant of a woman to her in an embrace to seek the solace and comfort of her best friend's affection. They had grown close over the past two plus years. MJ provided loving care to Liz on a nearly daily basis.

While the soup heated, Tori allowed her mind to wander back to the beginning. Claudia was the one who broke the news. "We've selected a long-term care facility in New Jersey, nearer to our home at the beach, so we can be sure she is well cared for until she wakes from her coma." Tori recalled her anger and frustration at the pronouncement. The trip from the home she shared with Liz in Pennsylvania was too long for Tori to make on a daily basis. She could mostly only see her on weekends when she'd make the drive, rent a room for the night, and visit both Saturday and Sunday. Finding a room for one night became difficult if not impossible once the shore season opened. Thankfully, she and MJ had become friendly by then, and the warm and supportive woman offered up her spare bedroom to Tori for a reasonable fee.

Initially, Tori felt resentful about the decision Liz's mother and father made to move their daughter closer to their home. However, once Liz was settled, she had to agree that the facility was lovely and provided excellent care. Besides that, Frank and Claudia paid for all the expenses of a private room, something Tori could never have afforded to do on her own. So she made the best of things, reached a peace with her 'in-laws,' and undertook the commute as frequently as she could.

When the nursing facility posted an opening for a vacancy in the pharmacy, MJ showed the flier announcing the position to Tori. "Look. This would be perfect for you. Why don't you apply?"

"I don't know. I'd have to sell our house and give Liz's parents half of the money before I could move. I can't afford to buy a place here until I sell that one. I probably won't be able to find anything I can afford with my share."

"Stay with me until you get things sorted. I have a realtor friend who'll find you something you can afford, I promise."

Finally convinced, Tori said, "What happens if I don't get the position?"

"You'll get it. I already put in a good word for you."

And so Tori's journey of relocation from Pennsylvania to the shore community in New Jersey began. The transition had been surprisingly simple. The move, beneficial in more ways than one, resulted in a raise in salary and after a brief period of adjustment, her job provided mostly tranquil evenings that suited her quiet nature. Being close to Liz was an added bonus. Her job required her to review reports, keep a running inventory and to track all the drugs ordered and dispensed each day. Some of these tasks she could do while sitting in Liz's room. Additionally, during her breaks, she was able to slip down to sit with Liz and pretend that things were normal even if for only ten minutes.

The chime on the microwave drew her back. Soup in hand, Tori returned to the table to join her friend who was waiting.

"Finally! My break is half over." MJ admonished.

"I know. Sorry. There was a woman ahead of me at the microwave who had three containers of something frozen she wanted to warm up. It took forever. That microwave is so old, I bet it's less than five hundred watts." Tori sat down and ate the first spoonful of her soup. "Umm. The soup is definitely up to your normal high standard."

"Thanks."

"So what's new?"

"Nothing...same old, same old. I went out Friday night. Met a nice guy...as usual, he's married to a woman who doesn't understand him." MJ grimaced. "You know what I say, they are either unemployed, in debt and looking for somewhere to crash, married to...well, you know, or about a foot shorter than I am." MJ was a gorgeous, nearly six foot tall hunk of woman who simply refused to consider dating anyone shorter than herself. "It always amazes me every time a five-foot-two-inch man comes up to me and asks me to dance. I have just one question. Why?"

"What does it matter? I'm glad I'm a lesbian. Height doesn't seem to be as much of an issue between two women."

MJ looked shocked. "Really? Hmm. Never thought about it in those terms. I don't know, though...I'd still like my guy to be someone I can look up to." A moment later, she asked, "You're not suggesting I switch teams, are you?" The ear-to-ear grin indicated she was only teasing.

"You know better than that. I'm just saying that maybe you'd have better luck if you considered looking up to him because of who he is, not how tall he is."

"Easy for you to say. You're only five-two. You look up to everyone."

"Yeah, especially you."

Their laughter slowly quieted and they ate their lunch, passing the time with idle chatter. Just before they had to leave, MJ asked, "What's bothering you?"

"What makes you think something is bothering me?"

"Because I know you. Something's on your mind."

"Maybe...I'm not ready to talk about it yet. I do have a question I want to ask you, though. I put some lotion on Liz today. I think she's lost more weight. She's so thin now, just skin over bones. I hardly recognize her body." Tears welled in Tori's eyes. "She never seemed to bounce back from the flu she had earlier in the winter."

"I'll mention her weight to the doctor." MJ shook her head. "It still doesn't seem fair that you can't speak to him about Liz's condition directly and have to get information second hand. At least her parents have given permission for you to get a daily update from the nursing staff."

"Yes. It's a small improvement." Tori sighed. "It's our own fault we're in this situation. Liz and I never got medical powers of attorney for each other. We talked about it. Somehow it always got put off. I guess being in our thirties at the time made us feel invincible." Tori rested her chin on her palm.

"Still, it's not fair. These privacy laws can be both a blessing and a curse." MJ stood, cleared the remains of their lunch, and heaved a sigh. "I've got to get back. Will I see you later?"

"Depends on how busy we are. I'll text you." They walked to the doorway where they would turn in opposite directions. "By the way, I won't be in tomorrow evening until probably around ten or so, just before I sign in to work. I have dinner plans."

MJ's eyebrows shot up. "And you wait till now to tell me? With whom?"

"A new friend. Nothing to be too excited about. I'll see you tomorrow when I get in. Maybe we can take our breaks together and get a cup of tea or something and I'll tell you about our meeting. It was funny in a way."

"Darn you Tori! I have to go. You better come prepared to spill your guts tomorrow night." MJ reached out and quickly squeezed Tori's hand. "See ya."

Chapter Six

MONDAY MORNING AT THE end of her shift, Tori followed her familiar route to Liz's room. Sue, one of her favorite nurses, was at the desk when she signed the visitor's log. She greeted her with a smile. "Everything okay?"

"No changes. She's resting peacefully. I was just in, administered her meds, and changed her. Enjoy your visit."

"Thanks Sue. MJ gone?"

Sue nodded. "Just left."

"How's your son doing?"

"Great. Just got notified he got a scholarship to his college of choice for basketball. He's on cloud nine. Me too, the money will be a big help."

"Congratulations. Best of luck to him." Tori tapped her hand on the desk. "I'm bushed, so I won't stay long."

Tori visited with Liz. She put the news on and struggled to stay awake as the host reported the latest crisis. Barely able to keep her eyes open any longer, she told her lover, "I'm tired, sweetie. I'll be back before I have to sign in for work tonight. I'll leave the news on for you." She leaned over and pressed a kiss to Liz's forehead. "See you later."

Less than an hour later, freshly showered, Tori slid between clean sheets. She tossed fitfully, guilt nagging her. She reached for the phone and dialed by memory. "Hi Mom."

"Hi honey. How are you doing? You sound tired."

"How can you tell I'm tired when I've only uttered two words? You're right, though. I am tired."

"Why aren't you sleeping, Tori? Is something on your mind?"

"I don't know...I mean you know I love Liz, right? It's just so hard to see her like this. A few short months from now, we'll mark three years that she's been this way. At first, I held out hope that she'd come back to me. Now, only her parents hold onto that delusion. Every day she withers. There's nothing left of her." Tori choked back a sob. "Sometimes, I...I wish they would have just let her go."

"Oh sweetheart. I'm so sorry. I know this has been impossibly difficult for you. Liz was so full of life and fun. You have to remember she's their baby. You've done everything you can to help her parents make the merciful choice. You've told them Liz's wishes. Because they're so resistant, you don't want to push them or you run the risk of having them cut you off from visiting her."

"I know. It's just that I'm so tired. I'm tired of being tired and depressed. I feel like my life ended the day she had her accident."

"You have every right to feel that way. In many respects, your life has certainly changed radically. Her accident caused some dramatic changes to both your lives. In some ways, more impact on yours than on hers, because you're aware of the changes. You're suffering every day. Fortunately for her, she is oblivious to her suffering and yours. You can be thankful for that much, I guess."

"I think I'm in trouble, Mom. I met someone. I mean there's nothing going on, I just met her. I'm so conflicted and I feel so guilty, even though I would never act on my attraction."

"Then you feel guilty because...?"

"Because I want a life. When I promised Liz my fidelity, I had no idea I would be the only one in the relationship." Tori blinked to keep the tears from rolling down her face.

"I don't know what to tell you honey. Maybe you should see a therapist. I know you made a commitment to Liz and still feel dedicated to it. You have to consider that the Liz you made a commitment to is gone and she won't be back. It's admirable you've devoted your life to her and until recently, it's been what felt right for you. You're in an impossible position. Maybe you need to review that commitment in light of the current situation. Just know that your father and I love you. Whatever you do, I support your decision."

"Thanks Mom. I love you too. I'll call you later in the week."

Tori finally got to sleep around eleven thirty. The alarm woke her at five. She got up and made herself a cup of tea, pacing the kitchen as she drank it, frequently checking the clock. At five thirty she selected black slacks and a simple off white, long sleeved shirt in a soft fabric. The outfit would do both for dinner with Bev and for work later. At a few minutes before six she checked her appearance in the mirror. The light coat of dark brown mascara helped emphasize her bright green eyes. She never wore lipstick because she didn't like the sticky feel on her lips, though she did dust her cheeks with some light blush. Giving a final fluff to her hair, she stared back into her own eyes in the mirror. "I hope you know what you're doing here." She wiped her sweaty palms on her slacks and got the wine from the fridge.

Tori extended the wine when Bev answered her knock. "Hope this will be okay. It's a nice, full bodied chianti that I thought would be good with pasta."

Bev checked the label. "Oh, nice choice. Come in. Give me your jacket."

"Umm. It smells good in here. Thanks for making dinner."

"Glad to do it. I appreciate the company. You're the first guest I've entertained." She laughed at Tori's expression. "Not the first ever, just the first guest I've entertained here. Come in and let me show you around."

They entered the living room. Tori, drawn to the ocean view, walked to the double doors that led to the balcony. The picture windows that wrapped around the living room gave a nearly one hundred eighty degree view of the ocean. Her unit was high enough that the building in front of her condo building only diminished the view on one side. "Wow! This view is amazing."

"Thanks. I'm lucky, aren't I?"

Tori raised her eyebrows in response. "I'd say so, yes."

"The place isn't huge." Bev looked around her condo evaluating it in her mind. "I love the view, and with the balcony, I have all the space I need. Through here are the two bedrooms." She led Tori down the short hallway. "This one is mine. It has a similar view to the one in the living room. This is the guest room. There's a peekaboo view out the one window there. Come this way, I'll show you the kitchen."

Tori loved the condo. The greyish brown walls provided sharp contrast to the bright white wainscoting and trim. The furniture looked comfortable and upscale. As they rounded the corner into the kitchen Tori was further impressed. White cabinets gleamed against a tan stone backsplash. Slightly darker granite countertops and stainless steel appliances attested to the recent renovation of the kitchen.

Bev checked the two pots, one filled with water and a second filled with sauce, perched on the restaurant style stove. She gave the sauce a quick stir.

"Impressive. You obviously like to cook."

"I do. I'm sorry to say that I can't take credit for the kitchen. The previous owner renovated it and I bought it this way. I'll admit that I do love this room because it's not only gorgeous, it's extremely efficient." Bev uncorked the wine and together they moved to the table where two salads waited. They sat down after Bev poured a glass for each of them. "To new friendships."

"Yes." Tori clinked her glass against Bev's. "This salad is beautiful...a true work of art."

"Thanks, I love salads. I added some dried cherries and walnuts. Hope that's okay."

Tori took a sip of her wine, set it down, and picked up her fork. "Absolutely. Very nice."

They made small talk as they ate their salads.

Bev exchanged her fork for her glass of wine, took a sip and asked, "So, how was your day?"

"It was okay. Mostly it consisted of my trying to sleep. Did you do anything exciting?"

Bev used her napkin to dab at her mouth. "Exciting, no. I did, however, see something I thought was great fun. I ran over to the food store, off island. The wind was really blowing across the causeway. I wish there was a place to stop on the bridge, because I could have watched the seagulls for hours. There were maybe eight of them just hanging in the wind. They were facing into the breeze with their wings spread, just hovering and having what seemed like fun. They weren't making any forward progress, weren't flapping their wings in an effort to get anywhere, just suspended there in the wind currents like a mobile. It's the coolest thing I've seen in ages."

"I've seen them do that. I agree with you, it is extremely neat."

"Excuse me a minute, I need to check the pasta." Bev gathered the salad plates and brought them to the sink. "Is it okay if I just serve us?"

"Please." Tori chuckled. "Don't stand on formality with me. If you do, it'll just make for more dishes to wash."

"Tell me how much you want." Bev dished up a portion of pasta, stopping when Tori told her to, and spread the sauce on top. "Cheese?"

Tori declined and Bev filled another plate with a serving for herself.

"Here, I'll get that one." Tori carried her bowl to the table where Bev joined her with her own serving.

"Umm. Wow! This is great." Tori wiped her mouth with her napkin. "I wish I had more time to cook. I'm actually not a bad cook." She shrugged. "It's just that, unfortunately, I rarely do it anymore. It's really difficult cooking for just one person, I think. Now, other than mooching from MJ, I generally have three types of meals..." She counted them off on her fingers. "Canned, microwaved, or take out."

Bev chuckled. "I'm glad you came over. I do cook for myself, because I prefer my own cooking to most restaurant food. There could be a rumor, however, that I can't resist a nice juicy cheesesteak once in a while, or a pizza every now and again, from that place on the boardwalk with those huge slices."

"Right. My favorites too."

"I used to cook sometimes. I'd be the first to admit that Liz was the better cook."

"Are you going to tell me about her? You've been pretty mysterious so far. I thought perhaps you had broken up, until yesterday when you told me you were spending the day with her."

Tori ran her hands over her face before she made eye contact with Bev. "I know. I'm sorry. It's just hard for me to talk about her. We were very much in love. The day it happened was pretty much like any other. We got up to the alarm, and she made breakfast while I showered and dressed for work." Tori dropped her eyes to her food and pushed the pasta around the plate with her fork. She glanced up, inhaled, and then exhaled a long breath before she continued. "We watched the news while we ate and talked about our plans for the holidays. She was running late and rushed out for work, I left soon after she did. I got busy at work. The last thing I expected was a call telling me about an accident. She was crossing the street to enter the school where she taught handicapped children. The driver of the car that ran her down was drunk. Seven thirty in the morning and drunk as a skunk. Can you imagine?"

"No, I can't. I'm sure it was awful." Bev waited as Tori paused gathering her thoughts.

"I rushed to the hospital. Because Pennsylvania doesn't recognize our relationship, all I could do was give them her parents' contact information. She had several broken bones and severe head trauma. They did everything possible and, at first, there was hope. The days turned to weeks, the weeks into months, and she never woke up..." Tori ran her hands over her eyes brushing away tears as she looked up. "The doctors ran tests and told us that there was no longer any hope. She was 'brain dead' they said. Her parents simply wouldn't accept it. The doctors asked us if we wanted to consider letting her go by removing support and donating organs. Her parents refused and made the decision to move her here, to the shore.

"I was devastated because the amount of time it took me round trip to travel here meant I could only visit her on weekends. Initially I did try coming midweek. Three and a half hours here, an hour to visit with her if I didn't hit too much traffic, some fast food for dinner, then the three and a half hour drive home. It was exhausting, and I only did it five or six times until I realized I couldn't do it and function at work the next day. As a pharmacist, I have to be on my toes...too much risk of error if I'm not rested and attentive to what I do. If all that wasn't enough, it became more difficult after the season here at the shore opened. In the off-season, I could rent any number of places reasonably for just a night. Once the season opened, most places wanted a two or three night minimum and they charged an arm and a leg." Tori paused long enough to eat a few forkfuls of the pasta.

"Is that when you decided to move here?"

"Not quite yet. I was fortunate that one of the nurses, MJ, who became my best friend, took pity on me and let me stay in her spare room for almost nothing. She's the one who told me about the posting for my current job. At first I hated the night shift. I don't mind it too much anymore. It allows me to keep an eye on Liz overnight, I'm free most of the day, and it makes it possible for me to spend time with her whenever I want during visiting hours."

Bev reached over and squeezed Tori's free hand, releasing it quickly. "I'm so sorry for you. It must be so difficult."

Tori nodded her head once. "It is. Like I told you, it's complicated. I'm paired and, in a way, not paired. I still take my commitment to her very seriously. In the beginning, of course, I was ecstatic that she was alive." Tori glanced out the window recalling memories. "Everyone told me that I was lucky because I could still see her everyday. Now, I can't help but feel guilty and ungrateful when I don't feel that way. In fact, I'm ashamed to admit that there are times lately, when I find it difficult to visit her knowing that, mentally and emotionally, she's been gone from me for nearly three years."

Bev shook her head. "I can't even imagine what you've gone through." Neither Tori nor Bev had eaten much of her pasta. They both took advantage of the lull in the conversation to eat some of their dinner.

"You know, at first, like Liz's parents, I held out hope that she'd come back. I mean you hear about those people waking from a coma after twenty years. I thought, you know, maybe..."

"What changed your mind?"

"Any number of things." Tori sighed. "Time, test results, watching her wither and waste away. Now... well, now I, uh, sometimes wish they had let her go." Tori leaned her chin on her hand and glanced over at Bev. Her eyes were bright with unshed tears. "I can't believe I told you that."

"I'm glad you did. It must be a difficult burden to carry that secret around." Her eyes, soft in their expression, glistened too.

Tori removed a tissue from her pocket, and blew her nose. She hoped that the smile she gave Bev appeared more cheerful than she actually felt. She gave a final sniff. "Liz was a voracious reader. She and I loved to read dialogue from lesbian romance novels to each other. She'd take one character and I'd take the other. We'd read the parts aloud and laugh at how corny some of the dialogue was. I loved her sense of humor. Personality wise, I'm a true scientist who has a tendency to be serious. She could always find a way to make me see the light side of things and could make me laugh with just a look. The worst part of this current situation is that Liz hated to be idle. She was extremely active, always doing something, both physically and mentally. Now, she can't even move. Sometimes I think that keeping her alive like they are doing is akin to torture. I know she'd hate it, just lying there hour after hour, day after day. It's one of the reasons I spend so much time there reading to her. I read her the newspaper every morning and we always have a novel going. I tell her most everything that I do, talk to her like I would normally do if things weren't...weren't like they are. It's hard sometimes, I miss having the other half of the conversation, her half."

Bev nodded her understanding. "I'm sure it's difficult for you. How often do her parents visit?"

"Liz's father can't stand to see her like this. He can only bring himself to come once or twice a month. Her mom...she comes a couple of times a week...every Sunday morning after church and whenever she can fit in a visit between club and lunch dates. If she doesn't make it on Sunday, she comes on Monday morning. Then maybe stops in later in the week. She reads her biographies and books on philosophy.

Sometimes she reads designing magazines to her. Liz hated biographies and I can see her crossing her eyes at her mother's choice of the philosophy books. She would despise those, too." Tori shrugged. "I figure it's only an hour or so a week, so I've never mentioned it. I grimace every time I look at the table next to her bed and see the bookmarked copy of the current book that Liz's mother is inflicting on her. I'm sure that book, *Good and Evil Compared and Contrasted*, is interesting to many people, unfortunately, it's definitely not one Liz would choose."

"So Liz's mother still thinks Liz will wake up?"

Tori shrugged. "I don't know. Sometimes I think her parents are coming to accept the reality that it will never happen. It doesn't matter now, because they've made this decision and will see it through. I would never describe them as flexible thinkers."

Bev was nearly finished with her pasta. "You'd better eat your meal before it gets completely cold."

Tori welcomed the break in the conversation and ate the remainder of her pasta with gusto.

Bev stood up to refill their wine glasses. Returning to her seat, she asked, "Did they approve of your relationship?"

"No, they never did. They had a hard time accepting that Liz was..." Tori stopped to reform her statement. "I mean is. You know, that Liz is a lesbian. The first few years were really rough. We met my senior year in college...moved in together when I graduated. She made the trip alone to her parents' home to tell them about us. It was just before Christmas. She assumed that after she told them they were going to refuse to ever see her again. Eventually, they came to transfer all the guilt for our relationship onto me. I obviously must have corrupted their little girl. Liz couldn't believe they'd ever be rude to me, so she convinced me to come with her on Christmas day to bring their gifts. It was ugly. They refused to let me into their home. As time passed, things settled down a bit. We eventually got to a point where we could all be civil to each other."

"How long have you and Liz been together?"

"The year we got together I turned twenty-four. Our anniversary is September eighteenth, so in roughly six months it'll be twelve years. Nine fabulous years before the accident and nearly three years of hell after." Finished with her meal, Tori used her napkin. "Thanks for dinner. I really enjoyed it."

Bev smiled. "Thank you, I'm glad you came. "I wonder, do you have much interaction with her parents now?"

Tori shook her head. "Not really. I'm pretty good at avoiding her mother. I know she's usually visiting Liz on Sunday morning or Monday, so that's easy to work around. Other times, she usually comes in just before lunchtime and I'm usually sleeping then. In the beginning, I had to beg to get information about Liz's condition. When her parents learned that I'd moved here and was coming so regularly, they finally agreed to allow the nursing staff to provide me with updates on her condition. Unfortunately, they still won't allow me to be involved in any of the conferences with the doctors, or to be involved in making any decisions about her care. So I remain informed but not involved, if you see the difference. At this point, I'm grateful that she has good care and although they say she's not conscious of her environment, if she's at all aware of her existence, she knows she's still loved."

"It's really unfair that you have no say."

"Yes, although it could be worse. At least I'm allowed to visit and I am informed of her condition. I just don't have any say in her treatment. Honestly, at this point, I don't know what I'd decide if the decision were mine. It's almost impossible to be in that position and to have to make that decision. We're lucky, in a way, that her parents can afford the best care for their daughter. I'm very satisfied and comfortable with the care and treatment she's getting."

"I appreciate you sharing all this with me. I know it was difficult for you."

Tori smiled. "It was easier than I thought. You're a good listener and easy to talk to. So, I wanted you to know my story right up front. I won't lie. I find you very attractive. If the situation were different…"

"I understand. Friends, right?" Bev stood, patted Tori's shoulder. "How about I clean up here, make some tea, and get dessert."

"Right, friends." Tori got to her feet. "Let me help."

Bev moved a container of cookies from the counter to the table. "I made Italian wedding cookies. So easy and so good."

"They're one of my favorites."

"Good. Are you up for a video?"

"Yes, anything."

"I picked up a couple of new ones and I have a bunch of old ones here, too."

Tori flipped through the selection of DVDs. "Meg Ryan fan?"

Bev blushed. "I admit that I am."

"Don't be embarrassed—me too. I love You've Got Mail. I love the way she walks, you know near the end, the scene where she walks down the street...it makes me laugh every time I see it. Can we watch that one?"

"Great choice."

At ten thirty, as they prepared to say goodnight, Tori zipped her jacket. "I'm sorry, I have to be at work in half an hour, so I need to go. Thanks for a great dinner and probably one of the nicest evenings I've had since I moved here."

Bev nodded. "I second that sentiment. Say, are you busy tomorrow? I think it's supposed to be nice again. Maybe another bike ride?"

"I'll need to sleep, first. I think I could be ready by two."

"Is that enough sleep?"

"I'm used to about five hours sleep. I'll take a short nap before I report to work tomorrow night. I'll be fine. I'm genuinely looking forward to it."

There was an uncomfortable moment when neither knew what the other expected in terms of a goodbye. Tori turned away and exited with a quick wave. "I'll call you tomorrow as soon as I get up."

Chapter Seven

TORI PARKED IN THE lot and raced up the back steps to her office making it in by ten till eleven. She punched in, reported to the pharmacy where she handled the urgent requests before sitting down at her computer to check e-mails and messages. Her phone beeped indicating she had a text message. She figured it would be MJ and felt pleased that she was correct.

'What time is break?'

Tori typed a quick response. *'Does an hour or a bit less work for you?'*

'Yes. I'll come to your office, more private. I have food and chips 4 both of us. You get water. Be prepared to spill your guts.'

Tori raised her eyebrow and muttered. "Just gotta love her."

"Come in." Tori responded to the soft tap at the door about twenty-five minutes later. They sat at the small conference table in the corner of Tori's office after MJ carefully closed the office door behind her. "Made it in record time, I see."

MJ stuck out her tongue. "Tori, I may never forgive you for making me wait to hear about your dinner."

"I don't know what's got your knickers in a knot about my going out to dinner. There was nothing to it."

"Tori. I've known you for two years now. In all that time, you have either been sleeping, working, or visiting Liz. Other than a couple of dinners out with me, I don't think you've ever taken any time for yourself. So give...what's up?"

"Nothing to tell, really. I met this woman in the food store. Her name is Bev." Tori debated about telling MJ about her guilty secret. In the end, she decided to reserve the decision about sharing that information, skip the confession, and start with dinner. She told her friend about meeting Bev in the market. "It was humorous, really. She was stuck, almost on her knees, her arms spread wide, barely managing to stop the apples from tumbling to the floor. I was her heroine, not once but twice, because I later loaned her money to check out. So she figured she owed me. There, that's all. Disappointed?" Tori looked away.

"You are so transparent. That's not the full story, is it?" MJ placed a sandwich in front of each of them as Tori uncapped the water.

Tori met MJ's eyes. "Technically, no. Dinner was actually our third da...uh, meeting. We went for breakfast and a bike ride Saturday." She exhaled a deep sigh.

"Is there more?"

"No, not really." Tori gripped the edge of the table to quiet her hands. "You know I love Liz, right?"

"More than anyone else alive, I'd say."

Tori sighed again, looked up, and ran her hand over the bottom half of her face. "I do still love her. It's just that I've been so lonely. I know I should be grateful because I still get to see her every day of my life; nevertheless, it's anguish. I miss her. I know that doesn't make any sense, does it?"

MJ stopped eating and leaned forward, giving Tori her full attention. "Oh Tori, of course it does. You've been living like a monk for almost three years. From what you've told me, before the accident you and Liz had a full and mutually satisfying life together. Why wouldn't you miss that?"

"I have a confession to make." Tori glanced around, buying time, steeling her courage, avoiding MJ's gaze. "Before I met Bev in the market, I saw her on the boards. She runs. I watch her. I don't know what it is about her that draws me to her. Every day that I can, I sit on the boardwalk and wait for her to show up. I watch her run in my direction and practically have to wipe the drool from my chin. After we pass by each other, I get into my car and come here to see Liz. Oh God, MJ. I'm a cheat and a liar and I don't know how to stop myself from wanting to get to know this stranger. No matter how many times I've told myself I'm not free, it doesn't make a damned bit of difference. That night we bumped into each other at the store and I finally met her, I thought maybe meeting her would put an end to my fixation with her. You know, I'd talk with her, maybe find out that she was boring, or unintelligent, or had bad breath and body odor. Anything...anything to break my fascination with her."

"I take it that didn't happen?"

"No, quite the opposite. I mean I was physically attracted to her before I even knew her. Now that I've met her, and find that she's really nice, it's worse, because she even smells nice." Tori looked down at her clenched hands. "I can't help feeling that I'm a shit, MJ. I mean I haven't done anything except lust in my heart. I just..."

"Okay, Jimmy Carter, eat some of your sandwich." MJ tapped the table to get Tori to look at her. "Don't be so hard on yourself. What you're feeling is perfectly normal. You've had three years to mourn the death of your partner. I mean you and I have already discussed this. The Liz you knew died almost three years ago. It's sad, I know. Truth is, without those machines she's hooked up to, her body would be gone too. Medicine is a wonderful thing. However, despite the best of intentions, we sometimes create unfortunate situations. Sadly, you're caught up in one of those instances." MJ took a bite of her sandwich. "You going to eat those chips?"

"No. My stomach is too queasy."

"By the way, what do you mean third date?"

"Get together, meeting...not date."

MJ raised her eyebrow. "Okay, what do you mean third not date?"

"I invited her over for ice cream the night we met in the market."

"I see." MJ gathered up the remnants of her lunch. "So, have you told her about Liz?"

"Yes. We've agreed we'll be friends, nothing more."

"Okay. Why?"

"What do you mean?"

"It's a simple question."

"Isn't the answer obvious? I love Liz. I won't cheat on her."

"If Liz had died on that day of her accident, would you feel you were cheating on her if you decided to date someone today?"

Tori looked off to the side, as she considered her response. "Honestly, I don't know how I'd feel. Probably not guilty knowing she was gone for three years."

"Tori. The essence of who Liz was, her spirit, her soul, is gone. Her body is being kept alive artificially. If we hadn't intervened with tubes and machines, her body would have died too. I can't tell you what to do. The decision has to be yours. I just don't think it's wrong for you to get some of your emotional and physical needs met. It doesn't mean you have to stop loving Liz. You know, you often criticize Liz's parents for not facing reality. Are you guilty of the same thing?"

Tears brimmed in Tori's eyes and she put her face in her hands.

MJ came around the table and pulled Tori to her feet. She sagged into MJ's embrace. "Come on, Tori. It's not the end of the world. You don't have to stop loving Liz to have a friendship with another woman. Even if that friendship ends up turning into something else. Feeling, wanting something more in your life, that's normal. It shows that you're human and still alive."

"I feel so guilty." Tori exhaled a shaky breath and sniffed back her tears.

"My telling you not to feel guilty won't make a bit of difference, no matter how much I wish it would. I have a friend who's a great counselor. Would you consider seeing her? She's easy to talk to, and maybe she can help you work through and accept your feelings."

"You're the second person to suggest that to me. My mother told me the same thing."

MJ smiled and gave Tori another hug. "It must be good advice then, don't you think?" She turned, gathered her belongings, and put her hand on the door handle. "If I don't get back to work the other nurses will give me the cold shoulder the rest of the night. You going to stop down in the morning to see Liz?"

"I think I'll go on my fifteen minute break later. I need to go home and get some sleep. I'm seeing Bev in the afternoon for a bike ride."

"Go have a good time. You deserve it."

"Thanks, MJ." As her friend turned away, Tori added, "Please send me your friend's number. I think I'll go see her."

MJ gave a quick smile before she exited, quietly closing the door behind her.

Chapter Eight

TORI GRABBED HER TABLET before sprinting down the steps to Liz's room. She quietly entered and settled in the chair at the head of the bed, her intention to read the headlines to her partner as she did everyday. She looked at the face of her lover and emotion overwhelmed her. She dropped her head onto the back of her hands she'd rested on the edge of the mattress. "Hi honey," she mumbled softly. She raised her head and stared at the face she loved, searching for any sign indicating an awareness of her presence. The incessant beeping of the monitors was the only sound in the room. "Are you in there?" Tears coursed freely down her cheeks. "God, Liz. I miss you. I will never stop loving you. It's just that I'm so lonely." A few minutes later she stood, kissed Liz's forehead and left for home.

***

Dressed casually, after her shower, Tori got her cell phone and texted Bev. *'I'm awake after some sleep, dressed, fed, and ready to go any time you are.'*

The reply came almost immediately. *'Great, you're earlier than expected. We've got a fabulous day for a ride...so looking forward to it. I'll meet you in your parking lot in a few minutes.'*

Tori already had her bike unlocked, her helmet on, and was sitting on the seat when Bev pulled up and beamed a smile. "Hi. Wow! It's really windy today. Good afternoon, by the way."

"Hey! Yes, maybe we should head into the wind so the ride home will be warmer."

"Good idea. Let's go." Bev asked, "Do you have a destination in mind?"

"No, not really. Let's ride up the boardwalk. Maybe we can make a loop around and head up onto the bridge. It should be a great view today. It's so clear."

"Wonderful idea. Let's go."

They pedaled for a half hour before they stopped for a drink. "The weather is glorious." Tori looked out over the ocean. "I can't say I really regret moving here. If the situation were different, if Liz's parents hadn't moved her to this town, I probably never would have thought to move to the shore. Now, I can't imagine living anywhere else."

"I can understand that."

"So are you going to tell me about yourself...how you ended up in New Jersey?"

"Later. Let's just enjoy the day. Do you mind?"

Tori shook her head. "Not at all. Shall we head up to the bridge?"

They pedaled up the steep incline to the lookout point halfway across the bridge to the mainland. With their bikes parked next to the fence, they walked to the overlook and leaned on the railing side by side. The wind blew down the street. Bev took off her helmet, pulled a cap from her pocket, turned into the wind, and put it on. Her jacket and pants flapped in the stiff breeze.

Tori's short ponytail held her hair in place as she pulled up her hood against the chill. She glanced up at the crystal blue sky. "Look at that." She gestured above her. Six gulls floated as if suspended on strings. The velocity of the wind was sufficient to keep them in the air without them even having to flap their wings. "I think they're just having fun."

"Wish I'd brought my camera."

Bev pulled her phone out of her pack, pointed it at the gulls, and took several shots. "I think I really need to record it, otherwise it'll look like a still shot of them flying." She flipped the slider on the phone and again pointed the camera at the gulls. "Can you believe it? They're still just hanging there, surfing the currents, like we talked about before. I love it."

They pivoted to look back toward the island. Tori pointed. "Look, there's the Ferris wheel near where we live. I love it at night, all the colors."

"Me too. I can't wait for the custard stand on the corner to open. I love their ice cream. The orange and vanilla twist is my favorite."

Tori flashed a wide smile. "Mine too. Another month and we'll be hurrying to get back to end our ride there." Tori checked her watch.

"Maybe we'd better get back. I'll need another shower and have to grab a nap before I go visit Liz."

"Sure. I'm glad you were able to come with me today. Think you could eat pasta again? If you do, I'd be glad for the company for a quick dinner. I know you don't have a lot of time, but you still have to eat. Maybe it would save you a few minutes."

Following a brief pause, Tori smiled. "Thanks. I'd like that, too. What time?"

"How about six thirty?"

"Good, I'll see you then." Tori mounted her bike and led the way back toward their condos. She returned Bev's wave when Bev turned toward her place, then locked her bike to the bike rack, used the back entrance, and took the stairs to her condo.

The phone was ringing as she entered her home. She checked the caller ID and punched the on button. "Hi, MJ. What's up?"

"I have that number of the counselor we talked about."

"Hang on, let me get a pen. Okay, shoot."

MJ read out the number. "Her name is Karolina Langston. She's a good friend. I think you'll like her. She's a straight shooter."

"Thanks, MJ. I'll definitely give her a call. I hope she can help me get a handle on how I'm feeling."

"Me too, babe. I have to run. Are we getting together for our break?"

"Absolutely. I'll probably just bring a protein bar. I'm eating dinner here earlier. Bev invited me for leftovers."

"Oh?"

"Oh nothing. Stop. I'll see you later."

Tori fixed a cup of tea and carried it into the living room where she settled in the recliner. She picked up her phone and dialed the number MJ gave her.

An efficient secretary took down answers to a series of questions and they agreed to a date for the following Wednesday afternoon at two for her appointment. As Tori pushed the end button she exhaled a long sigh. Hopeful that she could doze for the forty-five minutes before she had to get up and shower, she set the alarm on her watch.

***

Bev opened the door, her smile bright and welcoming. "Right on time. Come on in. Dinner will be ready in about five minutes. I made us small side salads. Did you get your nap?"

"No. I rested, though. Thanks for feeding me again. Maybe you'll let me buy you dinner sometime. You keep feeding me, I'd like to reciprocate."

"Deal. Who gets to choose the place?"

"You do, of course."

Bev rubbed her hands together and grinned. "Great! Come on into the kitchen." She turned leading the way. "I don't want to hold you up, so I need to get the pasta on."

Bev served the meal and they ate as they reviewed the highlights of their bike ride.

Tori helped clear the table. "I still can't get over those gulls."

"Oh, I almost forgot, wait till you see the video I shot." Bev got her cell phone and pushed a couple of buttons before she turned the screen in Tori's direction.

They watched the video together, sitting shoulder to shoulder. Tori willed the hands on the clock to move more slowly and secretly wished the video were longer.

"Can you send me a copy of this?"

"Sure. Give me your e-mail address." She typed the address into a quick e-mail and pushed send. "There we go. Now that I have your e-mail address I have someone else to forward all those annoying 'send this letter to a dozen people or you'll have seventy years of bad luck' letters to."

"I'm sure I don't have to tell you that you'll regret it if you do."

"Is that a threat?"

Tori laughed. "Worse yet, a promise." She laughed along with Bev. "I need to go. Can I help with the dishes?"

"No, I can take care of them. You go ahead. I have a few hours with nothing pressing to do before I have to call in." Bev led the way down the hall and held up Tori's jacket as she slipped into it. Reaching around Tori to open the door, Bev put her hand on Tori's back. The move turned the two women toward each other and they moved naturally to a brief hug.

Tori quickly pulled away. She felt her face flush with a combination of arousal and guilt and was unnerved by the quick physical response she had to Bev's brief embrace. Before she hurried away, she stammered, "Uh, thank you, again. I'll call you."

Chapter Nine

"Victoria Branningham? Please come in and have a seat." The diminutive, grey haired woman with beautiful dimples and a welcoming smile opened the door for Tori. Her eyes were blue grey, rimmed with darker lashes. "My name is Dr. Karolina Langston. Please call me Karolina. What should I call you?"

"My name is Victoria. I'd prefer that you call me Tori, please. Only my mother calls me Victoria."

"Ok, Tori. Although I sometimes work from a list of things I want to address during each session, I don't like to take notes during my counseling sessions. I find that it distracts me. I usually record our conversation so I have something to refer back to while I make my notes. Once I have made notes, I erase the recording. Is that acceptable to you?"

Tori nodded.

"Good. Let's start with you telling me why you're here."

Tori inhaled a deep breath. "I am having trouble sleeping."

"Is that the only reason you're here? If it is, have you consulted with your family physician?"

"No. I guess that's actually a 'no' to both questions. I think the reason I can't sleep is because I feel guilty."

"Tell me a little about why you feel that way."

"Before I do that, I should probably tell you that I'm a lesbian and my concerns involve and revolve around a lesbian relationship." Tori watched closely for any response from the counselor that she could interpret as negative or not accepting.

"Okay. Thank you for telling me that. Did you expect it would be an issue for me...perhaps you thought I might not approve?"

"I wasn't sure. Is it, an issue, I mean?"

"It might be, perhaps not for the reason you expect. You should know that I have little experience in that area. Despite that, I hope it will make you feel more comfortable to know I believe that love is love. I also doubt that your being a lesbian would limit my being able to help you. However, if you'd feel more comfortable with a lesbian counselor, I can refer you to a friend of mine. Perhaps if you tell me a little more about why you're here we'll be better able to make a decision about whether we think I can help you."

"Okay. My lover's name is Liz..." Tori explained about Liz's accident and her current condition. With some careful questioning from Karolina, she succinctly related the problems associated with her in-laws, and the difficulties associated with not having a say in her lover's medical care.

"So far I haven't heard anything that would indicate a reason you might feel guilty. It would seem that you've been extremely supportive to your partner and have managed to make the best of the situation. Can you explain more clearly why you feel guilty?"

"I've never cheated on my partner. Ever. For our whole relationship, I've never even had a thought about another woman." Tori glanced around the room while Karolina waited patiently for her to continue. "Until recently." Tori divested herself of the burden she'd been holding in, told about her crush on the runner, and how they'd met quite by accident in the market. "It's not even that I've met someone that I'm attracted to, although I suspect that's part of it. For the past few months, long before I ever saw Bev, I've been having a harder and harder time continuing the extended visits with Liz. I've faithfully spent as many hours of the day as possible with her ever since her accident. It's just so hard." Her eyes filled with tears, but she blinked them away. "I mean in the beginning I felt so relieved when she didn't die. There was hope then, at the beginning. As hope ebbed and drained away, I still felt thankful that she hadn't died." Tori plucked a tissue from the box on the table next to her chair and blew her nose.

Karolina steepled her fingers and furrowed her brow. "Do you still feel that way now?"

Tori again blinked away the new flood of tears that filled her eyes, refusing to give in to her grief. "Although I have shared some of what I've been dealing with, I haven't admitted the full depth of my feelings to anyone, not even to my mother or my best friend, MJ. I have shared some of my worries, but I have a hard time admitting everything I'm feeling, even to myself." Tori looked down at the tissue in her hands and in a hushed voice replied. "I'm very ashamed to admit it. The answer to your question about if I'm still glad she survived, is no, not always. Lately, there are days that it's all I can do to go in for my visit. I was feeling that way even before I met my neighbor, Bev, the woman I told you about, the one that I find myself attracted to. It's more about the fact that I hardly recognize Liz any more. She's down to skin and bones."

Tori glanced around the office as she analyzed which thoughts racing through her mind were most critical to share. "I don't actually blame Liz's parents for making the decision to continue life support. In some ways, I was relieved that the decision wasn't mine to make. Sometimes I look at Liz now, and I can't avoid wondering if the decision to keep her alive using extraordinary measures was a kindness after all." Her eyes sought the counselor's. "Sometimes I even feel angry. Not only at the situation...I'm ashamed to admit that there are days that I feel angry with Liz. I mean I surely know it wasn't her fault or what she'd wanted. I'm just angry that she wasn't more careful." She paused to formulate her thoughts. "Would you think I was horrible if I said that there are times I think it's cruel to keep her alive? Not only for her, but for everyone involved...her parents, me."

"I think it is quite normal to have doubts about those difficult moral decisions that have to be made. Over time, people have a habit of growing and changing. When you love someone and are in a relationship with them, those changes tend to be gradual. There's time to adapt, to accept, and perhaps to negotiate. Your circumstance is quite different. The change in your lover happened in an instant. Because you were in love with your partner, you really had no viable options other than to accept the changes. You seemed to do that in an admirable fashion. Now, years later, you find yourself rebelling against the unfairness of the situation. Are you familiar with the five stages of death and dying? I think it might be helpful for you to read up on the topic. The information is easily accessible on the web. Do you have Internet access?"

Tori nodded.

"Good." Karolina jotted down the information on a piece of paper and slid it across the desk toward Tori. "Look up this information and we can talk more about it if you'd like. We don't have enough time to get deeper into your issue of guilt today, I'm sorry to say. Although not specific to your situation exactly, I believe the stages they describe can be helpful and can be useful for the family and, when appropriate, the patient, in developing an understanding of the process. I do think that reading the information I suggested to you will help prepare us to better discuss your situation if you think you might benefit from working with me and decide to return. You present as quite open, willing and able to address your issues directly, and seem to be an introspective person who does a good deal of self-analysis. I believe we can make reasonably expedient progress in addressing your issues. Although I need to caution you that you are dealing with difficult moral dilemmas, something for which there is no magic bullet. You'll need to do some hard work and may have to make some difficult choices."

"Thank you. Yes, I think working with you will help me. Thank you for the reading assignment. I'll look it up. It'll make me feel like I'm doing something useful. When should I see you again?"

"Is this time a convenient one for you? I can see you weekly or every two weeks. It's up to you."

Tori sighed and tried for a smile. "I'd like to see you weekly. I'm eager to feel better. Sometimes it's so hard to..." Her brows furrowed as she struggled with how to finish the sentence.

Karolina smiled. "Don't give up. I know it's hard. The feelings you're having are very normal responses to an exceptionally difficult and abnormal situation. Nothing in our backgrounds prepares us for this type of loss. Although not specific to this exact situation, I think the information I suggested will help you recognize a normal progression of feelings and you'll be able to extract useful points that you can apply to your circumstances. Sometimes just knowing that others have responded the same way is reassuring and makes us feel better. Until I see you next week, be kinder to yourself and have some fun. From what you told me, your partner would want you to be enjoying your life and not feeling guilty about it."

"That's true. She was always trying to make me laugh and lighten up."

"My advice to you is to go get a massage, a spray tan, or have a fancy dinner out. Whatever gives you pleasure. And believe that Liz wouldn't want you to feel guilty about it."

"Thank you, Karolina. I'll see you next week."

Karolina stood up, plucked a card from the holder on her desk, and wrote her cell number on the back. "If you need me on an emergency basis you can leave me a message at this number. I'll get back to you as soon as I'm able. I'll see you at the same time a week from now. I assume my secretary, Janet, explained that the first appointment is an hour and forty-five minutes because we have a lot of background to cover and it sometimes takes a bit longer to hone in on a patient's specific issue or issues for discussion. Our next session will be fifty minutes. If at any time you feel you will need more time than that, please let Janet know and she'll schedule it as such. I leave extra time in my schedule for patients dealing with a crisis or issue that takes extra time."

"Yes, she explained that to me when I called to book my appointment. Thank you. I'll see you next week. I'm glad I came. I'll definitely do the reading before next week."

Karolina showed her out through a back door. "Please exit through this door. It helps maintain confidentiality. Turn left and the exit is at the end of the hallway."

Tori closed the door and followed the instructions, exiting the building two doors down from Karolina's office entrance.

Chapter Ten

TORI LEFT KAROLINA'S OFFICE feeling like she had divested herself of a heavy burden. As she opened the door to leave, she stood still for a moment inhaling several deep breaths, filling her lungs completely. It felt like she was inhaling the first full breaths she'd taken in weeks. The usual tightness in her chest was gone. She glanced up at the bright blue sky and blew a long breath out through her mouth. *I guess confession really is good for the soul.* Across the street, a small coffee shop beckoned to her. Hot chocolate in hand, she settled at a table in front of the window at the opposite end of the seating area from three boisterous young women drinking coffee.

She pulled out her cell phone, and keeping her voice low, called to check on Liz's condition. Only hesitating a few seconds after she finished, she made a decision, punched the address book icon on the phone's screen, selected Bev's cell number from the list, and began to type a text. *'I apologize...I know this is last minute. It's just that I was wondering if you might be available for dinner tonight around six? My treat. I just left the counselor who told me to go out and have a good time. You immediately came to mind.'*

Licking her lips after draining the last of the hot chocolate, she savored the taste of her treat. The chime indicating she'd received a text sounded as she was on her way to dispose of the paper cup in the trashcan. Her first instinct was to flip open the cover to see if it was a response from Bev. *No, not yet. I don't want to ruin the good feelings from my indulgence with bad news. If it's good news, I'll call and firm up a plan.*

Hurrying to her car parked a block away, Tori threw open the door and slipped into the driver seat. "Please make this a perfect day," she whispered clutching the phone to her chest. Tori selected the text from Bev and waited impatiently as it loaded.

'Yes, yes, yes! So glad you thought of me. For some reason I was having trouble facing another meal alone tonight. Where are we going?'

Tori thought for a second or two before she switched to the phone keypad to dial Bev. Without preamble following the hello at the other end, she said, "You get to choose. Casual or dressy?"

"You have to work later, right?"

"I do. And I want to stop in to see Liz. I haven't been there since this morning when I got off shift."

"How about we make it casual and save dressy for when we have more time, and neither of us has to work. Then we can have a drink or two. Okay?"

"Great suggestion. Who knew? Brains and beauty in one neat package." Later, replaying the conversation in her mind, Tori wouldn't know what possessed her to offer such a flirty response.

"T, you are a flatterer. How about we have dinner on the mainland, at Kirkpatricks. I'll meet you. I have to go to work after, and I can leave from there."

"T? Where did that come from?"

"Do you mind? I refer to you that way in my calendar. I guess I've just started thinking of you as 'T.' If you don't like it I can call you Tori, or better still, Victoria."

"Ha! T it is for sure, especially if Victoria is your alternative name of choice."

"So, Kirkpatricks at six?"

"That's fine. I was just thinking though. Since you're now calling me by a pet name, it's not very fair that you know my whole tale of woe and you haven't told me much about yourself at all. You keep promising next time, and next time has yet to come."

Bev relaxed into the chair, a smile on her face. "There's no big mystery. It's just not a very happy tale, so I prefer to leave it in the past where it belongs. If you really want to know, I'll reveal all tonight, abbreviated version only, before we move on to brighter topics. Deal?"

"Sure. To me, it seems I usually do most of the talking. Be forewarned...today you have to talk."

"I don't agree that you usually do most of the talking so I'm not sure how to respond to that statement. Instead, I'm going to hang up and go take a shower so you can stand to be in the same room with me. I'll see you at six."

"Absolutely. And Bev...I'm glad you're coming."

"Me too. Can you manage five thirty?"

"If I hurry. See you there."

***

Bev was waiting on the bench outside the restaurant entrance when Tori arrived at the restaurant. As she locked her car, Tori waved a greeting before hurrying across the parking lot. Bev, wearing a pale blue sweater that matched the color of her eyes, greeted Tori with a quick hug.

Tori said, "You look nice. If this is casual, I can't wait to see dressy."

"Well, I have to go in to work tonight, so I usually try to look professional. Sometimes I wear jeans if the weather is bad. Otherwise I shoot for business attire. I appreciate the compliment. Thank you."

Inside they asked for a booth and followed behind the hostess as she led them to their table and deposited menus for their use.

"I'm glad we agreed on this restaurant. I love the food choices here." Bev studied the menu briefly. "Have you ever had their fried shrimp? They're massive and so crispy. I try to ration how many times a month I allow myself to buy them. If I don't watch my school girl figure nobody else will."

"From my perspective I don't think there will ever be an issue with that."

Bev blushed and looked down at her menu. "What are you going to have?"

"I'm torn between the braised short ribs special and the shrimp. You made them sound so good."

"Let's get one of each and split them. That way we get to taste both."

The waitress took their order, noting their choice of salad dressings, drinks, and meal choice on her tablet. While waiting for the waitress to deliver their salads, they chatted about inconsequential topics. Once the salads arrived, confident they wouldn't be interrupted by a food delivery until they finished them, Bev asked, "Tori, I hope you don't think my asking you this question is inappropriate. On our last ride, you mentioned that you planned to talk to a therapist, and on the phone you said the counselor told you to go have fun. I wonder, what did you think of the therapist?"

Tori hadn't detailed the reason she was seeking therapy, she'd just dropped the fact that MJ recommended a friend of hers to talk to about her recent feelings of frustration and sadness. "I really liked her. She's easy to talk with and she made me feel like what I've been feeling is totally normal, even understandable. Have you ever seen a counselor?" Tori plucked a warm and yeasty smelling roll from the assortment in the basket.

"Yes. For a short time after my break up with my ex."

"It must have been a difficult breakup."

"It was. You asked for 'my story.' So here goes." Bev pursed her lips, gathering her thoughts. "Connie and I were lovers for eight years. When I met her, I'd just moved to the Washington area, from New Orleans where I'd attended college."

"D.C. or Washington State?"

"D.C., not that it's critical to the story. That roll looks good. Is there another like that one?"

Tori slid the basket of bread in Bev's direction. "So, D.C."

"Yes. I met Connie at work. We'd been talking for a few weeks over lunch and on our breaks. I was so homesick. She invited me for dinner and I jumped at her offer. She took me to a restaurant that served Cajun food and played Dixieland Jazz. I thought it was the sweetest thing anyone had ever done for me, and I fell in love with her at that exact moment. We moved in together within weeks of that night."

"Like the old joke?"

"You mean the one about what does a lesbian bring on a second date?"

Simultaneously they said, "A U-Haul." Laughing along with Tori, Bev finally settled enough to say, "Exactly."

"So was it good at first?"

"It was good for eight years. Of course, we had our issues. Connie was, after all Connie. She could be egocentric. Still, for the most part, we were basically happy. I didn't always approve of her business practices. She could be..." Bev pursed her lips and glanced up, searching for the perfect word. "I don't know how to describe it. Not really heartless, although she could be tough. To call her result driven, almost Machiavellian, to achieve her goals is probably the mother of all understatements." The waitress interrupted to ask if she could remove their salad bowls. They nodded and after she left to get their dinner, Bev continued. "We were very compatible...both active, with similar likes and dislikes. We had similar senses of humor, laughed a lot...had a great sex life. I couldn't imagine that anything could ever come between us."

The server brought their dinners. "We're not that busy tonight, so I had the chef split the order for you."

"That was very sweet, thank you." Tori said, giving the waitress a bright smile of genuine appreciation. "Wow! Look at all that food. There'll definitely be enough for lunch tomorrow."

The waitress smiled at the compliment. "I'll bring two take-home boxes my next trip back. Don't forget to save room for dessert. The short ribs are on special tonight. Dessert is included."

They dug into the food, quickly agreeing that the shrimp was their favorite. "Not that the short ribs aren't fabulous. It's just that the shrimp are amazing," Bev said. "They're delicious."

Tori agreed. "So tell me what happened that caused what sounds like a perfect relationship to end."

"Two words. Breast cancer. I got breast cancer. It devastated us. She never looked at me the same way, couldn't touch me intimately. Physically, I...I turned her off." Bev shrugged. "I came home after my surgery and discovered that she'd already moved into the guest room, allegedly to allow me to be more comfortable. I'll spare you the drama of the death knell and the recounting of all the tears I shed as it ended. Essentially, that was it. By the time I was well enough to return to work, she told me she was sorry...she just couldn't live with the damage from the surgery and the feeling of waiting for the 'other shoe to drop.' I...uh...let's just say I needed help. So there's a very long answer to your original question about if I've ever been to a therapist."

"What did she mean by waiting for the other shoe to drop?"

"I guess she couldn't live with the threat that my cancer would return. I've been cancer free for six years now. Statistically, I have no more chance of getting cancer again than you do or she does. I had the test and don't have the gene. Despite that, of course, it's been six long years of worry and wondering every time I went for a checkup. Only recently have I begun to believe that I really beat it."

The waitress returned with two Styrofoam boxes. "Here you go ladies. I'll be back in a few to take your dessert order and fill these containers with the leftovers for you when you finish. Do you want coffee?"

Bev shook her head. "Can you just refill my seltzer, please?"

Tori nodded. "Mine too, please."

Bev waited for the waitress to leave before she continued. "You asked about counseling. While all that happened I sought help. I found that just telling someone my story, admitting how I was feeling about having cancer, and having someone empathize with me, you know, validate my feelings, made me feel better."

"I'm sorry Connie hurt you so badly. What about since you broke up? Anyone else special?"

Bev looked away and shook her head. She exhaled a long sigh before she looked back to face Tori. "Remember that first night we got together and you told me 'it's complicated?' I have complications of my own. Ever since Connie found me so physically repulsive, couldn't touch me, I've not ever…you know, been intimate with anyone. I kind of figured if someone who supposedly loved me found me repulsive, who else wouldn't feel the same way?"

"I'd imagine any number of women would welcome a relationship with a smart, funny, and lovely woman like you."

"Thank you for saying that. Ironically, there was an up side to getting cancer, having to take time to recover…it actually gave me time to finish up the computer program I'd been working on since I got out of college. I finished it, marketed it, and as I mentioned, it's been financially very beneficial to me. I sold it for enough that, assuming I budget appropriately and invest wisely, I really don't ever have to work full time again. Trust me though, money doesn't buy happiness."

"Happiness can be elusive, for sure. I felt exactly like you did. I thought Liz and I would grow old together. I never figured on…on this. Not that the first two years of this reality were easy, it's just that I've been having an especially hard time the past few months. Seeing Liz wasting away with no hope of a future is something with which I've been really struggling. Short version, is that the counselor listened as I explained how I'm feeling and told me it was normal to feel that way. Then Karolina told me to go have fun. My first first thought was of you.

"I'm flattered."

Tori watched as the dimple appeared in Bev's cheek as she smiled.

"All finished here?" The waitress interrupted their conversation to put the remainder of their meals into the containers and take their dessert order. After she left Bev steepled her fingers in front of her lips, elbows resting on the table. "I'm glad we've become friends."

"Me too. It's not only nice to have someone to do things with, it's even better to have someone with whom I can share my thoughts and feelings with."

"Ladies, here's your dessert." The server placed the plate of bread pudding on the table between them and handed each a spoon. "Want anything else?"

"No, thanks, just the check," Tori said.

The waitress tore the slip of paper from her pad. "See you next time. Have a good night."

"You too. Thank you." Turning back to Bev, Tori said, "Shall we?"

They dug into the sweet treat. Tori finished her thought. "I have to say, talking to the counselor today and speaking with you tonight has made me feel less like I'm about to explode. Keeping all those feelings locked up tight has been making me crazy. Lately, I haven't been sleeping very well."

"Maybe you'll get a good sleep tomorrow morning. I won't bother you," Bev said.

"You're never a bother. I love it when you call and ask to do something."

"I feel the same. I'm so glad you called about dinner tonight. I think eating alone is the hardest part of being single for me."

"Bev, after what you've shared with me over dinner tonight, I want you to know that I think you are an extremely desirable and attractive woman. I find you fascinating. You're great company and I enjoy spending time with you. I'm glad we've become friends. Just know that from my perspective, if things were different, I wouldn't want to settle for just friendship."

Bev searched Tori's eyes, finally glancing away. Her gaze returned slowly. "I feel the same way. If things were different, I'd want more with you than friendship, too. You were right. You said your situation is complicated. I want you to know that I understand your commitment to Liz, and I'll never interfere with that. If she were healthy, I'm confident that the three of us would have been friends because I would never interfere in someone's relationship. From what you've told me about her, I would have liked her very much. Given the current situation, I hope there is a way that you can still make room in your life for me. I think we're good for each other. I know that I'm certainly having a better time living here since I met you."

"I feel the same. Living in this really heterosexually oriented community can be tiring at times. I sometimes feel like a stranger in a strange land, although I've never really felt any homophobia. My friend, MJ, is straight. She opened her home to me and has been so supportive. I love her kindness and acceptance."

"I think I read somewhere that, in our town here, lesbians comprise something like one tenth of one percent of the population. I'm amazed we actually found each other."

"It must just have been meant to be." Tori picked up the check, left a generous tip, and said, "I'd better get going. If I get a move on, I have time to read a couple of more chapters in the book I'm reading to Liz."

They walked to the parking lot together. "Thank you for dinner, T."

Tori smiled at the nickname. "No, thank you for joining me on such a last minute invitation."

"Let's avoid the need for that situation repeating itself again. How about we arrange now, for dinner tomorrow—my house, six o'clock, you can bring dessert."

"Deal. I promise to never turn down a home cooked meal." Tori grinned as she reached out for a hug. "I'll see you tomorrow night."

They each headed for their car. Just as Tori reached for the door handle, she heard Bev calling to her. Seconds later Bev caught up to her. "T, I was thinking. You know that I have lots of time on my hands. Do you think it would be okay if I went in to read to Liz sometimes? Maybe you could take me the first time or two."

Tori paused to quickly examine how she felt about that. She couldn't come up with any negatives for Liz because of Bev reading to her. "That's very kind of you. When would you want to do this?"

"I don't have to be at work for a couple of hours. Aren't you going to stop in to see her? I could come with you now, if it's okay."

Tori quickly glanced at her watch. "It's only seven thirty. Visiting hours are until nine. If you have a private room, they don't usually toss visitors out unless they're making a disturbance."

"I'll follow you." Bev touched Tori on the arm. "See you there."

Chapter Eleven

TORI DROVE SLOWER THAN she normally would so Bev could stay behind her. They pulled in and parked in the lot next to each other. Side by side they walked to the entrance of the nursing facility. Tori opened the door and held it for Bev.

As she entered the facility for the first time, Bev glanced around at the lovely lobby decorated in calming earth tones. An oriental rug, a soft green with cream and shades of beige mixed into the design, functioned as the base color scheme. Two beige leather sofas, matching one of the colors in the rug, and four coordinating armchairs, arranged around a square coffee table, provided a welcoming and comfortable appearing seating area for visitors.

Bev breathed in, anticipating and simultaneously dreading the usual unpleasant smell of disinfectant and urine common to so many facilities that took care of sick people. She was pleasantly surprised to find that the air smelled fresh and clean. They continued down the hallway past a beautiful antique looking desk that sat off to the side where the receptionist seated there greeted Tori by name.

"Good evening, Della Mae. This is a friend of mine, Bev McMannis. We're going to visit Liz for a little while." Tori signed in for both of them.

"It's a pleasure to meet you, Ms. McMannis."

"Please call me Bev. It's nice to meet you as well."

"Della, we're going to visit Liz, then I'm here for my shift. How's your mom doing?"

"Much better, thanks for asking. Her knee replacement has been a blessing. It was a tough go at first, thankfully she's doing great now."

"Glad to hear it." To Bev she said, "We'd better get going."

With a quick wave and a smile from each of them for Della Mae, Bev followed behind as Tori led them to the wing where Liz's room was located. The hallways presented the same appearance as a fine hotel, with lovely wallpaper, raised panel wainscoting painted in an antique white, and beautiful artwork displayed on the walls. At regular intervals along the hallways, armchairs flanked either side of narrow, rectangular tables decorated with seasonal flowers. *This place is obviously big bucks. I've seen five star hotels that aren't this nicely appointed. Liz is a lucky gal.* "This is a lovely facility."

"Yes, credit where it is due. Liz's parents wanted the best for their daughter, and they found it here. I enjoy working here, too. They treat their employees as well as their patients."

They rounded the corner and came to the nurses' station. Molly and Rose waved a cheerful hello. Tori greeted the nurses by name and introduced Bev before leading her down the hall. "This is Liz's room." Tori said, pausing in front of room number fifty-two.

Tori paused and took a deep breath before she led the way into Liz's room. As they entered, Bev glanced around the private quarters with a view of the bay. The decor, with walls painted a soft blue and furnishings similar in style to those Bev had seen in the hallways, created a relaxing ambiance. Bev stood at the doorway to give Tori an opportunity to see Liz alone first, waiting for an invitation to approach. Tori placed a kiss on Liz's forehead and fussed about with the covers, arranging Liz's hands along her sides. She leaned over and whispered something to her lover before she stood and invited Bev over.

"Honey, this is my friend Bev. I told you about how we met in the supermarket. She's offered to read to you. We agreed it would be nice for you to have company sometimes when I can't be here."

Bev looked down at the frail, pale woman in the bed, feeling unsure about proper protocol in this very odd situation. It felt very awkward as Tori addressed Liz and got no response, no indication that she was remotely aware of anything around her. She took her cues from Tori who spoke to her partner as if she understood her and placed her hand on Liz's. "Hi Liz. I hope we'll become good friends. I like to read, too. I'll try to pick something interesting enough to keep us both entertained." *This is so difficult. Normally, the person you speak to would say something back now.* With nothing coming back, Bev found herself babbling about books she generally found of interest. "Maybe Tori can help me pick something you'd like." She looked to her friend for help.

"Here, let's get these chairs and pull them up next to the bed." Once settled, Tori began a monologue about her activities of the day. Bev noticed Tori left out her visit to the counselor.

"So, Bev and I had dinner. You'd have loved the shrimp, Liz. They were so huge I had to take four bites to finish one of them."

MJ stuck her head in the doorway of Liz's room. "Hey there! Heard you were here."

Tori turned toward her friend. "Hey MJ. You doing another double?"

"Yes. We're shorthanded for another month. Maureen is still out on childcare leave."

"Come in and meet my friend." When MJ approached, Tori said, "MJ, this is Bev. Bev, MJ." Tori reached up to put her hand on MJ's shoulder. "She's my salvation. I don't know what I'd have done without her, especially after I first moved here."

MJ's eyes glowed with fondness as she replied. "Oh go on. We support each other."

"Bev kindly volunteered to read to Liz when I can't be here," Tori said. "I just introduced them."

"That's very nice of you, Bev. The more stimulation Liz has, the better for her." MJ turned to leave. "Sorry I have to run so soon. I need to get back out there to the nursing station. I have a break in fifteen minutes or so. If you're going to still be here, I'll stop back in."

Tori nodded, and Bev watched as MJ departed. "I like your friend, T. She's very nice. And tall..."

Tori laughed. "Yes, that she is. I tease her that she had to be that tall to house that big heart of hers. She's a phenomenal woman."

"Single?"

Tori glanced at Bev and nodded.

Bev raised an eyebrow. "She's very attractive."

"Yes, single, attractive, and straight."

Bev shrugged and Tori laughed. "We usually have a snack midway through our shift. When we can, we take it at the same time. I have more flexibility in my schedule than she does so I try to adjust my time to match hers. Her efforts to meet the perfect guy are fodder for our conversations during our 'meal' break."

"Well, there's her problem right there, trying to meet the perfect guy."

They shared a good laugh over Bev's observation. Tori grabbed a tube of lotion from the bedside table and applied it to Liz's arms, hands, and legs. "Just give me a minute. I always apply lotion to her at night. The air here seems so dry."

Bev turned away while Tori pulled the blankets down and tended to Liz. As Tori finished up and tucked the covers back in place Bev asked, "Is this the infamous book that Liz's mom reads to her?"

"That's it."

Bev picked up the book and turned toward Liz. "I think we can do better than this, Liz. I have a great book called, Watching Paint Dry, that could be more interesting than this one."

MJ returned in time to hear the comment and join in the laughter.

"Good one. I completely agree." MJ reached for Liz's wrist and checked her pulse.

"Anything or anyone new to report?" Tori asked MJ.

"Sadly, no." MJ walked to the other side of Liz's bed to check the monitors and tidy the bedding. "I assume Tori has shared with you my continuing search for the perfect man."

Bev glanced at Tori before she replied. "She mentioned you have difficulties finding someone suitable."

"After my disastrous marriage, I've decided I'm not going to settle this time. I've been through the gamut...bars, dating services, blind dates. You name it, I've tried it."

"I remember blind dates," Bev shifted in her seat to better see MJ. "What was your worst blind date experience?"

"Um...let me think. The worst, was probably back in college. My roommate fixed me up with this guy, George. Both of my roommates were there the evening he arrived to pick me up. My third roommate, Lucy, was everything I'm not, you know the type...petite, weighed about ninety pounds soaking wet, long blonde hair, cute, dimples. Well, you get the idea. Anyway, George and I went out for pizza. He was a good six inches shorter than me, and when I say we had no chemistry, it was more like vinegar and baking soda than any other chemical combination I can think of. The worst part of it was that he spent the entire evening asking me about Lucy, or Lusty Lucy, as he nicknamed her. I mean, really. At the end of the night, he tried to kiss me goodnight. When I declined, he handed me his cad and asked me if I would fix him up with my roommate."

"That was pretty brazen. What about you two? What was your worst blind date experience?" MJ glanced back and forth between Bev and Tori.

"Don't look at me. I've never had a blind date," Tori said.

In unison, MJ and Bev said. "Seriously?"

"Really? What about you, Bev? What's your worst?"

Bev laughed. "I have a winner too, although I'm not sure that I can top MJ's story. A friend of mine fixed me up with her brother." She saw the look of puzzlement on Tori's face. "Don't look so surprised. It was years ago...long before I figured out I didn't bat for that team and men didn't do it for me. Anyway, we were supposed to go out for dinner at seven. He didn't show, didn't call...so by nine I ate a salad and got ready for bed. I was in my PJs sitting in my living room when I heard the doorbell. I opened the door to find him standing there weaving to and fro, drunk as a skunk. He said, 'hello,' and promptly bent over and threw up on my feet."

"Oh my God!" Tori laughed. "You win for sure. I can see why you prefer women."

"Obviously that wasn't the only reason. No doubt, it surely turned me off of him." Bev paused thinking about her timing. "I would suspect this might not be the opportune moment to bring this up since we're talking about our worst experiences. Anyway, I have a friend I work with, a really great guy, that I think you might find interesting. His name is Victor and I like him very much. The fact that he works nights might make things easier for dating. His interests are varied. He's active in wildlife and animal rescue, loves to cook, has a quirky sense of humor, a great body, and I think he's very handsome."

"He sounds perfect. What's the catch? He's probably five feet tall."

"No, he's not...um...well there is one issue. Considering your vocation, I can't imagine it would bother you. He lost one leg below the knee while serving in Iraq. He wears a prosthesis. If I hadn't mentioned it, you probably wouldn't notice it immediately. I think, no, I know he's still a bit self-conscious about it. It took him several months until he told me about what happened. I know he's not been dating anyone because we've commiserated with each other about finding it difficult to meet someone of interest."

"Okay, you've successfully managed to avoid the question about his height."

"No, I didn't avoid answering your question, just saved the best for last. He used to play college basketball. He's like six-feet-five or so. In fact, I believe he'll even make you feel short. Imagine that."

"So when do I meet him? Not that I'm overeager or anything." MJ's laughter was light and melodic.

"I'll talk to him at work tonight and see if I can set something up."

AJ Adaire

MJ glanced between the two women. "Maybe you and Tori will join us for the first time, if he's interested? It might make meeting easier."

"Sure." Bev turned toward Tori a questioning look on her face.

Tori considered MJ's request, and after a few seconds delay, she nodded her agreement. "Sure. Sounds like fun."

Bev stood and gathered her jacket from the back of the chair. "Speaking of work, I'd better get going. Liz, I'll see you tomorrow and we'll read a bit. MJ, it's a pleasure meeting you. I'll set everything up through Tori." She glanced at Tori, thanked her for dinner, and gave each of them a grin and a quick wave as she left.

Tori took Liz's hand giving it a squeeze. "I'd better get upstairs too. My shift starts soon." She stood up and turned to MJ. "I should be able to meet with you during your break. I'll call you after I see what I have on my schedule tonight. I'd prefer we do it later, if possible. I'm still stuffed from dinner."

"Sure. I'll try to arrange things so my break is later. I can text you a time as soon as I figure out what needs to be done and what time I can take my break."

Tori turned toward the bed and leaned over to place a kiss on Liz's forehead. "Oh, MJ, Liz seems warm to me. Can you check her?"

"You know I will. I'll text you later about where I am in the rotation for my break and let you know then how Liz is doing."

"Thanks. I'll see you later." Tori took the stairs to her office. Twenty minutes later, she read the text from MJ giving a time for their meeting and stating that Liz's temperature was a few tenths elevated and they would be carefully monitoring it.

***

Three hours later MJ showed up in Tori's office. She sat at the table and unpacked her meal as Tori came around the desk to join her. She opened the protein bar she'd taken from her reserve in her desk drawer. "That's it?"

Tori centered the protein bar on top of her napkin. "Yeah, I'm still full from dinner. I'll stop on my way home in the morning and get a breakfast sandwich."

MJ took a bite of her sandwich and stared at Tori while she chewed, waiting for her to speak.

"What?"

"So?" MJ raised an eyebrow. "You know what."

"If you're referring to Bev, we're friends. That's all. I've been honest with her. How much more honest could I be? I even introduced her to Liz. I've kept no secrets."

"Honesty doesn't always stop feelings." MJ popped the top on her soda and took a swig. "There's a spark, a connection between the two of you."

"Are you accusing me of something?" Tori's eyes searched MJ's for her reaction.

"No, of course not." MJ reached across the table and squeezed Tori's hand.

"I love Liz. You know that. I would never cheat on her." Slowly and deliberately, Tori fiddled with the wrapper on the protein bar, finally tearing it open and taking a bite. "Bev and I talked about it tonight over dinner. She knows exactly how I feel and where I stand. We've both admitted, that if things were not as they are, there might be a potential for us to have something different, something more. But I made a commitment to Liz and I intend to keep it."

MJ set down her sandwich. She exhaled as she leaned forward and pinned Tori with her eyes. "Honey, we've talked about this before. Forgive me if you think I'm being insensitive, but I'm talking to you as your friend here, not as a nurse. The possibility of Liz recovering is miniscule. After all this time, even if she did improve, she'd be so impaired that there would be no hope of you ever having any semblance of a normal life. Her brain damage is too extensive. The fact that she's still alive is only attributable to two factors. One, she was in good physical condition at the time of the accident and, two, that she's had extremely good medical care. The majority of people in her condition would have passed away many months, if not years ago. She's already had several close calls with pneumonia and infections. Nobody would ever fault you if you got involved with someone. Although your life has been dramatically impacted, you have to accept that she's the one in that bed, in that condition, not you. Between work and visiting her every day, you spend fourteen to sixteen hours a day here, even on weekends. I'm sorry, it's just that we've had this conversation before and you know that I worry about you."

"I know. I'm okay." Silence spread between them as they each took a bite of food. "MJ, I saw your friend, the counselor. I liked her very much. Thank you for the recommendation. We were having a similar conversation to this one. I, uh, lately..." Tori sighed and looked away. "I'm ashamed to admit that recently I sometimes find it hard to be with

Liz. It's becoming burdensome, at times, carrying on a one sided conversation. I feel like I don't have anything to talk to her about. Then I feel guilty, so I come even more often."

"As if that's possible."

"Well, still. I come, and I watch her and I think about how much she would hate being like this. Lately, I sometimes feel like Liz is dead, even though I can see her there in the bed. And I feel guilty because I'm having these feelings."

MJ swallowed and patted her mouth with her napkin. "The Liz you knew is gone, sweetheart. It doesn't mean you have to stop caring. Maybe you just have to care differently."

Tori absorbed that thought. "I know that she's gone. She's still my partner. I made promises to her." The phone rang, disrupting the all too serious conversation. "It's Bev," Tori said after checking the caller ID. A smile appeared on her face as she punched the answer button on the phone. "Hey there. To what do I owe the privilege of this phone call?" She listened as Bev spoke. "Oh really." Tori glanced over at MJ.

"What?"

"Oh, I think that could work."

MJ leaned forward trying to hear what Bev was saying. The conversation went on for another twenty or so seconds. "I'll ask her." Tori turned to MJ. "Bev wants to know if she can give Victor your phone number. He'd like to talk to you before we get together. Are you available Saturday night for dinner?"

MJ nodded.

Tori gave Bev the phone number. "She says she can make Saturday night." She listened for a few seconds as Bev told her how much she was looking forward to getting together. "No, I won't forget I'm seeing you for dinner. I'm looking forward to that, too." Just as Tori said goodbye, MJ's phone rang.

"Hello? Oh, yes. How are you, Victor?" MJ glanced over at Tori. She listened for a bit and laughed. "I'm sure we'll figure it out." She grew silent again as she listened. "That's very nice of you. Yes, I think that will be fun. I appreciate your calling and asking me in person. That was very considerate." A pause. "Yes, see you Saturday."

"What was so funny?"

"Victor. He said he couldn't figure out which of you was 'Yenta,' you know the matchmaker."

"I know who Yenta is. Remember, this wasn't my idea. So if it goes south, you can't blame me. Bev is in the hot seat for this one."

"I thought it was nice that he called to invite me to dinner himself and didn't play whisper down the lane from Bev to you and then to me. Something different, too, he's making all of us dinner. I don't think I've ever had a date cook for me. He has a nice voice too...deep and kinda sexy. Yum!"

Tori chuckled and shook her head. "Well, we all have something to think about for Saturday."

MJ looked up at the clock. "I'd better get back to work before they fire me."

"Fat chance. But I need to get busy, too. I'll see you on my way out."

AJ Adaire

Chapter Twelve

SATURDAY EVENING, TORI PICKED up Bev a half hour before they were due for dinner at Victor's house. They stopped on the way to pick up MJ and made their way there. Victor's home was a small Cape Cod style house located about ten miles north of their town. He welcomed them, bestowing a quick hug on each of them. "Come in, come in."

"Vic, this is my friend Tori and this is MJ. Ladies, my friend Victor."

"I'm glad to finally meet you both. I've heard a lot about each of you. I feel like I know you already."

"I always hate it when someone says that. It makes me wonder why my ears haven't been burning." Tori tugged her right ear for emphasis. "I guess my ESP is failing me."

"Trust me, I've only told him the good things," Bev joked. "We can gossip about the rest later, now that he's met you." Glancing over the contents of the room she said, "Vic, you got a new chair. I like it. I think the three of us could almost fit in it."

Victor laughed. "Thanks, I think. I finally found a chair that's comfortable for me." He turned to MJ. "You are the only one I trust enough to sit in my chair and not make fun. Bev, before MJ and Tori make themselves comfortable, would you mind giving them a tour while I open the wine?"

"No problem. However, I don't promise not to raid the underwear drawer to answer that age old question about boxers or briefs."

With a cocky smile, Vic reached for his belt buckle. "That's unnecessary. I can answer that question very easily."

"No," screamed Bev. "I'll behave, I promise. Come on ladies, before he carries out his threat." Bev led the group toward the stairs. MJ watched a grinning Victor walk away. Unobserved by the others, she let her eyes travel appreciatively over his extraordinary physique before she followed her friends.

Upstairs, Bev asked MJ, "So, what do you think? I told you he was tall, handsome, and nice."

"And big." MJ grinned. "You forgot to mention those shoulders. I watched him go through the doorway into the kitchen, curious to see if he'd he have to turn sideways to fit through. Yum."

Tori shook her head. "So shallow."

"Please behave. He's really nice and tall. Don't forget tall."

"It's interesting," Bev observed. "The night I told him about you and mentioned you were tall, he became really interested in meeting you. Like you, his preference is obviously for someone near to his own height. It's a match made in heaven."

Bev finished the tour of the house, ending up back at the counter separating the kitchen and dining room.

Victor grinned at them as he placed a glass of wine in front of each of them. "So, did you finish talking about me?"

"Everything about you is big, including your ego," Bev said.

"Tell me I'm wrong."

"You're wrong," they said in unison before they burst into laughter.

"Ladies, the salads are ready. Please join me."

They settled at the dining room table, passed around the dressing, and began enjoying their salads. MJ turned toward her host. "You have a lovely home. How long have you lived here, Victor?"

"Two years, give or take. I lived in a rental room for a couple of months when I first got here. Finally, I decided I liked living near the ocean, and I bought the house."

Looking at Tori, he asked, "Where are you from originally?"

"Pennsylvania, about two hours northwest of Philly."

"What about you, MJ?" Victor put his fork down to focus on MJ's response.

"I'm a local girl. Never lived more than two miles from where I live now. I grew up, and got a job right back in my hometown. I trained for nursing in Philly and returned here right after graduation."

"I am thankful for the medical care I had when I was injured, especially the nursing care. It takes a special person to be a nurse, I think. Your parents must be proud of you."

MJ smiled. "I just followed in my mother's footsteps."

Victor smiled and looked at MJ. "Then I know I'll like her already."

They finished the salads and passed the empty bowls towards the head of the table. Victor stood, gathered the plates, and carried them to the kitchen. He returned with a large tray of lasagna, which he portioned out. "There's obviously more if you want it."

MJ licked her lips and dabbed at her mouth with her napkin. "This is delicious, Victor."

"Thank you for cooking for us. We've all agreed that it's an unusual and pleasant change to have a man invite people for a homemade dinner. In our experience, men usually take their guests out for dinner."

"I'm glad I pleased you with the invitation. I hope I don't disappoint you when I tell you I did buy the dessert. There's a wonderful bakery down the street. I got us an amazing, cinnamon-walnut sour cream coffee cake. So save room."

After talking about their jobs, dinner conversation was a mixture of discussions about world affairs, local politics, and entertainment news. After the meal, they moved to the living room. MJ and Victor graciously endured gentle teasing from Bev when MJ declined Victor's generous offer to sit in his new chair.

"Come on T, I'll show you the patio." Bev took Tori's hand and pulled her toward the back door. "Victor has a lovely garden."

"I can't take the credit, I pay someone to take care of it."

Bev and Tori went outside while Victor and MJ continued to get acquainted. "It looks like you've made a good match, Bev."

"That would be nice, wouldn't it? They are both such nice people." There was a lull in the conversation until Bev said, "How long do you think we have to stay out here? I'm freezing."

"I'm glad you said that, me too. Come on, I have the car keys." They went around through the side yard and got into the car. Tori started the engine and cranked the heat to high. Once the car was warmed up, they turned it off and chatted until the air cooled again. "Shall we retrace our steps and return from the back?"

Bev laughed. "I can't believe this. The lengths friends will go to..."

Victor and MJ barely noticed the two women as they came inside. Because they seemed to be having a serious conversation, Bev pulled Tori into the kitchen. "Let's give them a few more minutes."

A short time later, Victor and MJ came to the counter and peered into the kitchen. "What are you two doing hiding out in here?"

Bev teased her friend. "Giving you a chance to get acquainted and ask MJ out on a real date."

"Ha. You could have come back five minutes after you left." His eyes crinkled as he smiled broadly. "We're going to see a movie tomorrow evening. I'd ask you to join us, but it would only be because I was being polite."

"Okay, on that note, I think it's time for us to head home." Bev poked Victor in the side and made a face that caused everyone to laugh.

Victor sent each of them home with a serving of lasagna and a piece of the cake. As everyone hugged goodbye at the door MJ got a kiss on the cheek from Victor, for which she endured five minutes of good-natured teasing after they settled in the car. MJ's comment about how quickly Tori's car heated up garnered a chorus of vigorous laughter from her friends.

"So what did you think of him, MJ?" Tori pulled from her parking spot and pointed the car toward home.

"He's got a great sense of humor, handsome, tall... I think he's too good to be true. You know, he told me about his war injury and how he lost his leg. Then he pulled up his pant leg and showed me his prosthesis. He said that he wanted me to see what I was getting myself into if I accepted his invitation for a date. Losing his leg has really shaken his confidence. He doesn't believe anyone would find him attractive or interesting now that he's 'damaged goods,' as he put it."

"Were you able to convince him that wasn't true?" Tori asked.

"Not completely. I'm hopeful, that given the opportunity, I will. Thank you, Bev for introducing me to him. He seems like a wonderful person."

The rest of the ride home they replayed the highlights of the evening until they dropped off MJ at her home. Tori stopped in front of Bev's condo and waited for her to unclip her seatbelt. Bev gripped the door handle but didn't turn it right away. "One disadvantage of working nights is that right about now, I'm coming fully awake."

"I know what you mean. Will you try to go to sleep now, or stay up a while?"

"I'll probably have some hot chocolate, then I'll read for a bit until I get sleepy. Care to join me?"

Tori thought about the offer. "I'd appreciate the company and the hot chocolate. Your place or mine?"

"Let me get my book. I'll be over in a few minutes. I want to change into warm ups first."

"I'll leave the door open for you. I'll put the kettle on to heat and get changed, too."

"See you in a few." Bev gave a wave and turned for her place.

Tori drove home and, finding all the on street parking taken, parked the car in her assigned spot.

Chapter Thirteen

TWENTY MINUTES LATER, BOOK in hand, Tori settled on the couch. Bev opted for the glider rocker opposite as they sipped their hot chocolate.

Bev set her mug on the coffee table, carefully centering it on the coaster. "That's so good, it really hits the spot, doesn't it?"

"Um hmm. It does."

"You've been quiet all evening. Are you okay?"

Tori shrugged a shoulder. "I guess so."

"Want to tell me what's on your mind?"

Tori ran her fingers through her dark, wavy hair and briefly intertwined her fingers at the back of her neck. Exhaling a sigh, she rested her forearms on her knees, leaning forward. She raised her eyes to meet Bev's patient gaze. "I was just thinking that this is the first evening since I moved here that I haven't spent with Liz."

"How does that feel?" Bev slipped out of her shoes and tucked her feet under her.

"I was just trying to figure that out. I mean, I did go to see her before I picked you up. Molly and Rose were on duty tonight. I think Molly is doing a double, so she'll be there overnight. If I can get some sleep a little later tonight, I'll get up early in the morning and go in to read her the newspaper."

"Okay, all that's fine. You haven't answered the question yet."

Tori's eyes wandered around the room taking in the sterile surroundings. "You're right."

Bev waited for Tori to finish her thought. Tori didn't continue, so she nudged. "I like being right. What exactly am I right about, that you didn't answer my question?"

"Yes." Tori smiled. "I know, about that and about your previous observation concerning my condo. You know, when you told me that there were no clues in my home about my life, no pictures of my life with Liz before her accident, no pictures of my parents, no collection of my favorite objects or artwork."

Bev exhaled in frustration as Tori took a sip of her hot chocolate using it to hide her grin. "I'm sorry, I'm not trying to be difficult. Okay, what I'm feeling...it's just that I'm, uh...not completely sure how I feel about taking a night for myself. To answer your question, guilt is a big part of how I'm feeling. I think I feel guilty, selfish, and maybe a little sad that I feel that way. I feel..." She stopped mid sentence to inhale, and pursed her lips in thought. "I feel tired and boring. In addition, I just looked around here and realized, that when you told me there were no clues to who I am in here, you were one hundred percent right. Truth is, I don't live here. I sleep here, I bathe here, and on rare occasions I eat here. But I don't actually live here." Tori took the last sip of her drink. "I stopped living my life the day Liz had her accident. Since that day I've been existing, surviving, not living."

"How long have you felt this way?"

Tori looked at her watch. "Maybe forty-five seconds."

"What do you mean?"

"I've felt this way for about forty-five seconds, since you asked and I attached labels to my emotions. No, that's not totally correct. I've been feeling guilty for a while now, maybe months. Guilty that I sometimes dread having to go there to visit and talk to Liz, knowing she won't respond in any way. In my mind, I know that she's gone. I just can't get my heart to admit it. Even if there were a miracle and she woke from her coma tomorrow, the Liz I knew would be gone. Her mind, her spirit, the essence of who she was...all gone." Her eyes filled until they could no longer contain the tears. Two huge drops tracked down her cheeks before Tori gave in to the tears she'd rarely allowed herself to shed since Liz's accident.

Bev moved quickly from the chair to sit next to her friend, pulling her close as Tori sobbed on her shoulder. Tori sat up, reached over, and pulled a tissue from the box on the end table next to her. As she wiped her eyes, she leaned back against Bev, seeking the comfort of her embrace. "I'm a mess. Why do you even bother?"

"Because I like you. You're kind, caring and loyal, and because I'm lonely, too. Because someday I may need to cry on your shoulder...that's what friends are for." To lighten the mood, Bev pretended to brush tears from her shirt. "Because it's a new day and I haven't had my shower yet."

Tori sniffed and gave a wan smile. "Sorry about that. Do you want a dry shirt?"

"No. I'm just teasing you." Bev leaned back pulling Tori's arm. "Turn around and let me hold you for a minute or two." Tori did as instructed, resting her head on Bev's shoulder. "Are you comfortable?"

"Yes, thank you." She sighed again, this time more out of contentment than frustration. "This feels good. I feel so selfish to be enjoying myself earlier tonight, and again now, with you."

"You think being selfish is a bad thing, I assume."

"Don't you?"

"Not always, and probably less so now than before I was ill. Although I believe in giving back, I also think that taking what I need from life to maintain a core level of happiness is what I should strive to do, otherwise I'd simply be wasting my existence. Maybe my cancer diagnosis, and the thought that my life might end before I'd had the opportunity to live it fully gave me a different perspective. Life is a precious gift. I believe it should be lived completely, fully, and happily. Taking what I need to do that is, in my opinion, just doing what I should be doing. Taking more than I need, *that* I might consider selfish...taking less, wasteful of my gift of life."

"I think I'll have to learn that balance." Tori rested her head, relaxing into Bev's embrace. "I feel exhausted. Dealing with feelings is tiring." She exhaled a long sigh. Moments later she lost her struggle to keep her eyes open.

Tori's deep breathing revealed that she was asleep. Bev glanced around and spotted a throw on the back of the sofa. Reaching her arm behind her, as slowly as possible, she pulled the throw over them and shifted to a more comfortable angle. Still asleep, Tori adjusted her position, turning to slide further up on Bev's chest, she slipped her hands around her back at the waist, and cuddled against her.

Bev inhaled the clean scent of Tori's hair and wrapped the sleeping woman in her arms. *If the reason for this affection weren't so sad, this would be nice. After nearly six years, it feels good to be close to someone like this. She's comfortable with me now, fully clothed. How would she feel if we were naked? Maybe not so comfortable, eh? Connie couldn't stand looking at me, and she supposedly loved me. I guess it's a good thing that Tori and I agreed that we'll just remain friends. She's not really free anyway, and she's made it clear that her first and only priority is Liz. It's admirable, for sure that she's remained steadfast all this time, knowing that the person she was in a relationship with will never come back to her.*

Forty-five minutes later, Tori sighed before giving a start. Suddenly she awoke and sat up. "Oh, I'm so sorry."

"Please don't be. I genuinely enjoyed being able to do that for you, and glad that you trusted me enough. To me, it was a gift."

Tori cupped Bev's face with her palm. "To me as well."

Chapter Fourteen

FOUR DAYS LATER, TORI found a parking space about a block away from Karolina's office. She was about ten minutes early, so she took her time walking to her destination. There was a short wait before Karolina opened her office door and invited Tori in.

Tori slowly settled into the chair opposite her and Karolina smiled and welcomed her. "So, tell me, how was your week?"

"It was interesting, in many different ways. I did the reading assignment you suggested."

"What did you think about it?"

Tori adjusted her position in her seat, leaning back as she relaxed into the conversation. "It was one of the interesting things that comprised my week. I've never thought about what has happened since Liz's accident in a chronological way before. I also read that not everyone progresses through the stages in order. I believe that was true in my case. I think I started with bargaining after which I went through denial. Therefore, I didn't follow the order as the articles delineated it. Unfortunately, I think I'm stuck at the depression stage."

"What makes you think you're stuck?"

"Maybe stuck is an incorrect word choice. It's just that I haven't moved through that stage."

"What do you think it is that's been holding you in that place?"

Tori thought about the question. It was not something she'd really considered. She'd recognized her failure to move through that stage, although had given no consideration as to why. "I'm not sure. I'm sorry."

"No need to be sorry. Maybe we can work to figure that out. I think the time you came for your first visit you told me you were feeling guilty. Would you like to examine those feelings?"

"Yes, if it will help me."

"Good. I think it would be beneficial to continue our discussion about it." Karolina rocked back in her chair. "What does guilt mean to you, Tori?"

Tori studied the ceiling for a few seconds, organizing her thoughts. "Well there's guilt in the classical sense, like if you break a law or a rule, commit a crime or some other offense to society. You might be found guilty in that sense. Or, even if not caught, you might feel guilty because you did something you felt you shouldn't have done, or conversely, something you should have done and didn't."

"Okay. That's very good. You have defined guilt in the classical sense. Focus on the latter part of your definition where you said guilt was a feeling related to doing something you should not have done, or should have done. Now, from my favorite source, me..." Karolina waited for Tori to look up and smiled. "You touched on what I think we should focus on, guilt as an emotion that occurs when someone believes that they haven't lived up to a societal standard."

Tori's brows furrowed. "I don't understand."

"Let's take the definitions one at a time." She pulled up the word guilt on her computer and queried Tori based on the definition she found there. "Have you committed an offense?

"No."

Karolina nodded. "Okay, how about a crime, or done anything wrong that violates a moral or judicial law or a standard we live by as a society?"

"I don't think so." Tori shrugged. "Perhaps, if anything, I've failed to live up to what I perceive is what's expected. None of the rest." Tori met Karolina's gaze. "I've been a loyal partner to Liz. Since her accident, I've spent every spare minute I have with her, supported her as much as possible." Tori looked down and studied her fingernails. "Recently, I've had a hard time continuing to do that, to give her that much time, to focus all my attention on her. I feel empty, like I just have no reserve left to continue as I have been. That's where my conflict comes from. I feel like I should continue to do what I've been doing for Liz. I should continue to spend most of my day with her, to be sure she has stimulation and, you know, to be there for her. If I fail to do that I would feel in violation of what the proper thing to do is, or maybe what people, what society expects of me."

Karolina glanced at the ceiling as she tapped her finger against her lip, composing her thoughts. "Ah...should, one of my favorite words. *Should* is the root of many evils. What does the word should mean to you, Tori?"

Tori considered the question. "I guess we use the word should to express the sensible or right thing to do."

Karolina smiled. "Right or sensible in whose opinion?" Karolina emphasized the last three words by poking the desktop with her index finger as she said them. "Whose 'should' is it, Tori, that you must continue to be involved at the same level you have been in Liz's care and day to day life? Is the 'should' your own? In other words, do you feel other people expect it of you, or do you expect it of yourself and are failing to meet your own expectations?"

Tori didn't answer right away, as she usually did.

After a reasonable length of time, Karolina said, "It's okay if you can't answer that question just yet. You can think about it and we can address it next time."

"No. I think that it's a mixture of both. Mostly, I think it's my own expectations of what I should do." Tori humphed. "Should..."

"All right. So you have a set of standards for yourself, based upon a combination of what you think others expect of you, and what you expect of yourself, correct?"

"Yes, I believe that's true."

"Have you ever considered that your expectations are too stringent, or that you have set standards that are too difficult to maintain for an extended period of time? Think about it. Perhaps initially, one could or should expect that you would want to be at your lover's side after an accident as often and as frequently as possible. Six months pass, her condition worsens and hope begins to fade for a positive recovery...you don't adjust your standards. A year passes, then another, and again no adjustment. I think you might find it helpful to examine the possibility that your guilt or internal conflict stems in part from the fact that you haven't adjusted your responses to several new sets of stimuli over the past nearly three years. I suspect your guilt might be stemming from your being unable to maintain what might have been expected to be a short-term response on a long-term basis." Karolina closed her laptop. "You told me that you are not the one legally responsible for Liz's care, her parents are. How much are they doing? Could they do a little more so you could pull back a little?"

"So, you think I should be spending less time with Liz?"

"What I think you should be doing is not the least bit important. It is more important what you think. That's your assignment for this week. Okay?"

"Yes."

Karolina glanced at the clock. "Now, we're growing short of time for this session. Is there anything you want to address?"

Tori nodded. "Yes. I've been seeing quite a bit of Bev. We're becoming good friends. She asked to meet Liz because she wants to read to her. So I took her there and introduced them. I think having her there when I visit Liz sometimes might help by facilitating conversation. I mean at least there's another person responding. Now it's not always a one sided dialogue. She's only come twice so far. Her being there seemed to make visiting less..." Tori shrugged. "I guess the word I'm looking for is stressful. Bev's a very kind and sensitive person. I like her very much. Having another friend has been a boost to my spirits."

Karolina nodded her approval. "I'm happy to hear that."

"I actually took Saturday night off. Bev arranged a blind date between my friend, MJ, and her friend, Victor. Victor cooked all of us dinner and we had a nice time."

"How do you feel about doing that?"

"It was the first night I've taken for myself since I moved here. I really enjoyed it, but afterward I felt guilty and selfish, of course." Tori quickly related the conversation she had with Bev about being selfish and Bev's perception of selfishness.

"I think she raises some valid points for you to consider, don't you?"

"Yes." Tori smiled. "You know, thinking is hard work and takes a lot of time. I suspect I'm probably feeling a bit less guilty because I don't have enough time to fit it in."

Karolina and Tori's laughter brightened the mood of the session. "I guess we'll view that as forward progress then and ask you to do some more thinking. Okay, as we discussed, this week I want you to consider the expectations you've set for yourself and your 'shoulds.'" Karolina made air quotes around the word 'shoulds.' "Think also about the source of your guilt, consider whose shoulds are causing those feelings. Finally, if you can, take some time for yourself and do something you enjoy, even if it's only taking a nap during the time you would normally be at the nursing center. Go out for dinner, see a movie, sit in the sunshine, whatever will give you pleasure. The objective is to give yourself permission to do this and not feel guilty about it, or at least feel less guilty about it."

"Okay, I'll try."

"Don't try, do." Karolina stood. "This was a good session. I hope you will find it helpful as you give it some more thought. See you next week."

AJ Adaire

Chapter Fifteen

NO TIME LIKE THE present to start my assignment. Tori left Karolina's office, got in her car, and drove home instead of heading for the center. She stuffed a few dollars into her pocket and headed up to the boardwalk finally settling on her favorite bench. It was a glorious day, with a bright blue sky, comfortably warm temperature, and the sound of the ocean to soothe her. Two gulls perched on the lamp post above her and called out a loud protest about some imagined slight. She leaned back, closed her eyes, and turned her face up to the sunshine. Relaxation flowed through her as the sun warmed her.

Replaying her conversation with Karolina, her mind churned with thoughts about selfishness, expectations and shoulds. *Have I set unrealistic goals for myself?* She thought back to the time when Liz's parents moved their daughter to the center. *I only saw Liz on Saturdays and Sundays, maybe a total of between twelve and fourteen hours per week. Was I comfortable with that?* She recalled feeling frustrated that she couldn't see Liz more often during the week. The trips she made midweek were too harrowing and she'd given up on making them after a few weeks. Once she got her in-laws to agree to allow the nursing staff to give her updates on Liz's condition, she made it a point to check in everyday, by phone. She usually called them in the morning before work, either at lunchtime or dinnertime, and always before she went to bed. She still missed Liz back then. But they had friends who invited her to dinner or stopped by their house for a quick visit. She recalled playing cards with them and going to cookouts. *I had a life then, despite the fact that Liz was hospitalized. Other than MJ, and now Bev, I haven't made any friends here, nor have I done anything fun on a regular basis. I remember going to the bird sanctuary in Cape May and feeling pressure to get back. When did I become so rigid about spending so much time with Liz? I remember thinking it was sad that her parents didn't come very often and they lived so close. Was I trying to prove to them or to someone that I cared for Liz more than they did? When did that translate into guilt, if I missed a visit or didn't stay as long as usual?* Tori didn't bother to open her eyes when she felt someone sit on the bench.

"T, you asleep?"

The familiar voice and scent brought a smile. Tori turned and stared into Bev's beautiful blue eyes and felt her spirits lift. "Hey, you. What are you doing here?"

"I was going for my run and saw you sitting here sun worshiping. What's happening?"

"Not much. Just doing some thinking. I saw Karolina today. She gave me a couple of assignments. Although I know it didn't look like it, I was working hard on them."

"Want to share?"

"Not just yet. I'm just starting to put together some thoughts. Maybe when they're better organized I'll take advantage of your offer."

"Fair enough, whenever you're ready. So, you heading in to visit Liz soon?"

Tori glanced at her watch and sighed. "I guess. I think I'll grab a quick sandwich or burger before I go in."

"Want some company? Maybe we could grab something together and afterward I could come with you to read to Liz. I have an e-book on my tablet that I've been putting off reading for longer than I should have."

Tori noticed the use of the word should. "Putting off...how come?"

"I bought it a long time ago. I bought it...well, let's just say years ago and leave it at that."

"What's it about?"

"It's about a woman who loses her partner to breast cancer. The blurb says it's a story that deals with the woman's rebirth after the event. I thought it would give me a better perspective. I guess the thought of it sounded a bit too depressing at the time. I don't think I got past the first couple of pages."

"Why now?"

"I don't know. I mean, I met the challenge, didn't I? I survived. So the book that I was so afraid to read after I was diagnosed shouldn't hold me hostage anymore. So I figured I'd start it and see how it goes."

"Why read it at all?"

"I like the author and I bought it because I wanted to read it. More importantly, I started it. I don't think I've ever left unfinished a book I started. I know it probably sounds a bit compulsive, but I'm very disciplined about that."

"I see." Tori paused. "You know, Bev, if it will make it easier for you, we can take turns reading. If the beginning is hard for you, I can read that part. I finished that story Liz and I were reading, so it'd be a good time to start a new one."

"Sounds good. Want to take me up on my offer and start today?"

"Sure, let's go grab a bite to eat, then we'll give it a shot."

They went to a family restaurant on the main street of town where they split a hoagie and a salad. Tori stopped home to change before she drove to the center. Bev was already in Liz's room when Tori arrived. She paused at the door to eavesdrop.

"So, Liz, this is a book I bought some time ago, just before I was diagnosed with breast cancer. I had a partner then, named Connie..."

Tori withdrew and went back to the nurses' desk to get an update on Liz's condition. Satisfied that all was well, Tori returned to Liz's room, tapped at the door, and entered.

"Hey, Tori, there you are. I've been telling Liz a little about this book. Liz and I have been waiting for you so we can start the story. We agreed this had to be better than the one on the nightstand, even if the first few chapters are depressing."

Tori laughed. "I'm sure. Do you want me to begin?"

"Yes, that would be nice."

Tori started the book. At the conclusion of the first three chapters, Bev took over and read three more chapters. Looking up, Bev said to Tori. "This is pretty good. I can't believe I let this story intimidate me for six years. It's not even about the actual death of the woman, more about the aftermath for her partner. I think I initially read the first paragraph or two and just couldn't go any further."

"You should celebrate the conquering of your fear."

Bev laughed and cast her eyes upward. "Give me a break. We read a book, we didn't conquer Everest." She closed the e-reader, and stood. "I think I'll let you spend some time alone with Liz. I'm going to meet Victor for a coffee before we go to work. I want to get the details about how things are going with MJ."

"Give me a call later, okay? I'll get the scoop from MJ and we'll compare notes and see how we did." Their laughter mingled. "Say hello to Victor for me. Thanks, too, for visiting Liz and reading with us. It was fun."

"My pleasure. We can continue the story tomorrow, if you'd both like." Bev stood and walked to the door giving Tori a quick wave. "Goodnight."

Tori returned the wave with a smile. She turned back to Liz. "Well, that was fun. I hope you're enjoying the story as much as I am. I didn't realize it was a romance. You'll like that." Tori told Liz about her day, again skipping her visit to Karolina. Forty-five minutes before she had to report to work, she stood. She brushed her fingers along Liz's cheek. "I'm off to work. I'll see you later." She waved to the staff as she passed the nurses' desk and took the stairs to her office. With over a half hour until she had to sign in, she unlocked the door and adjusted the shades in the window facing the hallway so that light came in through the shades while no one could see in. Thankful she had some time alone to review her thoughts, she made her way around her desk and sank into her chair as she exhaled a long breath and allowed her thoughts to wander.

Tori's cell phone buzzed indicating she had a text message. Probably MJ wondering what time we're getting together for break. She pulled out her phone to check. A rush of pleasure washed over her when she discovered that the message was from Bev.

'Hi...thinking about you and hoping you have a good night. If you have time, give me a call later.'

From memory, Tori typed in Bev's number on her desk phone, waiting patiently as the connection went through and the phone began to ring. Bev answered on the third ring. "Hey T. Glad you called. You at work or still with Liz?"

"No, I'm in my office. I wanted a few quiet minutes to think a bit. Your text saved me from myself." Tori felt sure, that through the tone of her voice, Bev would know she was smiling.

"You didn't have to call me right back."

"I know that. I wanted to. I always enjoy talking to you. It's a bright spot in my day if I get to talk to you."

"Really? I'm glad. Mine too. So have you made any more progress on your assignment from Karolina?"

"Funny you ask. I came up here to spend some time doing just that before I had to start work." Tori turned her desk chair around to look out the window at the parking lot. The stragglers for the night shift were hurrying to make it into the building as quickly as possible.

86

"So let's hang up so you can have your alone time."

"I'd rather talk to you. It's a lot more fun than trying to figure out my assignment."

"Anything I can help with?" Bev switched the phone to her other ear and saved the file on her computer. "I don't mean the offer to be nosey. Sometimes, I think, it helps to bounce things off of someone else."

"Well, I'm not sure what you can do, even though I appreciate the offer. I have to figure out why I'm feeling so guilty and how I managed to get myself into this box I find myself living in."

"Can you explain in a bit more depth? I'm not sure I understand what you mean. What makes you feel guilty?"

"Time. Time I spend with Liz and time I don't. Lately, I'm having some difficulty being here, yet I feel guilty when I'm not. I'm trying to figure out my shoulds."

"Shoulds?"

"Yeah, you know...like 'How did I come to figure I should be spending as much time as I do with Liz?' and 'Why do I feel so guilty when I no longer enjoy doing so?' I love Liz, so why am I having such a hard time being with her?"

"T, I can't imagine anyone thinking you don't love Liz. You've been so dedicated to her. So much so that it's sometimes to your own detriment. When was the last time you had a vacation?"

"Vacation?" Tori repeated the word as if it were foreign. "Um, about six months before Liz's accident."

"And that was what...three years ago?"

"Roughly, give or take."

"Everything I've ever read says that an illness is often more difficult on the caregiver than the person who is ill. So, the best thing the caregiver can do for the person they are caring for, is to take care of themselves first. It's like that thing when you travel on a plane with children...they say if the oxygen masks drop down, you should put it on yourself first, before you strap the mask to the child. Maybe you're having trouble being there has little to do with Liz or your feelings for her, maybe it's happening because you're just worn out."

"Interesting observation. I'll give that some thought. Thank you for your input. Having your perspective is helpful."

"I'd better get back to what I'm doing and you're about to start your shift. Call me later if you have time."

"Thanks Bev. I'll call you back around three, when I take my break. Take care." Tori depressed the switch hook, continuing to hold the phone in her hand as her thoughts raced. She replaced the receiver, reluctant to break the connection, and turned toward the window. Her mind drifted to thoughts of being wrapped in Bev's arms. *It felt so good and so right. How could anything that felt so right be so wrong? It would be wrong on so many levels. Wrong for me, I'm already committed to Liz. Wrong for Bev, she'd just end up getting hurt. Still, we fit together so perfectly.* Tori recalled looking up at Bev's lips. They looked so soft and kissable. *Oh God!* Tori moaned softly. *I'm really in trouble here.*

Four hours later, MJ appeared at Tori's office door. "Ready for break?"

"Yes. More than ready." Tori put aside the inventory she was working on. "Have you heard from Victor?"

"As a matter of fact I have. We did the movie on Sunday. He's so nice. I really enjoyed our time together. We're going out again this weekend, probably just for a movie and pizza. You and Bev want to come? He said it was okay to ask you."

"That's very generous of him...let me think about it and talk it over with Bev. Don't you think you should get to know him one on one? You already had Bev and me hanging around on your first date."

MJ shrugged. "We don't mind. He's very comfortable to be around. I don't feel like this will only be our third date. The comfort level I feel with him is amazing. Being with him...it's like I've known him forever. Besides, we all have fun when we're together. I love the way Bev and Victor tease each other. I can't thank Bev enough for introducing us. You know, she's a great person..." MJ arched her eyebrows.

"And?"

"That's all. Nice."

"She is."

MJ drummed her fingers on the table. "Okay, are you being deliberately obtuse? What's up with you two?" MJ asked.

"Nothing. We're friends. That's it."

MJ began unpacking her meal. "You're really great together. I'm glad to see you doing things with her. I think she's good for you. She makes you laugh, and that's always a good thing."

"I know." Tori took out her protein bar and opened her bottle of water. "MJ, do you think I spend too much time with Liz?"

"I'm not sure how to answer that. I think you have to decide what's right for you. You know from experience that we have patients here who have no one come to visit them, others have visitors monthly, weekly, and then...there's you and Liz. She's an extremely fortunate woman to have you care for her the way you do. I'm not saying you're wrong to spend so much time with her, please don't misunderstand me. It's just that, sometimes, I worry about your health. I think it is extremely difficult to maintain a positive attitude under the circumstances. You've been told that she'll never recover, yet I think some small part of you still believes otherwise."

"Yes. At first I believed that without a doubt. Now, I think I'm accepting that the Liz I knew is gone and will never come back to me. I just can't walk away from her."

"I don't think anyone expects that. However, you spend your entire life here at the center. 'Your entire life' are the key words in that sentence, in case you missed them. With 'your' being the most critical. Work, time with Liz...where is your life, Tori?"

Tori searched MJ's face for more insight about what she wasn't saying. She found nothing but caring and kindness there. "I'll be honest with you. I'm only beginning to admit all of this to myself." Tori's eyes filled. "Can I tell you something else?"

"Anything. You know that. What's wrong?"

"I don't know if wrong is the right word for what I'm feeling. I feel conflicted, I guess. You know I've been spending time with Bev. Well. Uh..."

"Come on Tori. Spill it. Just say what you're feeling. I'm not Judge Judy. I won't pass judgment on your feelings."

Tori reached out and squeezed MJ's hand. "I know you won't. I'm just now coming to accept what I'm feeling myself." Hesitating at first, she finally blurted, "I think I'm growing dependent on sharing time with Bev." Tori searched MJ's face for a reaction.

"Is that a bad thing?"

"I'm not sure yet." Tori exhaled a long breath and rested her chin on her palm. "I look forward to spending time with her. I feel alive with her. I laugh with her. And, when she comes to read to Liz, we have fun. It's just so different having her there with me."

"Well, of course it is. It's good that your time with Bev is fun and that your visit with Liz is fun. Nothing wrong with that."

"I guess." Tori glanced away, disappearing into her thoughts.

Silence hung between them.

Enough time elapsed that MJ finished the last bite of her sandwich. Her gaze conveyed an expectation of more explanation. With none forthcoming, her patience gave out. "Is there more?"

Tori pulled her mind back to her friend. "She held me."

MJ leaned forward waiting for Tori to tell her more.

"That's all. I cried and she held me. It felt so good. I've missed and needed that so much." Tori wiped her hands over her face. "It would be so easy to love Bev, to fall into her embrace, to..."

"I hear a 'but' coming."

"Yeah, of course you do. I'm not free, MJ. I have Liz. And because of that, I wouldn't only be unfair to Liz, I'd be unfair to Bev if I got involved with her." Tori toyed with the ring on her ring finger that matched the band that Liz wore. "I'm not a cheat. At least I have never thought of myself as being able to cheat. Liz and I promised each other our fidelity. At the time, I never imagined I'd be facing a life with Liz like this." Tori ran her fingers through her hair, stopping half way through and supporting her head in her hands. "Obviously, I'm having a hard time here." She released her head and looked directly at MJ and gave her a wan smile.

"I'm sure you didn't. Who would?"

"It could be so easy with Bev. I could just lose myself into the moment with Bev. It would be great to be with her. I was drawn to her before I even met her, used to watch her run. And now that I know her..." Seconds passed. "If I did anything with her though, afterward..." Tori shook her head, emptying her mind of the vision of making love with Bev. "There would still be Liz. She'd still be here in the center, and I'd be a liar and a cheat. And guilty, let's not forget guilty. We both know it's my middle name, don't we?"

MJ laughed. "You amaze me. All this serious talk, and you end it with something that makes me laugh. "I love you Tori. Wanting Bev is so human. She's a wonderful person. She obviously cares for you. She's fun, vibrant, and alive, not to mention hot. And that last part came from a straight woman. I do wonder, though, how much of what you're feeling is guilt, and how much is sadness over the realization and acceptance of the fact that the Liz you knew died in that accident."

Tori stopped to consider MJ's question having not contemplated it before. "I'm not sure."

"That's okay. You're going to be feeling a whole mixture of feelings. I've seen it many times. It's best to accept that you're growing into a new kind of relationship with Liz. Maybe you need to examine and adjust or change the rules, the expectations you have, and to recognize that sometimes there are growing pains associated with change."

"What will people think if I change what I've been doing?"

MJ looked puzzled. "You mean will they think negatively about you?"

"Yes."

"I don't think they'll think anything negative at all. I think the behavioral expectations you have are your own and no one else's."

"Thanks MJ. I appreciate your honesty."

"You can always count on that much from me."

"I know that. Thanks for listening and not condemning me. I feel a bit better now that we've talked. So, what's new with you?"

MJ folded up her lunch bag. "Well now that we've got you sorted out, let's talk about that hunk a hunk of burning mankind, Victor. Umm, umm, umm...oh baby!" She tried to rub her hands together while still holding her lunch bag.

Tori laughed at her friend. "I owe you that much, I guess."

Chapter Sixteen

"COME IN TORI. HOW are you?" Karolina returned to her seat behind her desk and waited for Tori to settle in the chair opposite her.

"I'm doing okay. You'll be pleased to know I took your advice. On Saturday evening I again went out with my friends."

"And how did that feel?"

"It felt good to be with people and it felt a little bad at the same time."

"Okay. You said bad, not guilty."

"Don't get too excited." She smiled. "I think I felt bad because I felt guilty." Tori gave a small chuckle and shrugged. "I thought about the 'shoulds' this week, a lot. I even talked to Bev and MJ about it." Tori related the conversations she'd had with her friends about her feelings and her assignment.

"So have you come to any conclusions?"

Tori tipped her head. "To some extent. I think I've concluded that I'm the one who is imposing the standards upon myself. I'm feeling guilty because I expect more, expect better of myself, and I think that's why I'm feeling the way I do. I'm letting myself down."

"I see. And..."

Tori looked at Karolina's kind face, seeing the support she needed. "I'd like to change."

"Ah. Change. Change is difficult for a number of reasons. Sometimes we resist it ourselves. Sometimes we meet resistance from others when we try to do it. Even if everyone around us is in favor of us changing, the path is not always straightforward...it zigs and zags. There are moments of brilliance where it appears that we are racing to achieve the goal, and then backslides that make us want to surrender to our old ways. So, how do we accomplish change? First, and probably most important, is setting realistic goals. Do you have a goal or goals in mind?"

"I think so."

"Good. We can talk about them in a couple of minutes. First, I need you to tell me a little more about Liz. What was she like?"

"In a word, wonderful. She had a fabulous laugh. We laughed a lot. She was always into something new."

"Describe her in five adjectives."

"Hmm." Tori took a few seconds to organize her response. "Okay. Tender, generous, unselfish, caring, and...um...fun."

"No negatives?"

"No."

"So she was perfect?"

"Nobody is perfect. I think she was perfect for me."

"So you never fought or disagreed?"

Tears welled and spilled from Tori's eyes. She reached for a tissue and struggled to compose herself.

Karolina waited for Tori to compose herself. "What just happened?"

Tori looked up, took a deep breath and exhaled slowly. "We rarely had cross words. Most of the time we only fought about her parents, and how much they disapproved of our relationship. Mostly that was centered around the holiday. That morning of her accident, before she left for work, we were talking about her parents coming for the holidays. We were arguing about it really. It was the first time that I ever remember her leaving the house that she didn't kiss me good-bye. She was really pissed that I told her if her parents were coming to stay for the holiday, I was going to go home to visit my folks. We'd talked so long that she was running late." A sob burst from Tori. "It was my fault she got hurt. I made her late."

Karolina handed Tori several tissues and waited for her to regain her composure.

"I've never told anyone that before. I've been so guilty about it. It was my fault."

"No. It was an accident."

"I made her late."

"No, Tori. You and she had a disagreement. She chose to stay for the disagreement, for the discussion about it. She could have asked you to wait to discuss it later. She was an equal partner in the decision to stay to argue about it. You did not cause the accident, Tori. You were not responsible for Liz getting hurt."

"I think that, initially, I couldn't accept that it was nothing more than an accident. When it first happened, I vacillated between being angry with her, then with me, blaming her for not being careful enough and me for making her late. If I wasn't blaming her, I was assuming the total responsibility. Like maybe the accident was punishment for my being selfish and not understanding that she wanted her parents to visit." Tori sniffed, wiped her eyes, and her nose. "I finally settled on the fact that her accident was completely my fault, you know...that if I hadn't delayed her that morning, fighting. If I hadn't wanted my own way, she wouldn't have needed to be careful because she'd already have been at work at the time of the accident."

"Thank you for sharing that with me, Tori. I'd like to remind you, again, that we each make our own decisions. She had a choice to stay and discuss your issue or leave for work in a timely fashion. Remember that one critical point—she made the decision. Today, that decision and who made it is irrelevant. What happened is a fact of life. You can't go back and change it. You are living in the here and now. It's time to forgive both her, and yourself for whatever part you feel you played, whomever was responsible, and whatever happened, so you can move forward with less guilt." The timer on Karolina's desk gave a gentle ping reminding them there were only five minutes remaining in the session. "I'm sorry, Tori. Unfortunately, our time is up for today. We made good progress today at getting to the basis for some of your guilty feelings. I'd like to see you before next Wednesday, if possible. I have an opening on Friday if you'd like to continue our discussion."

Tori nodded. "Please."

"I'll add you in. In the next couple of days, I'd like you to think about trying to let go of those guilty feelings. I can tell you it won't happen in two days...still, you have to start somewhere, and the business of forgiving yourself for any guilt, real or manufactured, over the accident is, I think, a good place to begin."

"How do I do that?"

"Do you have any ideas that you think might help?" Karolina asked.

"Maybe confessing my secret to someone would help. I also think that I need to tell Liz, to apologize to Liz."

"Those are two good ideas. And don't forget yourself in this process. Listen to your inner voice and be gentle and compassionate with yourself. The person who most needs your forgiveness is you."

Karolina paused to let Tori absorb that concept. Tori nodded and Karolina continued. "You need to grant forgiveness to yourself, Tori. I know that's a tall order, and it may seem a daunting task. Just remember every journey starts with just one small step. We talked earlier about setting some goals. You said you had some in mind. In your spare time, begin thinking about what you want to achieve. We'll start with them next time." Karolina smiled. "We made good progress today. I'm sorry we're out of time."

"That's okay. I think I need some time to process all we've discussed today. Thank you for seeing me again on Friday."

"You're welcome. Until then, be gentle with yourself, and don't forget to do something fun."

Tori laughed and replied, "I don't know how I'll fit it in."

***

Sitting in Karolina's small waiting area on Friday afternoon, Tori paged through the list of e-mail messages on her cell while she waited patiently for Karolina to open the door and invite her into the office. At last the door opened. "Tori. Welcome. Come on in."

Tori returned the greeting, entered the office and sat down.

"Tell me about how you're feeling. How have the last two days been?"

"Busy." Tori flashed a quick smile. "I've done a lot of thinking and some research into Liz's condition. On Wednesday, after our session, I asked for some references from MJ and I did a lot of reading about the potential for recovery from Liz's type of injury. In reading about conditions similar to hers, the first thing I discovered is that it's amazing she's still alive and that one of the infections she's had hasn't taken her life. I found some sobering statistics regarding recovery. Liz is six years older than I am, so she's now forty-three. Considering her age, her potential for recovery without permanent and pervasive delays, is considered statistically irrelevant. Not that I didn't know this on some level...it's just that reading case studies on it were extremely sobering.

"I recalled that, back in the beginning, the doctors described some of this, although they were hopeful at the time for recovery. I think I just forgot or discounted some of what they told us, was simply unwilling to believe it, and I put the possibility she'd end up like this right out of my mind. Reading and seeing the statistics in black and white, was...overwhelming. I think the most damning sentence I read was the one that described her condition as personality death. Even if she were to miraculously recover from the coma, the Liz I knew, the Liz I loved, is gone." Tori paused to gather strength as her eyes filled. "I'm slowly coming to accept that fact. I think, on some level I'd always believed, I always hoped, that if she woke up she'd at least still know me, still love me. I didn't care that she might be paralyzed. That's not important. I just wanted Liz back...to be able to talk and share things the way we used to. I'm finally beginning to believe that's never going to happen."

"How does that change things for you?"

"I think it's helped me begin to accept that this situation is a reality, a permanent way of life. I'm not living a nightmare that, some morning, I'm going to wake up from to discover it's been a bad dream. Some of what we discussed on Wednesday is helping too. I apologized to Liz and told her I hoped she'd forgive me for whatever part I played in the accident. Told her how sorry I was we fought and that I didn't get to kiss her good-bye. I told her how sad I felt that the last words we exchanged were angry ones. Then, I talked with MJ last night and told her my secret. You know about my feeling that Liz's accident happened because I'd made Liz late that morning." Tori made quote marks with her fingers.

"How did she respond?"

"Much the same way you did. MJ told me many of the same things."

"How did you feel about telling her?"

"Afraid, guilty...isn't guilty my middle name? God, I'm so tired of feeling that way." Tori humphed. "MJ was great, as always. She held me while I blubbered about how I was afraid she'd hate me when I told her." Tori smiled. "I told Bev, too, just before I came here."

"Her response?"

"The same. She said she could understand why I might feel as I do. While she had cancer, she did a lot of what she described as positive affirmation while she was recovering. She taught me a bit about it, and despite not having enough time to finish our discussion, I can see where it could be beneficial. She's going to help me develop my affirmations later. She thinks I can use them to help me forgive myself."

"I like that and believe it will be very helpful for you. You are making amazing progress. Did you get a chance to think about your goals?"

Tori nodded. "A bit. I think if I accept that Liz's condition is permanent, or at least ongoing, I know I can't continue providing the same level of support I've been doing. I feel horrible admitting it, but

I'm just drained. I sometimes feel I'm so depleted that I have nothing more to give, not only to Liz—to anyone. I feel depressed and boring. I know, probably have known on some level for some time now, that I need to take more time for myself. So my first goal is to give myself permission to do that, to have some fun. Liz was always a generous partner. She wanted me to maintain my individual interests. Unlike many lesbian couples who are joined at the hip, we each had separate interests as well as shared ones. She wanted me to pursue my hobbies and my individual friendships. She believed that we would enrich each other's lives that way and would each continue to grow. After her accident, I think I forgot about that. Recalling it will, I think, help me to allow myself to take some 'me' time."

"I agree." Karolina glanced at the time. "Consider, too, that you are not the only support that Liz has. You've told me the nursing staff, especially your friend MJ, is very good to Liz. Now she has Bev, too. And her parents obviously care."

Tori rolled her eyes.

"I'm sure they had to face many of the same feelings you are facing now. They've dealt with it in their own way and have come to their own peace."

"I know. I shouldn't judge." Tori chuckled. "There's that word again."

Karolina smiled as she nodded. "Shoulds rule our lives. Both our own, and those of friends and others who always think they know what is right, that their way is the better way, or even the only way."

Tori nodded her agreement. "I used to worry that while I wasn't there, Liz had no stimulation. Bev has been visiting Liz regularly and is reading to her when I'm not able to be there. Sometimes, we read to her together. That's actually fun. It makes me feel better about cutting back on my visits a bit. She's picking up some of my slack."

"Have you established goals regarding your frequency of visits?"

"No. I don't want a rigid schedule. I think sometimes I'll feel better than others about not going in as often as I have been. I'd like to allow myself the option of changing it up, maybe to sleep in if I feel I need to, or to go somewhere special, should an interesting offer present itself." Tori shrugged. "Foremost, I want to not feel guilty about it, when I take time for myself."

"Good job, Tori. You've set reasonable, attainable goals for yourself. You've given yourself permission to be flexible depending on your feelings, and know that sometimes this change will feel right and sometimes it won't. Remembering Liz as a generous person who loved you and wanted you to be happy will help with the guilt."

"I hope so. I know that, as painful as it is for me to make changes, I can't go on like I have been. I've become an unhappy person, someone I hardly recognize and don't like too much. I'm glad I came to see you. I know that we discussed the fact that progress would not be a straight path forward, but rather a zigzag journey with some retracing of previously traveled ground. Still, I feel I've begun to make some progress and I feel more comfortable. Thank you for helping me."

"I'm glad you're feeling that way, Tori, and that our discussions are helping you." Karolina glanced at the clock. "I'm afraid our time is up for now. I'll see you next week at our regular time?"

"Yes."

Karolina stood and walked with Tori to the door where they said good-bye.

AJ Adaire

Chapter Seventeen

TORI LEFT HER SESSION and drove over to the center to visit Liz. She had just settled in when her phone rang. "Hi Bev, what's up?"

"I'm here with Victor. He has a question he'd like to ask the two of you. Well, the three of us technically, although I already know the question."

"Now I'm really curious. MJ isn't on duty right now, she won't be in until later. I can probably get together with her and call you back during one of our breaks."

"Good. You seeing Liz?"

"Yes, till I go up to my office."

"I won't keep you then. Talk with you in a little while. I hope you'll think his idea is a good one."

"Tell me and your suspense will be over."

"Nope. Later. It'll give you something to wonder about. Bye."

Tori could still hear Bev chuckling as she disconnected the call. She realized she was smiling. It felt good. She placed a call to MJ who picked up on the second ring.

"Hey, what's up?"

"Hi. Have you been in touch with Victor today?"

"Of course. Why?"

"What did you talk about?"

"Um, let me think. Nothing serious, just general chat about his days...or should I say nights at work. Oh, yeah, he said he wanted us to all get together again and was working on making some arrangements for, possibly, next weekend. He wanted to keep his plans a secret until he could be sure about availability."

"Hmm, interesting. He seems like he's putting a lot of planning into this mysterious event he wants the four of us to participate in. He wants us to call him back. Are you free and interested in calling him later when you get in?"

"Am I free? For Victor, of course I'm free. I'm definitely interested. Now I can't wait to for the call and to see what he has in mind."

***

Around one o'clock Tori sent a quick text to MJ to assure they would meet in time to place the call to Bev and Victor.

Time seemed to crawl. Tori would have been willing to bet she'd checked her watch a hundred times before MJ showed up for their dinner break. She always chuckled to herself when she called the break their dinner break even though it usually did involve food. At three in the morning, dinner it definitely was not.

At two forty-eight MJ arrived at Tori's office door. "Hey! Your cryptic text said to not be late for our break...here I am. So what's happening?"

"I'm sure you remember that we have a phone call to make, right? But I know you can get so involved in what you're doing that you lose track of time. So I wanted to be sure you'd not be late."

MJ chuckled. "Fat chance for that when it involves talking to Victor!"

Tori used her phone to make the call. The phone rang and Bev answered right away, putting Victor on speaker. Tori did the same. After brief greetings all around, Victor took control of the conversation. "Hello ladies, and Bev too."

The sound of the smack Bev gave Victor and the sharp, 'Hey!' retort made Tori and MJ laugh. "Hello, Victor," they replied in unison.

"I'll make this quick because I know you're both working. I thought we all had such a nice time at dinner and the movie last weekend maybe we could all do something together this weekend. I'd like to suggest a day trip on Saturday, over to a little river town about an hour from here, called Millersville. A friend of mine runs a riverboat. She wants to take a shakedown cruise before her season opens next week. It'll just be her, a skeleton crew comprised of her husband and teenaged son, and the four of us. She's full of knowledge about the area and we'll get to hopefully see lots of birds as they start nesting. Before the cruise, I thought we could get lunch at the old pub there in town after we do a little window-shopping. The business district is only a couple of blocks long, but they have some unique gift shops there. Anybody game?"

MJ looked to Tori, her desire to accept the invitation clear from her expression. Tori couldn't refuse. She gave a small nod of agreement and MJ gushed an acceptance for both of them before Tori could change her mind.

"What time would we be back?" Concern about leaving Liz all day made Tori doubt her agreement to join the group.

Victor responded quickly. "Do you need to be back here by a specific time, Tori?"

"Not for any reason other than to check on Liz here at the center." She figured that either Bev or MJ would have told him the circumstances, so didn't feel a need to explain any further.

"Okay let me think." Victor thought out loud. "If all goes as planned, the boat trip should be over by four and I see no problem with getting back here before six. Will that work?"

"That'll be fine for me," Tori replied. "I can pick up a sandwich and spend the rest of the evening reading to Liz."

Bev jumped in. "If you wouldn't mind company, T, we could take turns reading to Liz again. I've enjoyed it when we've done it before. Just tell me if you'd rather not have company."

"I'd love company, Bev. Reading to her together with you, Bev, is fun. And Victor, thanks for understanding."

"Hey, since the two of you are deserting MJ and me, you'll miss out on a meal. MJ will you join me for dinner?"

"I'd love to have dinner with you Victor, anytime. The whole day sounds wonderful." MJ's excitement and enthusiasm for the event were evident in her voice. "Thanks for arranging everything for us."

Bev took advantage of the gap in conversation to say, "I have to get back to work. T, I'll call you later, okay?"

"Sure."

"MJ," Victor asked, "Can you stay on the phone to discuss our dinner plans?

"Sure, I have time left on my break."

Bev and Tori said goodbye, leaving Victor and MJ chatting away about their dinner plans.

"I hate to let you go Victor, I could talk to you all night. I have to get back to work, however." Hanging up, she turned to Tori. "He has to be the most considerate man I've ever met. He's amazing. He has a fantastic sense of humor, is a wonderful conversationalist, listens to my perspective about things, and is respectful of my opinions." MJ's eyes sparkled.

"You forgot big," Tori added with a laugh.

"I can but hope, you dirty girl."

"I meant tall, you idiot."

"I didn't. Gotta run." The sound of her laughter followed MJ out the door. Two seconds later, she leaned around the doorframe. "Oh yeah, he's picking us up at nine on Saturday. I told him that would work. You'll have time to see Liz before we go."

"Perfect, thanks."

"I know that being away from Liz makes you uncomfortable. We always have fun when you and Bev come along, so I'm glad you've agreed to go with us."

"Thanks. It's okay, really," Tori's genuine smile lit her face. "Karolina wants me to start taking time for myself, to take some breaks, and to have some fun. This definitely fits the bill."

"Victor is excited you and Bev are coming, too. We're both looking forward to spending the day together." MJ turned to leave, then turned back hanging half way in the door. "I really like this guy, Tori."

"I know. I like him, too. He's very special."

"I've got to run or I'll be late. See you tomorrow."

Chapter Eighteen

SATURDAY WOULD PROBABLY GO on record as one of the ten best days of the year 2012. The morning temps were in the mid-sixties with the weathermen forecasting afternoon highs in the upper seventies, low humidity, vivid blue skies, and zero chance of rain. Tori visited Liz and read her the paper before rushing home to shower and change. She was sitting on the bench in front of her condo building enjoying the color of the clear, cloud free blue sky and warm sunshine on her face. Her three friends pulled to a stop at the curb and called out a greeting.

Victor dazzled Tori with a bright, even-toothed smile. "Going our way?"

"I certainly hope so, otherwise getting up as early as I did was a wasted effort."

Victor laughed. "It'll be worth it, I promise. We've got a great day. You're in the back."

Bev pushed the door open. She had to stifle a laugh when Tori looked dubiously at the few inches of legroom remaining behind the driver's seat.

"Victor, I don't think my feet will fit behind you in the space you've left me without taking off my shoes."

"Sorry sweetie. I forget sometimes that I have my seat all the way back." Victor slid the seat forward an inch. "How's that, better?"

Bev grinned as Tori rolled her eyes and said, "Yes, I brought my shoehorn with me."

"Everyone's a critic," Victor replied good-naturedly inching the seat forward another half inch. "If I move forward any more, I won't be able to operate the pedals. Come on, time's a wasting. I have a hot dinner date tonight." He reached over and squeezed MJ's hand causing her to return a warm smile. He had to release MJ's hand briefly to shift. Tori noticed that once he got the vehicle moving, he reached over and took it again.

Happy and lighthearted chatter filled the ride to their destination. Once they arrived, they strolled the street of the tiny town poking through the little shops. Bev took a slew of photos. At one point, she set the camera on a wall, and used the automatic timer to take a group shot of the four of them. Bev joked as she showed the photo to the group, "T and I look like little people compared to you two."

MJ guffawed. "You two are little people compared to us." She looked at Victor, a contented smile on her face. He took her hand as they led the way down the street.

Tori and Bev gave the new couple some distance so they could talk privately. Bev gestured with her head at Victor and MJ's joined hands. "Do you ever envy straight people their ability to do that without worrying that someone will disapprove?"

"Hold hands?" Tori shrugged. "I don't think I ever gave it much thought. As a teacher in a school district that's pretty parochial, Liz was never out, so it was never an expectation I had with her. How do you feel about it?"

"I have personally never felt the need to do that. I'm not against it. It's just never anything I got used to doing. Connie was never very physically demonstrative. She liked sex, but never was a cuddler."

"You seem physically...uh...how shall I put this...warm, and welcoming of physical contact."

"Oh, definitely. It was always an issue between Connie and me. Not that I don't enjoy sex, but I love lying in bed talking and touching, arms and legs entwined...or with my partner holding me, or me holding her. In some ways that's more enjoyable and intimate than the sex act itself. When Connie and I got together the sex was hot, but as we lived together, I came to realize I needed more. I needed that affectionate intimacy from her. It was never something she was comfortable with, especially after I got sick."

"I'm so sorry, Bev, that you didn't get everything you wanted from your life with Connie. You deserve better."

"Thanks. That you understand means a lot to me. I think affection is so important to me because of my mom's early departure from my life. My father was more likely to give me a salute than a hug."

Tori put an arm around Bev's shoulders and pulled her closer until their sides touched. "Hugs are always available from me."

Bev turned and wrapped her arms around Tori's waist, pulled her close, and gave a squeeze. Bev leaned back, sought and held Tori's gaze. She brushed a stray strand of hair from Tori's brow, sliding it behind her ear and allowing her fingers to linger on Tori's cheek. The moment was electric between them. Bev was the first to recall they were standing on the street. She pressed her palm against Tori's cheek.

"Thanks. I appreciate that. Come on, we're falling behind. Those two and their long legs, I feel like we've been walking double time as they lope along." Their gaze held for a few more seconds before they dropped their arms and hurried to catch up.

After touring the town, the group ate lunch and reported to the dock where they met Victor's friends Tina and Tony and their son Seth. The cruise up the river was fascinating. Tina talked the entire length of the cruise, relating the history of the area, folk legends and stories, as well as pointing out several egret nests and two bald eagle nests.

"This river is critical to migrating shore birds, raptors, songbirds, fish and other wildlife." A short way down the river, Tina pointed to an eagle sitting below the nest perched high up on the tree above him. "Watch," she said. "That male has a habit of trying to distract people's attention from the location of his nest. He'll draw our attention away." A few short minutes later, as if on cue, the eagle majestically spread his wings and sailed down from his perch effortlessly gliding above the surface of the water. He looped back around to return to his spot in the tree after they had passed the nest. Bev could hardly contain her excitement as she snapped photo after photo, first of the eagle, and then of several egrets fishing along the river.

"Look, there's an otter family near the bank." MJ pointed toward the edge of the water.

Victor wrapped his arm around her waist. "They are so cute. Have you seen how they open their food using a rock on their stomach?

MJ laughed. "We must watch the same animal stories. I just watched that series on television last week where they showed the otters raising their family."

"You're lucky, it's not often we see them." Tina was filled with knowledge, and the information about otters' breeding habits, diets, and other interesting tidbits of information related to their lives flowed from her.

As they returned to the dock, everyone expressed disappointment that their river adventure was coming to an end. They agreed that, because of the trip, they'd all enjoy learning more about the migration habits of the various birds and waterfowl they'd observed.

In the car on the way home, they argued about what was the most exciting part of the journey. Tori and Bev said in unison, "I loved seeing the eagles."

Victor signaled to change lanes. "I liked seeing so many different species of waterfowl, a couple of which I'd never seen before."

Eventually, they all agreed the pair of river otters they had seen frolicking on the river bank were the most fun and made all the more special when they learned how rarely they were seen on the cruises. All too soon, their day together concluded as Victor dropped Tori and Bev at Tori's parking lot. They waved farewell as Victor and MJ pulled away. Tori and Bev agreed to grab a quick sandwich before heading back to visit with and read to Liz.

By ten they were both yawning. Tori closed the e-reader and tilted her head toward the door. "Shall we head for home?"

"Absolutely. Although it was a wonderful day, I'm exhausted."

"Me too." Tori parked the car in her spot and they walked together toward the corner.

"I'm going home, Tori. Thanks for coming today, it was fun." They stood facing each other each unsure how to part. "Can I have a hug?"

Without hesitation, Tori stepped forward, opened her arms, and Bev melted into the embrace. "I don't know why I feel so needy tonight. I could stay here wrapped in your arms all night." Bev slid her hands from Tori's back and pushed against her waist, separating them. She put her palms on Tori's elbows, sliding them down toward Tori's hands. "Thank you." She quickly turned and jogged across the street toward her building.

Tori watched her go, sighed, and turned toward her place.

***

"So what have you been doing about your assignment to do something fun?" Karolina asked.

Tori smiled as she recalled the trip with her friends. "I think you'll be pleased. Last Saturday, Victor, MJ, Bev, and I went on a river excursion. I've never done that before. We saw all sorts of birds, and even saw a family of otters." Excitement was evident in her tone as she described their boat ride and the other aspects of the day. "At the end of the day, Bev and I stopped by to read to Liz."

"How does that feel to be with Liz and Bev at the same time?"

Tori thought for a moment, trying to clarify her feelings. "At first, you know, that first night, I was nervous. After a short time, though I felt okay. Bev is a natural with Liz. She genuinely seems to care for her. Now, it's comfortable. Her presence has made it more fun, more light-hearted to spend time with Liz."

Before the session ended, Tori asked, "I wonder if we can talk a little about the parting hug I shared with Bev on Saturday?" She related to Karolina the information Bev had divulged earlier in the day about her relationship with Connie. "After she told me about Connie, Bev requested a hug before we parted ways. So, I complied with the request, and I gave her a hug."

"How did you feel about it?"

"It was nice. It felt like mostly friendship."

"Mostly?"

Tori pursed her lips as she analyzed her feelings about the incident. "I can't deny my attraction to Bev. It would be extremely easy in the heat of a moment to forget I'm in a committed relationship. She's warm and witty. We laugh and talk and support each other. And, if you could see her, I mean who wouldn't be attracted to her? No doubt, she's someone I could definitely fall for if I wasn't already in a relationship." Tori bobbed her head, "Yup. Really easy."

Karolina sighed. "You know I usually try not to give advice like this, but I don't want to see you get into a potentially destructive situation."

"You don't need to warn me, I'm fully cognizant of the risks. I've promised myself that I will remain faithful to Liz and I will. Bev knows that."

"You're speaking of sexual faithfulness. What about emotional faithfulness? It would seem that you are walking a fine line between friendship and something more meaningful with Bev."

"I know. She and I need to talk about it some more, to get things out in the open. I think, on Saturday, Bev was trying to tell me that affection is more important to her than sex. That we could skirt that fine line of my remaining sexually faithful if she and I could be more physically, not sexually demonstrative."

"Do you feel the same way?"

"I don't know. Like you, I think it could be a slippery slope. Neither of us has had sex in a long time. If I were completely honest about my feelings, not only am I physically attracted to her, I genuinely like her. It would be so easy to fall in love with her." Tori heaved a heavy sigh as she glanced at the ceiling for an answer. "So, the question remains, can we draw a line in the sand that neither of us will cross? I don't know. Perhaps a more critical question is can I stop myself from falling completely head over heels in love with her? Even if I commit not to act physically on my feelings, it feels a little dangerous."

"What do you think you'll do?"

Tori again looked at the ceiling still hoping to find the answer there. "I have no idea." She sighed. "I've promised myself that Liz will always be first. If I get more deeply involved with Bev, from square one, she's already 'the other woman' and if I don't abandon Liz, just by the nature of the relationship, Bev will always be second in line in my life."

"She needs to know that."

"I know. I've said as much to her already."

"You've been making wonderful progress, Tori. Just be careful you and she don't create a situation where you and or Bev end up getting hurt." The timer sounded indicating that the appointment was over. "Same time next week?"

They agreed to meeting at the regularly scheduled time and Karolina walked Tori to the door.

Chapter Nineteen

MJ AND TORI MET in Tori's office for their usual dinner break. As they shared their meal, talk drifted to the topic of MJ and Victor's relationship.

"I have a personal question to ask you," MJ said as she arranged her meal. "You know that Victor and I have been dating pretty steadily since we met. But we've still not, uh...you know..."

Tori smiled, as she gently supplied the words MJ was having trouble getting out. "You mean you've yet to move your relationship to a more physical level."

"Well, yeah. I mean we still haven't had sex. He seems to be enjoying our time together as much as I am. "We've been out several times since we went on the river cruise. We always meet for dinner before our shift starts. He walks me to my car and opens the door for me. I get in and he leans in to give me a kiss that curls my toes. Trust me, there's nothing wrong with his lips. Then he backs away and we each go to work." MJ hesitated. "I love him, Tori."

"Have you told him yet?"

"No. I don't want to scare him off." MJ fiddled with her sandwich.

"Do you think when he lost his leg he lost his ability to, you know..." Tori made a gesture involving an erect index finger that she allowed to limply drop. She raised a questioning eyebrow?

MJ laughed. "You're so bad! I'm talking to the wrong person here. What do you know about it anyway?"

Tori scratched her ear and arched her eyebrow. "We lesbians never have a problem with erectile dysfunction." She elevated two fingers, on her right hand then popped up a third, "And, size is never an issue."

"You're filthy. I always thought you were such a good girl, too." MJ finally took a bite of her sandwich as Tori chuckled softly.

Tori grinned, a mischievous twinkle in her eyes. "I was a good girl. I'm an even better woman." The two best friends laughed together. "I'm sorry to make light, MJ. I can't believe you haven't gotten close enough to figure out if all mechanisms are a go." Tori smiled at her friend. "Seriously, maybe he just respects you. Plus, Bev said his confidence was really shaken after he lost his leg."

"He has no reason to feel that way, he's perfect. I mean..."

Tori's phone rang, interrupting MJ's story. Tori checked the caller ID. "It's Bev." She pushed the answer button and delivered a cheery hello.

Tori listened as Bev talked. "Yes, we're having our dinner break, and yes, MJ is here with me. Hang on I'll put you on speaker." Tori punched the speaker button. "Okay, shoot."

"Good evening ladies." Victor's deep voice filled the room. MJ responded to the pleasant surprise with a huge grin and a wink at Tori. "I'm sorry it took so long to get this arranged. I wanted to do it sooner, but...well, all that's not important. I've got things straightened out now, I think." He paused. "I'm making a mess of this. Let me start at the beginning. Friends of mine, Robin and Lauren, own a bed and breakfast in Cape May. The season doesn't really get under way for another couple of weeks yet, not until after Memorial Day, so they're willing to give me a break on staying there. All I have to do is make them dinner. I was wondering if you two, and Bev of course, would want to join me there for this Saturday and Sunday. I thought we might make the trip down to Cape May Saturday afternoon. We can stay at the B & B my friends own, and maybe tour one of the mansions on Sunday before we head back. I know you'll need to check your calendars so I don't expect an answer this minute. Maybe you could let me know by noon tomorrow so I can let Robin and Lauren know to expect us or not."

The trip sounded like fun. *Maybe I can visit Liz Saturday morning before I leave and then spend some time with her before my shift on Sunday evening. If I do that, at least I'll only be leaving Liz alone less than thirty-six hours. Part of that time, on Sunday, Liz's mother would normally be visiting with her daughter anyway. Can I live with that?*

MJ's eyes implored Tori to say yes.

"I think that's doable." Tori glanced at MJ. "What about you, MJ?"

MJ exhaled a long, quieting breath before responding. "We all had such a great time last time, I'd love to do it again."

Bev chimed in. "I guess I'd better go along and make sure Victor conducts himself as a gentleman. After all, he'll be surrounded by all those women."

Tori laughed. "True, but only one of them needs protection, the rest of us are all lesbians."

Bev continued to tease her friend. "Yeah, how about that Victor...how come all your close friends are lesbians?"

Not allowing Bev to get to him, Victor responded with characteristic good humor. "I'm just trying to show you all what you're missing."

There were a number of comments from all of them with the end result being laughter.

They made all the arrangements before Victor said good night. "I hate to run but I've got to get back to work." MJ gathered the remains of her dinner. "I've gotta get back to work, too." She flashed a happy smile at Tori and hurried out the door.

Bev asked Tori, "Do you have a few more minutes?"

"Sure."

Tori punched the button to disconnect the speaker. "Ok, it's just me now. Funny you called just now. MJ was just talking about Victor as the phone rang. She's head over heels for him."

"He's nuts about her, too. Unfortunately, he's still hung up about his injury. He's afraid to move forward with her because of his leg. Maybe being together for an extended amount of time in a romantic setting will give them a chance to talk about it."

"This was your idea wasn't it?"

"I'll never tell."

"I can't imagine how someone like him would lack self-confidence. I mean he's so personable, good looking, has a great sense of humor..."

"Don't let MJ hear you talk about Victor like that. She'll be concerned you're going to jump the fence, switch teams, and be competition for his affection."

Tori laughed. "Like that would ever happen."

"I don't know, you're making me jealous."

"You've no reason to feel that way...you've not heard all the nice things I've said about you." Tori grinned, enjoying the banter.

"Sure, I bet. Anyway, as for Victor, I can relate to his dilemma. I know exactly how he feels. Since Connie's rejection I've never, uh, been intimate with anyone. I just feel so self-conscious."

"No offense, but your ex, Connie, should be euthanized for stupidity and insensitivity. Your scar is only skin."

"You haven't seen it."

"No, but I have an appendix scar that I would stack up against your scar any day. My surgeon must have been operating without his glasses that day he took out my appendix."

Bev barked out a laugh in response to the unexpected comment. "You're too funny. Despite how much I'd love to talk longer, Victor needs some help. Oh, did you get permission for me to work on the database? I've been thinking about the problems you have with your software program for your reports and drug tracking. I'll be finished up here soon. I'd like to stop by and take a look at the program you use for inventory and reporting."

"It's just something the previous pharmacist here developed with the IT guy. I gave him a copy of your resume and letters of reference and told him you were doing the work gratis. The program is not something the center bought or anything. He told me he would welcome someone with your expertise to spruce up the interface. He gave me an unlocked copy of the program for you. Before we start to use it he wants to review the changes you suggest. Do you think you could make it more user friendly for me?"

"No doubt in my mind. The program I'm supporting now uses the same platform. In all modesty, I'm a bit of a wizard with it."

"I'll see you soon. It'll be a welcome treat."

Approximately an hour later, Bev arrived at Tori's office. Tori showed Bev the software program she was using and demonstrated the problems she had with it. They completed the assessment of the needs Tori had that the database program was not meeting. Bev promised that she could fix everything, meet every requirement Tori had, and then some. "What can I do in exchange for you? Anything...name it."

"Anything? Really?"

Tori crossed her heart with her finger. "Anything."

"Okay, I'll let you know. Now don't forget, you promised anything."

"You're scaring me just a bit. Yes, I promise."

"Okay, I'm going home and get to work. Can you free up some time on Thursday night for me to show you the program?"

"You'll have it ready that soon? It's only a few days."

Bev stood and patted Tori on the shoulder. "The basics are already there. All I need to do is write a few new user forms and make a couple of report forms and you'll be good to go. Set up a meeting with your IT guy for Thursday so I can show him the changes we want to make. Once he agrees, I can show you and we can do a test run."

"Will there be a lot to learn?"

"No. And it won't affect the basic program that you and the other pharmacists use. It'll just enable you, specifically, to get the information you need out of the already existing information."

"That sounds perfect."

"I guarantee you'll be pleased. Oh, I have some good news. Remember, I told you I had a possibility of selling my program to a couple more companies?"

Tori nodded. "Yes, did you hear something?"

"Yes. I have an appointment in two weeks to make a sales pitch to them."

"Oh, Congratulations! How long will you have to stay? I'm kind of getting used to having you around."

"Maybe two weeks, initially, a bit longer if they buy. I'll gather all the information, figure out what they need and how to meet their requirements, then come back here and work on the programming." She smiled. "I'll miss you too much if I'm gone too long."

"Right." Tori gave a nervous laugh.

"It's true. Your friendship has become very important to me." Bev turned and walked to the door. "I'd better get out of here so you can get some work done. See you later today?"

"I'll call you later, after I wake up."

"Okay. Dinner?"

Tori agreed. "We can decide what and where then."

"Sounds good." Bev waved and closed the door behind her as she left.

Tori felt the emptiness of the room wrap around her. Bev's departure always left her feeling lonely.

AJ Adaire

Chapter Twenty

SATURDAY MORNING BEFORE THE trip to Cape May Tori visited with Liz and read her the paper before hurrying home to pack. Tori, Bev, MJ, and Victor began their journey to Cape May shortly after. After greetings were exchanged, Tori shared her enthusiasm about the new interface Bev wrote for her work program. "I can't tell you how great it is. It cuts the time to do my final report by half, and once I become really comfortable with it, it'll only get faster. She wrote a new form for me to input all the information I need to record. Everything is in one place, where before I had to move between several screens to gather the data I needed. She fixed it so that the data is pulled automatically. All I have to do is run the program, print the reports, and analyze them."

Victor agreed with Tori's praise of Bev's abilities from his perspective. "She's the best, for sure."

"Okay, let's change the topic. I'm not used to this much praise. I'm glad you're pleased, T, but let's talk about what we're seeing tomorrow." Bev said, her face a delightful shade of pink.

"We're going to tour some of the old houses." Victor reached over for MJ's hand and gave her a quick smile. "Lauren and Robin arranged for us to tour a couple of the other Victorian B & Bs tomorrow morning. Tonight I'm making dinner. This afternoon, when we get there, we can walk the mall shopping area. I may cut out a little early so I can get dinner started."

"I can help slice and dice," MJ volunteered.

"I'd like that." Victor glanced over at MJ and smiled.

A short time later, they pulled into the parking lot of the Feather Bed & Breakfast owned by Victor's friends. Once they had the bags unloaded and introductions complete, the group gathered in the dining room where Lauren and Robin had lunch waiting. The dynamic couple entertained the group with humorous stories about their business.

"People are endlessly entertaining," Robin offered. "Just last year, we had a man who stayed three days then refused to pay the bill. He complained that the bed was too high. We ended up giving him another night free along with a stool. Sometimes the path of least resistance is the best. Otherwise people post bad reviews on the Internet."

Lauren stood and gathered a pile of plates. "You'd better get underway. Cocktails will be served starting at five, followed by dinner at six, courtesy of Victor."

"Come on everyone, grab your bags and I'll show you to your rooms." Robin led the way down the hall followed by the group of friends. "Victor, you're in here. This is the Garden Room." She swung open the door to reveal a room done in cream wallpaper with dark green vines. "I gave you our only king-sized bed. I figured you'd like the extra room. And the shower in here is big enough to hold a square dance in. MJ, you're next door here, in the Rose Room." She opened the door to find a lavishly decorated room. "You can see from the decor how the room got its name." Victor and MJ dropped their bags in their respective rooms and trailed after the others to see Tori's and Bev's rooms. "To keep you all in this wing, we put the two of you in these adjoining rooms that have a shared bath. Hope that's okay?"

Tori said, "The rooms are lovely"

Bev quickly agreed. The accommodations are perfect. Thank you."

Each room had a double bed, wainscoting painted a crisp white, and bedspreads done in navy blue. The upper half of the walls were painted a serene, coordinating shade of a lighter blue. Nautical themed pillows decorated each of the beds. "We call this our Water Suite. She walked to the back wall of the first room and opened the French doors to reveal a fountain trickling water down a rock wall, and ending in a small pool of water. A glider sat next to the fountain. "The other room opens onto this private patio too."

"It's lovely, Robin. Thank you."

"I'll leave you to your afternoon. Since Victor is cooking for us tonight, Lauren and I have a rare afternoon to ourselves and are taking the few hours off for some alone time. If you need anything, our assistant will be around. Her room is in the other wing at the end of the hall. See you all around five."

The group bid Robin farewell and agreed to meet by the front door in ten minutes.

"I need to check out the kitchen. I want to be sure I have everything I need to prepare dinner." Victor looked at MJ. "Anyone care to join me?"

MJ reached out and grabbed his hand. "Your able assistant would be pleased to join you."

"And then there were two." Tori gestured between herself and Bev who responded with a laugh.

"Gee it sure got quiet all of a sudden." Bev followed Tori to the patio.

Tori looked at the splashing fountain. "Does that thing make you want to pee?"

"You're too much," laughed Bev. "This place is beautiful, isn't it?"

"Yes, lovely." Tori bent down to sniff one of the potted flowers. "Um...Robin mentioned they bought the place in a run-down condition and refurbished it themselves."

"Victor helped them a lot. He is not one to toot his own horn, but I think he has spent a lot of time here and has helped out quite a bit. That's why he gets to stay here for reduced rates. They aren't charging him for any of the rooms this weekend, but he supplied all the food and is making dinner. I told him we'd supply the wine tonight. Hope that was okay."

"Sure. Thanks for offering that, Bev. Maybe in addition to the wine, we can find a little gift for them this afternoon."

Ten minutes later, Tori and Bev waited at the door for Victor and MJ. "I think they're in the kitchen. I'll check." Tori went down the hallway and peered around the corner. Victor and MJ were in a passionate embrace, lips locked together. They broke for air and as MJ's eyes opened, she spied Tori. Behind Victor's back, MJ waved to Tori to go.

Tori returned to Bev. "I think Victor and MJ have plans for the afternoon different from what we originally arranged." She winked.

"Finally." They gave each other a high five. "I thought he'd never work up the courage to make a serious move."

"We'll have to see who it was who made the first move. I can't wait to hear. My money is on MJ."

They walked from the B & B to the shopping area, bought a chance on a new car in support of a church fundraiser, and purchased T-shirts. In a cute little gift shop, they found a brass lantern they thought would fit in with the decor in the Water Suite and purchased it for Lauren and Robin. They found a very unusual wooden watch that they thought

Victor would like and bought that for him in appreciation for him arranging the weekend. Surrounded by their purchases, they sat on one of the benches on the mall, sharing a bag of candied nuts and enjoying the beautiful weather. Wine in hand, just before four o'clock they headed back to the Feather Bed & Breakfast, freshened up, and joined Lauren and Robin for cocktails. Fifteen minutes later, MJ showed up, eyes bright. Tori and Bev exchanged a look when they noticed the whisker burn she sported on her face.

Lauren made a cocktail for MJ. "Victor is putting the finishing touches on dinner. We, uh, ran into a bit of a delay, so dinner might be a little later than we thought."

Dinner was an enjoyable event with conversation moving quickly from food to politics, and then to the history of the B & B.

"We bought the place not realizing what a complete mess it was and how much work we'd have to do." Lauren volunteered. "I don't think we'd have been able to ever finish without Victor's help. He's an amazing guy. We hardly knew him when he started to help us."

"Just shows how desperate I was for friends after I moved here. Someone I worked with took a look at my size and recruited me."

Robin patted Victor's shoulder. "Can you imagine anyone so nice? He gave us so much time we sort of adopted him as a big brother. Then we found out he could cook."

Lauren smiled at her partner. "Good thing Robin had already married me, or I might have proposed to him myself."

Robin laughed and squeezed her partner's hand. "Not after he wanted to name the place 'The Peeing Fountain B & B.'"

"Hey that was an improvement on some of the names you came up with when we first moved in here," Lauren poked her partner. "We stayed in the fountain room for the first month while we worked on some of the other rooms. At the time, the fountain ran continuously. Every night, we'd be exhausted and would literally fall into bed, the last thing Robin would say to me was, 'Why doesn't that fountain make you want to pee?' Then she'd say, 'I think we should call this place The Incontinent Fountain.' Robin had a new name for the fountain every night from The Peeing Peregrine, to the Piddling Puffin. I got to the point I couldn't stand it anymore and, as a surprise, I had the electrician put in a switch to turn the thing off." She turned toward Tori. "You'll find the switch next to the light switch near the headboard in your room, by the way."

Tori laughed. "I wondered what that switch did, and am very appreciative of the information. I'm afraid I agree with Robin on the sound the fountain makes."

As the enjoyable evening started to wind down, Bev and Tori presented their hosts with the gift they'd selected for them. "Bev, MJ, Victor, and I appreciate you sharing this wonderful weekend with us."

Tori and Bev, knowing MJ and Victor would want to be included in the gift for their hosts, had added their names to the card. MJ subtly winked and nodded her appreciation to her friends when Lauren acknowledged all of them for the gift.

Robin said, "Thank you all for the lovely gift."

They all pitched in to clean up the dishes and put the dining room in order.

"We've arranged the tours for you that Victor requested," Robin said. "They start at ten o'clock tomorrow morning. Breakfast will be ready at eight-thirty."

"Thank you, ladies." Victor stood and stretched. "Feel like a walk, MJ?"

"Sure. Let me get my jacket."

Tori gave her two friends a smile. "I'll see you in the morning, you two. Have a nice walk. I'm tired, I think I'll turn in."

Bev nodded. "Me too. I need a shower first though. Have a nice walk, you two."

***

A few minutes later, Bev stuck her head in Tori's room. "Do you need the bathroom before I tie it up taking my shower?"

Tori ended her phone call and shook her head. "No, I'm good."

"Everything okay?"

Tori grinned. "Yes. I just checked with the nurse's station. She's okay. All systems normal."

"Good. I'll be done in a few minutes." Bev closed the door to the bath that linked their two rooms.

Tori opened the French door to the patio and sat on the glider. It was a beautiful night. She looked up at the sky sprinkled with a million twinkling stars and thought back over the lovely day she'd shared with Bev, MJ, Victor, and their hosts. A smile played on her lips as she recalled the wonderful time she'd spent with Bev. She liked that they could chatter on endlessly about things and then equally enjoy the periods of comfortable silence. They touched so easily and naturally. As she turned off the shower, the thought flashed through her mind that less than twelve feet away Bev was standing naked, wet, and warm from her shower. Her body responded to the thought as she struggled to push that image from her mind. She shook her head, physically trying to deny herself the thought and the desire. Tori jumped when the door opened and Bev stood in the doorway wrapped only in a towel. "Oh God," Tori groaned.

"T? You remember your promise to me that you'd do anything I asked to repay me?"

Tori shook her head side to side. "Oh, Bev. I..."

"No. Wait. Please. It's not what you think. I'm so uncomfortable about being naked in front of anyone since my surgery and well, you know, after what Connie said to me. I was wondering if you'd look at my breast and tell me what you think. As much as I'd love to, I swear I'm not coming on to you and have no ulterior motives. I'll admit that there are times that I wish you weren't so loyal to Liz, but I've given you my word that I won't do anything to disrespect that vow you've made to her." Bev stood and waited. "I don't trust anyone but you to be honest with me, T. Please."

Tori moved slowly through the door, her eyes on Bev's as if searching for any source of insincerity. "Okay. I believe you. Let me see." She steeled herself to keep her expression neutral, no matter what Bev revealed. More than anything she didn't want to react in any way that would deepen the pain Bev's previous partner had inflicted on her with her hurtful words, a pain that had lasted way too long.

Bev closed her eyes and dropped the towel to her waist, knotting it there. She stood perfectly still.

Tori saw Bev's nervousness evidenced by her increased rate of breathing. Tori moved closer. Her eyes feasted on the site of Bev's naked breasts, her body betraying her by immediately responding. As if it had a will of its own, Tori's hand reached out and traced the two inch long, slightly indented, red and puckered scar on the side of Bev's exposed breast. It was all she could do to hold herself back from cupping Bev's breast with her palm when she saw the nipple respond to the tender touch on the jagged scar. Bev's lips parted in anticipation.

Tori exhaled a ragged breath and dropped her hand to her side.

A look of pain crossed Bev's face and tears filled her eyes.

"Look at me Bev. It's just a scar, sweetheart. We all have them. Some are visible, some aren't. Your previous lover was a hurtful bitch who couldn't have loved you if that little nick sent her packing. My appendix scar is much worse. Look."

Bev's eyes slowly opened to meet Tori's soft gaze.

Tori unzipped her pants and lowered them to expose her own appendix scar. She turned Bev to the bureau mirror. They stood, side by side, reflections staring back at them. "See. My scar is much worse."

Bev laughed and shook her head. "I've been lusting for you since I met you. Never once, in my wildest imagination, did I ever think our first time being undressed together would be standing next to each other comparing scars in a mirror."

"You've been lusting for me?" Tori said as she zipped her pants.

Bev pulled the towel up to cover her breasts and secured it. "Yes, I have, you idiot." She put her arms out and Tori stepped into her embrace wrapping her tenderly in her arms. "I've been fighting hard not to fall in love with you T. I know you can't love me back. It's okay. Whatever you can give me will be enough. Your friendship is enough." When she felt Tori's tears on her shoulder, Bev pulled back seeking Tori's eyes. "If I get dressed will you let me hold you?"

Tori nodded.

"Get your PJs on and get into bed. I'll be right back."

Tori was already in bed on her back, tears still silently leaking from her eyes by the time Bev returned. "I can't stop crying. I don't know what's wrong with me."

"Slide over and let me hold you." As Bev's arms pulled her close, Tori began to quietly sob. Bev held her until she quieted.

"Oh God, I'm a mess." Tori pulled away, sat up, and got a handful of tissues from the night table. "I'm not sure who I'm crying for, Liz, me, or you who's stuck in this limbo with me." As she wiped her eyes, then her nose, she chuckled. "Bet this little display has made me a lot less desirable as an object of your affection."

Bev joined in the laughter. "Not even a remote possibility. Feel better?"

"I guess. I'm sorry." Tori blotted the last of her tears. "I don't want you to think I don't want you. That couldn't be further from the truth. I care very deeply for you and you have a beautiful body, including both of your breasts. It was all I could do tonight not to touch you intimately."

Bev responded by giving Tori a squeeze. "It's okay. Really. This is a difficult situation, and I want you to know that I admire you for your

commitment. I've grown to care for Liz, too. She's just so vulnerable."
Bev kissed Tori softly on the cheek. "You okay now?"

Tori nodded as Bev propped herself up on one elbow. She reached out and traced Tori's lips with her finger. Exhaling the breath she'd been holding, she shook her head. "I'd better get out of here. I'll see you in the morning." They slid from the bed and walked toward the bathroom. Before leaving, Bev turned, placing her hand on her breast. "So the scar isn't a big deal?"

Tori hesitated for a fraction of a moment then reached out to cup Bev's breasts. "They're beautiful, just like you are." Tori's yearning for more was nearly palpable. She closed her eyes, gathering strength to drop her hands and step backward, increasing the distance between them. "Now, get out of here before we do something we'll both regret tomorrow."

***

The next morning, Bev and Tori joined their hosts for breakfast. Robin handed Tori a note from MJ. Tori read it silently then passed it to Bev who chuckled. "Skipping breakfast, eh?"

"Yeah, and they'll be joining us after the bed and breakfast tours for the trip home." They looked at each other and smiled. "Phew, finally," Bev said, pretending to wipe her brow. "We'd better not tease them, at least not today."

"Agreed." Tori passed Bev the bread basket of homemade muffins. She took one and spread a generous dollop of butter on each half.

"I might even let Victor off the hook entirely, knowing he's been so nervous about taking their relationship to the next level. Although if I were in his shoes, I'm not sure I'd have dragged us along as witnesses."

"Maybe it wasn't planned, and nature just took its course." Tori broke open her own muffin and imitated Bev's action. "Whatever happened, I'm happy for both of them."

The remainder of the day sped by. After the tours, they returned to the Feather Bed & Breakfast for a late lunch where they found MJ and Victor sitting on the front porch swing with clasped hands. They waved as Bev and Tori walked up the steps toward them.

"How were the tours?" MJ asked, a big grin on her face.

"Amazing." Tori answered. "Did you have a good rest?"

"Um, yes." MJ glanced over at a bright red Victor. "We were up late, um talking, um, so we decided to sleep in this morning."

"That's nice," Bev added. She turned toward Victor. "I have a hard time waking up at a normal time because of working the night shift. It's hard to reset our clocks sometimes."

Victor stood up and reached down for MJ's hand. As she stood next to him, he put a protective arm around her shoulders. "Okay, thanks for being tactful and not teasing us, but let's get this elephant out of the middle of the room. We're in love and proud of it. Besides that, we both want to thank you for introducing us. For your maiden venture as matchmakers, you two did an amazing job." He dropped his arm from around MJ and wrapped the two women in a huge bear hug, ending by kissing each of them on the top of their heads. "Now, let's go eat so we can get home. Tori, I know you're probably eager to get under way." He reached back for a stunned MJ's hand and led her inside, leaving Tori and Bev standing there with bemused expressions on their faces.

"So, that takes care of that," Bev said adding a chuckle.

"I guess so. Come on before the two of them eat all the food. They must be famished. Remember, they didn't have any breakfast."

AJ Adaire

Chapter Twenty-one

DURING ONE OF THEIR afternoon excursions, early in the summer, Tori and Bev stopped by the local bookstore. Bev held up a book. "Look, T. This is a fun cookbook. *Sixty Scrumptious Summer Dinners.*"

Tori came up behind Bev and leaned over her shoulder to look at the picture on the cover. Before replying, her eyes closed just a brief second longer than customary for a normal blink, as she allowed herself an extra few seconds to inhale the fresh scent she'd come to identify as Bev's. "Hmmm. Too bad."

"What do you mean?"

"Well, don't you think the author missed a prime opportunity there?" Tori glanced at the author's name. "She missed her chance to make a great alliteration. You know, *Sixty Scrumptious Summer Suppers.*"

"Come on! You're impossible." Bev turned and placed her hand on Tori's shoulder and briefly pulled their bodies together as they shared their laughter. Their comfort level with the intimate contact might instill a suspicion, in a casual observer, that they were lovers, at least until Tori smiled and stepped back taking the book.

"I'll make you a deal. I'll buy the book and all the food if you'll prepare each of the dinners for us."

Bev stuck out her hand. "Deal." Her eyes twinkled. "That'll be fun. What's more, it means you'll have to eat dinner with me every night I cook."

"It'll be my sincere pleasure."

True to their deal, Bev started on page one of the book and cooked each of the meals in order. On weekends, they would go out for dinner, order takeout or Tori would cook. On weeknights, Tori would take a nap before dinner, if Bev didn't need her help dicing ingredients for their meal, Tori would take a nap before dinner so she could stay awake overnight. Then she'd wake and eat dinner with Bev. As they dined together, they'd discuss their activities of the day, which more and more frequently they'd spent doing something active.

***

Bev hummed an ABBA song as she prepared their dinner. She was halfway through the cookbook they'd bought. She set the table before going into the living room to wake Tori from her nap. She sat on the edge of the coffee table and studied the sleeping woman. The tension line between Tori's brows, usually present in her expression when she was awake, was softened in sleep. Her full lips were slightly parted and begging to be kissed.

Tori's lids fluttered open and her green eyes fixed on Bev. Tori moistened her lips as she forced herself to keep breathing, when Bev leaned forward and reached out to brush Tori's bangs aside. Bev traced her finger down the crease in Tori's forehead then brushed the back of her fingers against Tori's cheek then lightly across her lips.

Tori took Bev's hand in her own and kissed Bev's palm before she sat up, breaking the moment. "Are you okay?"

"Yes. I'm fine. It's just that you looked..." Bev shrugged. "You looked so kissable."

"Bev," Tori said, her tone conveying a mild admonishment.

"I know I promised you we could just stay friends. Forgive me? It's sometimes just so hard."

"Yes. It's not easy for me either."

Bev stood taking both of Tori's hands and pulled her to her feet. Tori held her breath as Bev took her face in her hands and leaned in. Bev turned Tori's face from side to side as she placed a tender kiss on each cheek before releasing her. "Friends, right. Come on, my friend, let's have dinner."

The moment of tension between them passed. Bev turned and led the way to the kitchen where Bev presented the meal she'd prepared. Chicken salad with walnuts and fresh blueberries purchased from a local blueberry farm.

"Umm! This is great, Bev." Tori smiled as she glanced around Bev's condo. There were souvenirs of their days together everywhere she looked. Shells and other objects of interest they'd collected from the beach. Propped in the corner was the rainbow-striped umbrella they used when they chose to nap on the beach in the afternoon.

Bev studied Tori. "It must have been a good nap. You look rested."

"Yes, I'm feeling good lately."

"Is it okay if I come with you tonight? I don't feel like being alone, and I'd like to finish that book I'm reading to Liz. If you'd rather be alone with her, I'll understand. I can come in later, when you go up to your office."

Tori brushed her hair behind her ear. "No, I'd love the company, and I'm eager to see how that book ends. We always have fun reading to Liz. Besides, I won't see you tomorrow until dinnertime. I have my appointment with Karolina. So it'll be great to have your company tonight."

***

Tori was continuing her regular counseling sessions with Karolina and felt that, although she still had guilty feelings at times, she had mostly been successful in reducing feelings of being sinful. She entered Karolina's office, took a seat in her usual chair, glanced around the welcoming office, and smiled at the woman she'd grown to trust and care for over the past several months.

"It's nice to see you smiling. You look rested," Karolina said after returning Tori's smile. "How are things going?"

"Good." Tori paused, considering. She nodded slowly. "Really good. I've been able to attain a more comfortable balance in my life, and am able to take time daily from my visits to Liz, sufficient to build in some enjoyment for myself. I'm comfortable that I'm devoting the appropriate amount of time that I 'should' to my partner." Tori emphasized the word should with air quotes. "I'm still doing the daily affirmations Bev helped me develop. I think they're helping to keep me feeling centered."

"That's wonderful, Tori. I'm pleased and proud of your gains."

Tori beamed, then chuckled. "Yes, me too!" She shifted in her seat. "You know, something odd about all this? I feel now, that there is more to share with Liz. I find myself often describing things I've found on my walks or bike rides with Bev. Bev frequently accompanies me to read to Liz, or just to sit and quietly talk about current events and entertainment news at her bedside. There's laughter too, during our discussions there, something that was sorely missing from my solitary visits with Liz. It's hard to laugh alone, you know," Tori grew silent, her brow furrowing as she recalled her dinner with Bev.

"I see a frown. What are you thinking about?"

Tori described the near kiss she and Bev shared the night before. "It was Bev who was strong this time. We seem to take turns having moments of strength and weakness. I have to say that Bev has been true to her word and never pressured me for more than friendship despite the constant hum of sexual tension between us."

"And what do you see happening as a result?"

Tori shrugged a shoulder. "Right now, we're both holding strong to our promise to continue our relationship as friends. I can't foresee myself cheating on Liz, but I'm saying that here in your office far away from the temptation that is Bev." She smiled and shook her head. "I don't know. It's my plan to stay faithful."

Tori talked about her upcoming week as their session was winding down. "Time seems to fly. Oh, before I forget, I won't be able to make our Wednesday session next week. I have to go home to see my mother and father. Mom is receiving a teacher of the year award at the assembly on the opening day of school, and I want to be there to support her. I'm taking two days off, and will leave Tuesday afternoon so I can attend the award program on Wednesday, September fifth. I'll come back on Thursday in time for my shift."

Karolina leaned forward on her desk. "Good for you. That sounds like it fits right in with your goals...a meaningful event for you to attend, certainly a valid justification for missing a visiting day with Liz. How are you feeling about it?"

Tori's arms relaxed on the armrests of the chair. "So far okay. I mean I've been away for the weekend trip to Cape May, but that was only half an hour away."

"How would it feel to invite MJ or Bev to come home with you? They both give you good advice and could provide you support and comfort if you begin to feel anxious."

Tori tapped a finger against her lips. "MJ will be working, but Bev might be an option. I'm sure I'll be okay about it for all the reasons we've discussed. I feel like I'm doing much better managing my life and my visits to Liz. I really want to be there for my mom and I know with one hundred percent surety that Liz would want me to go. I like your idea for a different reason, though. I think it would be fun for Bev to meet my family and I'd enjoy having company for the ride. I think I'll ask her."

"Good. Don't forget to keep my card handy. You can reach me anytime you need me. However, after what you've told me today and the progress I've seen you make the past few months I'm confident that won't be necessary."

As the session ended, they confirmed Tori's next appointment. "I'll see you on September twelfth, then?"

Tori nodded her agreement as she tapped the date into her phone's calendar.

* * *

On Tuesday morning, the day of her planned trip to her parents' home, Tori visited Liz at the end of her shift, read the paper to her, and did her nails. She'd already explained the reason for her trip earlier. At eight fifty, Tori yawned and stretched. It had been a long night as she tried to do her regular job and get ahead in preparation for her time away. She stood to caress Liz's cheek and place a kiss on her forehead. "Be well, my love. I'll see you in a couple of days. I know you'd want me to go." *The last sentence is meant more for me than for Liz. Still, it's true and I'm going to hold onto that thought.* Tori squeezed Liz's hand. "See you soon." She gave one last look back before heading to the desk to be sure the staff knew not to expect her the next day and to double-check that they had her parents' phone number and to remind them to call her on her cell number rather than at home or work. She'd spoken to Liz's mother over the weekend, informing her that she wouldn't be in to see Liz on Wednesday.

Claudia promised to stop in to check on her daughter. "I can read her more of that interesting book we're working our way through."

Happy that Claudia couldn't see her rolling her eyes, Tori said, "I'm sure she'll be glad for the visit." Before leaving the building, Tori sent a quick text to Liz's mother with her contact information at her parents' home and thanked her for visiting Liz in her absence on Wednesday.

Bev had expressed her pleasure at the invitation when Tori had extended it and jumped at the opportunity to join Tori for her visit home. It was her suggestion to pick Tori up after work the morning they left. "You can catch some sleep in the car on the way there, then catch a nap later, after we arrive. I'll be fresh because I can sleep overnight." That was the plan they'd agreed upon and Bev was already waiting for

131

her as Tori emerged from the center on Tuesday morning. Bev sat in the driver's seat of Tori's car and greeted her friend warmly as Tori slid into the passenger's seat.

"This is weird, being a passenger in my own car."

"Think you trust me enough to go to sleep?"

Tori tipped the seat back and closed her eyes. "I'm going to give it my best effort." She yawned. "You're clear about the directions?"

"I am. I'll wake you just before we get there. I promise to keep the speedometer under eighty-five."

Tori's eyes snapped open.

Bev laughed. "Only kidding. I'm a good long distance driver, honest. You can rest easy. Trust me." She reached for Tori, running her hand down her arm to grip her hand. Their eyes met.

Tori gave a quick squeeze to Bev's hand. "Believe me when I say I do."

Bev slowly pulled her hand away and trailed her fingers up Tori's arm. Tori sighed and closed her eyes again.

***

"T, wake up, we're here."

Tori felt Bev lightly stroking her arm again. Enjoying the sensation, she kept her eyes closed as long as she dared. *If I don't open my eyes soon, maybe she'll try mouth to mouth. Oh, stop!* Reluctantly she placed her hand over Bev's hand that was currently raising goose bumps on her arm and causing the hair at the back of her head to stand on end. Tori opened her lids to find Bev's blue eyes inches away, brows furrowed with concern. Tori struggled to refrain from leaning forward the few inches to brush Bev's slightly parted lips with her own. Bev's breath was sweet, smelling of the spearmint gum she'd been chewing.

"You scared me. I called you several times and got no response. You were really sleeping soundly."

"What you were doing to my arm felt so good, I didn't want you to stop," Tori admitted candidly, not fully awake enough to have her defensive filters firmly in place.

"There's no reason it has to stop. Touching can be part of friendship, can't it? We've touched before. I've even held you before, remember?"

"Yes, I know. This felt different, made me want...more."

Time froze in place. Bev licked her lips.

Tori groaned and shut her eyes. "Please, I need to sit up." Tori opened her eyes. Bev was still only inches away. Tori gently pushed her back and raised her seat back into a more upright position. "We can't do this, Bev."

Bev reacted as if she'd been struck. "I'm sorry. For just a second there I forgot." She turned away and placed her right hand over her left breast above her heart as if to protect both.

Realizing the root of Bev's concern, Tori gently turned Bev's face toward her, but Bev kept her eyes lowered. "Don't. Please. This has nothing to do with you and your surgery. I told you that would never matter to me, and I meant it. This is one of those 'it's all about me' situations. Really. Look at me." Bev raised her eyes to meet Tori's. "You and I agreed on friendship, and you know why. It's all about me and Liz."

"I know. There are all kinds of friendships though, including friends with physical benefits. Why can't we have that much? Don't we deserve that? Fate threw us together. Was it all just a cruel joke?"

"Bev, please. I won't deny that, physically, there is nothing I'd enjoy more than making love with you. But mentally, emotionally, I know I can't do that. It would destroy us and end our friendship because I'd never forgive myself. I'm sorry."

"You're right...you are. I know it." Bev leaned over, brushed Tori's hair back and used her palm to pull Tori close enough to allow her to place a soft kiss on the cheek nearest her. "I'm sorry. It's just that, sometimes, I wish we could have more." The sound of Bev's laugh was unexpected. "Now who's being selfish, wanting more than she deserves?"

"You deserve it all. And so do I. You know I'm not the one to give you that right now, Bev. It seems we have to keep having this discussion even though I told you in the beginning that I wasn't available."

"I know that. In the beginning all that was so abstract, wasn't it? It was easy to imagine us just being friends. That was before I..." Bev shrugged. "Before I developed deeper feelings for you. Now I get into my bed at night, and you invade my mind. The thoughts I have for you aren't exactly friendly thoughts."

Tori leaned her head back against the seat, closed her eyes and exhaled a long breath. "I know. I have feelings for you too, feelings that aren't always only friendly. In fact, I have a confession to make." Tori told Bev about her guilty pleasure, how she used to sit on the boardwalk and watch for her. "And that was before I even knew you."

"Really? Thanks for telling me that." Bev reached for Tori's hand, pulled it into her lap and cradled it in both her hands. "It goes a long way in boosting my confidence and making up for your heartless rejection earlier." She emphasized the word heartless, and smiled, softening the criticism.

"I told you..."

"I know, it's not me, etcetera."

Tori withdrew her hand after giving a gentle squeeze. "Come on. I want you to meet my folks. We'll have lots of time together this weekend to talk about things. Let's go get unpacked and settled."

Overnight bags in hand, Tori led Bev up the walk of her parents' home. She opened the door and yelled, "Anybody here? I'm home."

Frantic barking preceded a small white ball of fur that launched itself at Tori's thighs. Tori dropped her bag and stooped to lift the excited little Westie into her arms. She fended off kisses as she nuzzled into his fur. "Hello Bert, I missed you too." The little dog stopped wiggling and finally settled into her. She kissed him on top of his head and tucked him under her arm. "Let's go find our people, shall we?" That set off another whole onslaught of wiggling. Tori set the little dog down. "Let's go see if they're in the kitchen."

They headed through the living room and past the dining room toward the kitchen. "Wonder where they are? Mom was supposed to have early dismissal today, and I figured Dad would be home with her. Oh well, let's get settled in." Tori led the way back to the front door, dodging the little dog as he darted in front of her. "Bertie, heel. I'm afraid I'm going to step on you." Obediently the little dog fell in step at her side, tail wagging a mile a minute as he gazed up lovingly. Tori reached down to pat his head. "Good boy. I'm glad to see they haven't totally spoiled you and that you still have some manners."

Returning to the door, they picked up their bags and Tori headed down the hallway with Bev a couple of paces behind. As Tori turned the corner into her room she came to a sudden halt causing Bev to run into her. "What the hell?"

"What's wrong?"

"My room. Look." Tori stepped aside to allow Bev access.

"It's beautiful," she said after glancing around. The room was painted a soft shade of blue with crisp white trim. Navy blue drapes hung at the window. In the center of the room was a queen-sized bed covered by a white quilted spread with scalloped edges. Spread across the top of the bed, blue accent pillows matched the color of the walls. "Gorgeous, in fact. What's wrong with it?"

"It's not my room." Tori turned abruptly and strode across the hall to what used to be the guest room. "They've commandeered the guest room, turned it into an office, and converted my room into a guest room." She turned around and looked at her old room. "This will never do."

"Tori what's wrong?"

"I'm sorry, Bev. I didn't know they did this. I'll sleep in the living room on the sofa. My old room had twin beds. They didn't even tell me they did this."

"Is that what has your knickers in such a knot? For God's sake, T, it's only two nights. We'll survive. With your mom retiring they probably thought it was a good time to make some changes. Besides, how often do you come here? They have a more functional use for it and you're certainly not often enough for them to keep your room intact."

Tori picked up Bert and sighed into his fur. "At least they didn't get rid of my dog."

"He's yours?

"Yeah, mine and Liz's. When she had her accident, they took care of him for me. It was supposed to be short term. Unfortunately, after I moved to the shore, between working and visiting Liz I wasn't home enough to keep him with me. It would have been unfair to him, although I still miss his company. So they agreed to keep him for me. Now, I couldn't pry him away from them if I wanted to, not that I'd do that to them."

"Have you calmed down now?"

Tori picked up Bert and sat on the edge of the bed scratching his ears. "I guess. It was just such a shock. I'm sorry I had a melt down. I kinda felt home would always be home, you know. Wonder what they did with my stuff?"

As if on cue a voice called down the hallway. "Victoria, we're home. Where are you?"

"I'm in here Mom." Tori yelled back.

"Come out here. Your father and I brought you lunch."

Bev grinned at the use of Tori's full name.

"I know what you're thinking. You can just wipe that grin off your face and come meet my parents." Tori put Bert down and turned toward the door. "And don't even think of calling me Victoria," she shot back over her shoulder.

"Okay Victoria, let's go, I'm hungry."

Tori stopped and faced Bev, one eyebrow raised. "Knock it off. Everybody has parents who can't be trained. I bet your parents call you Beverly and there's nothing you can do about it either."

"No, nobody calls me that." Bev abruptly turned toward the door. "Come on, I think someone mentioned lunch."

Leading the way to the kitchen, Tori thought about Bev's strange response to their gentle teasing and made a mental note to ask about Bev's parents. *Strange, now that I think about it, she's never mentioned them. We haven't really talked much about our families.*

"There she is! Hi sweetheart." Tori's mother swept her daughter into a warm embrace.

"Don't hog her all to yourself. Give me a chance too," Tori's dad said.

Bev watched Tori's interaction with her parents with curiosity. It was so different from her family dynamic. Tori's father had a deep and soothing voice. He sounded like a radio announcer. She listened, smiling as he welcomed his daughter home.

"Mom, Dad, this is my friend Beverly McMannis. She prefers Bev."

"Hello, 'she prefers Bev,'" Tori's dad teased. "I'm William, the father of Victoria who prefers Tori. Most folks call me Bill. I won't tell you what my wife calls me."

"Dad...behave. Bev, this is my mother, Mona."

"I'm pleased to meet you both. Thank you for letting me come along for Tori's visit home. She's very proud that you're receiving the Teacher of the Year Award. It's a wonderful honor."

"Why thank you, Bev. That's very kind of you."

Impatient to find out about the changes, Tori blurted out, "Mom, what happened to my room and my stuff?"

"We updated things. Do you like it? We wanted to surprise you. I saved everything. It's all in the attic. When you're ready for it, you can have it. This is a more efficient use of space. I intend to tutor some students in the new office, so we had to make that room single purpose instead of doubling as a guest room. We thought having a nice room with a queen-sized bed for your visits to us, as well as for other guests, would be nicer than those two old twins and that horrible futon we've had in the office for years. You know that sleeping on that thing was torture of biblical proportions and even more uncomfortable to sit on."

"The room is beautiful, Mom, but..."

"I know how you hate change, Victoria. Trust me, you'll get used to it." Her mother's years of combined experience as a teacher and as a parent told Tori that further protests would be futile. Besides, for as often as she got home for overnight visits, her mom was right, it was a more functional use of space.

"You're right, Mom. You and Dad did a great job. The rooms are beautiful."

Tori's mother nodded and patted her daughter on the shoulder. "Come, eat before your hoagie gets soggy. Now Bev, I want to hear all about you. You sit here next to me."

Chapter Twenty-two

THE GROUP SETTLED AROUND the dining room table. "We got these hoagies from your favorite place, Nico's Deli." Bill said, looking in Tori's direction.

"I know. I saw the bag. I'm sure they're still good as ever." Tori grinned at her parents. "Thank you."

Mona focused her attention on Bev. "Tori tells me that you two have become good friends. How did you meet?"

"Tori rescued me at the market, not once but twice." Bev told the tale of how they met and subsequently became friends."

Bill jumped in, continuing the line of questioning while Mona took a bite of food. "So, you're a local girl, then?"

"Um, no, I'm a transplant, too."

"Where did you grow up?"

Bev turned toward Mona. It was apparently her turn to ask questions and Bill's turn to chew. If they kept it up she might starve to death. Bev took a bite of her sandwich to give herself a chance to form a response. "My father always told me I was a citizen of the world." She smiled. "I was an Army brat, born in Texas, and raised everywhere and nowhere."

The friendly inquisition continued. Bev hated talking about her childhood. To avoid further specific questions, Bev gave a quick summary. "Both of my parents passed away before I was in high school. I lived with my grandmother until I went to college. Sadly, she's gone now, too." She looked to Tori for rescue.

Tori, who hadn't heard any of Bev's background was reticent to change the direction of the conversation. Bev realized no salvation was coming from Tori and took her revenge at her the first opportunity. She shot her friend a mischievous grin. "So, tell me, was Tori always the perfect daughter she is today?"

"Did she tell you that whopper?" The look of pride on Bill's face told Bev that the answer to her question was definitely yes.

Tori wiped her mouth and hands. "That was a great treat, thank you. I need a quick nap, if you don't mind. After working all night, the two hours I slept while you drove us here wasn't quite enough. I'm dragging. Bev. You want my car keys? You can take a run around town if you want, or you can wake me in two hours and I'll give you the grand tour. I'm sorry, I'm bushed."

"She can wait for you." With a mischievous smile, her mother added, "I can keep her busy showing her pictures of you as a baby. I have that array of school pictures I can show her, too."

"Oh, great!" Turning to Bev, Tori said, "You, my friend are on your own. Wake me in two hours and I'll show you where my mother has inflicted her years of torture upon her students."

Mona raised her eyebrow at her daughter. "You're just jealous I couldn't teach you." She turned to Bev. "Teaching relatives was not permitted by district rules, so she wasn't allowed to be in my classes."

"I leave you to fend for yourself, Bev." Tori stood. "Thanks, Mom and Dad." She gave each a hug and kiss before heading to the guest room for her nap.

"I'll help you clean up," Bev said, standing.

"Why thank you, dear." Mona gathered several plates from the table and Bev collected those remaining along with the silverware.

As they washed and dried the dishes Mona tried to tactfully obtain information about how her daughter was coping with Liz's situation. "Look. Tori and I are very close. Still, she doesn't tell me everything because she doesn't want me to worry about her. Of course I still do. It's what mothers do."

"She's lucky to have you to share things with. I wish my mom was still around to talk to."

"I have to be honest with you, Bev. Tori has told me you and she are just friends. However, she obviously has some feelings for you or she'd never have brought you home."

"I can't speak for her. I will tell you that if things were different, I'd want more than friendship with your daughter. Like she's fond of saying, things are complicated."

"She'll never walk away from Liz."

"I know that. I respect that about her. I wish..." Bev couldn't understand why she suddenly wanted to share her pain with Tori's warm and empathetic mother. It was her normal habit to hold her heartache and grief inside. "I won't deny that part of me wishes things were different. We're clear about where things stand. Friends, and that's all. Although I know Liz comes first in her life, I'm not willing to sacrifice enjoying a warm and supportive friendship with Tori just because she has a partner."

"Come out to the porch. You can tell me about yourself." Mona steered Bev toward the porch, with an arm wrapped around her shoulder.

Bev didn't know how it happened, but before long she found herself telling Mona about her cancer and all the pain surrounding the end of her relationship with Connie. "Despite what she told me, I suspect that my scar was not the only reason she left, because Connie was showing off a new girlfriend a day or two after she moved out. That fact, combined with the cancer treatment and scar, left me in such a very vulnerable place. Her leaving really destroyed my confidence. So, as I said, Tori's loyalty to Liz is a trait I admire in your daughter. I wish my previous partner had demonstrated more of it. I care for Tori very much. The only thing I can promise is that I'll never hurt her intentionally. If our friendship ever moves to a different level, we both are exposing our hearts to equal risk of being hurt if Liz's condition improves. I suspect the rewards of taking that risk would prove very worthwhile. Still, it remains to be seen where we'll end up. The least I'm hoping for is a growing friendship."

"Thank you for your candor Bev. If ever you need someone to talk to, I'll be here for you." Mona patted Bev's hand.

Bill came into the room. "Am I interrupting?"

Mona shook her head. "No, not at all."

Bev smiled up at the handsome man with a kind face and warm grin. "We were just getting acquainted. Were you a teacher, too?"

"Oh Lord, no! Never in a million years. I ran a small printing company. Retired three years ago. I can't wait for Mona to be finished so we can do some traveling, maybe spend some time over at Tori's, help by visiting Liz to give our daughter a break once in awhile. Liz was a great girl."

Bev nodded. It was at that moment that it struck Bev how many lives in addition to Liz's that drunk driver had impacted. She checked her watch. "I'd better go wake Tori. She said two hours and by the time I get in there and wake her she'll have had at least that."

***

Bev could hear the sound of Tori's soft and rhythmic breathing as she entered the room where Tori rested. She was on her back, the covers neatly folded over her breasts, with her hands folded over her stomach. Bev watched Tori sleep, grateful to be able to stare unobserved. *She's even neat when she sleeps. I wonder what she'd do if I kissed her awake. No, I want her to be fully aware of what's happening should that ever happen...it's surely a temptation though.* "T, wake up," Bev called softly.

"Do I have to?" Tori mumbled with her eyes still closed.

Bev settled next to her friend, clasping their entwined fingers with her right hand. "No, you don't have to. However you might want to give it some serious consideration since your mother still hasn't shown me that collection of your school photos yet."

Tori's eyes flew open. "Wow! You play rough." A slow smile curled her lips. Bev released Tori's hands and moved to sit up and rub her eyes, trying to force herself awake.

"Please...that woman out there makes me look like a lightweight. Your mother could get Bonnie to rat out Clyde. She's some kind of cross between Mother Teresa and Jessica Fletcher."

Tori laughed. "Imagine growing up with her. Jessica knew I was gay long before I ever told her, and Mother Teresa loved me anyway."

"She and your dad love you very much."

"I know. I'm lucky to have them. They love Liz too. They more than made up for her parents' disapproval of us. Liz loves them a lot." Tori slipped her hands behind her head so she could study her friend's face as she responded to her question. "So, did she pump you for information?"

"Like I said, she has a way of making you want to tell her what she wants to know without her asking. I think her real mission was to be sure of my intentions. She's worried about you, concerned that we might be working on an 'us.' She worries because of Liz."

"Ha! Don't we all."

"What are your plans for the rest of the day? I'm sure you'll want to call in. Is MJ on duty this afternoon?"

Tori shook her head. "Unh uh. She wasn't scheduled for today. You never know with her. She rarely turns down a request to work if someone calls in sick at the last minute. Although now that she has Victor, she's a little less willing to work so many extra shifts."

"I'd better let you get up. I have to admit that lying in bed talking is something I love to do." Bev stood up and walked to the door. "See you out there in Cabot Cove."

Tori laughed. "I just need a few minutes. I'll get dressed and see you out there." She flipped the covers back and stood up just as Bev turned back to add a comment.

Bev couldn't stop herself from allowing her eyes to sweep appreciatively over Tori's body clad only in a pair of briefs and a lacy bra. "Sorry. I'll tell you later." Bev turned away and hurried down the hallway. *She has a tattoo. Who knew? I wonder what it says.* Her pulse was still racing as she rounded the corner and entered the living room where Tori's father sat reading.

"Hello Bev. My wife is freshening up before we all sit down for cocktails. I hate to drink alone. Now that you're here I don't have to wait, nor do you. What'll you have?"

"What are you having?" Bev usually avoided conversations with men her father's age. Tori's father allowed her little freedom to avoid what appeared to be the inevitable, since they were the only two people in the room.

"I'm an old fashioned man of simple taste, so just some rye and ginger. You?"

"That sounds good."

Bill made quick work of preparing the highballs, handed Bev her glass and took a seat opposite her. "So, I suppose my wife has concluded the first stages of the inquisition. You appear to have survived and don't look any the worse for the experience."

The unexpected statement surprised Bev so much that she barked out a laugh.

Bill's hearty laugh melded with hers. "I guess by your reaction my statement was accurate. Good. Now I can relax. I hate it when that job is left to me. Frankly, it's why I disappear if someone new shows up. I'm not very good at getting the answers to questions she wants to know about." Bill took a sip of his drink. "So, what would you like to talk about?"

Bev thought about Bill's participation in the questioning over lunch. She decided not to bring up his strong abilities to hold up his half of her initial interrogation and opted to change the subject instead. "I noticed some interesting bird photographs in the hallway. Did you take those?"

"I wish. Victoria took them. She has a good eye, don't you think?"

"I do. They're beautiful. It's sad she doesn't display any of her work in her apartment. Does she only take photos of birds?"

"No. They were our favorites. She enjoys taking pictures of all kinds, but seems to have a special gift for photographing birds. Victoria and I used to do a lot of hiking. She has such patience to wait for exactly the shot she wants."

"I think that's true of her life. She's a very patient and kind person. You and your wife raised a wonderful woman."

"Thank you."

Laughter and the sound of footsteps indicated that Tori and Mona were coming to join Bill and Bev.

"So, Dad, are you plying my friend with liquor? Watch him, Bev. He's more subtle than mom, but he'll soften you up with a couple of drinks and have you spilling where you store the family jewels before you know what happened."

"I don't believe a word of that, T. We've been having a perfectly illuminating conversation about you, actually."

"Really? He was just getting you to let your guard down."

"Want a drink, pumpkin?" Tori's father stood up, ready to fix drinks.

"No, thanks, maybe later. I think we're going to take a little ride around town to see all the hot spots."

"You will be home for dinner, right?"

"Absolutely. Be back by six." Tori turned to Bev. "Want to take a tour of the town where I grew up?"

Bev leaped to her feet. "I'd love to."

Chapter Twenty-three

THE TOUR OF TORI'S SMALL town began downtown. Tori drove, leaving Bev free to tune in the radio to a station of her choosing. "Oooh, this is one of my favorite ABBA songs."

Despite it not being her favorite choice of music, Tori felt her spirits lift and she soon found herself bouncing along with the infectious rhythm of the music. Tori pulled to a stop. The main intersection had four stop signs instead of a light. Tori pointed at the food mart, pharmacy, and hardware store that comprised the downtown area of her hometown. "These are our anchor stores." Her deadpan delivery of the funny line caused Bev to laugh with delight.

Pointing at an ad in the window Bev said, "Look at the window. The lottery is worth sixty million dollars. Want to get a couple of tickets and split the winnings?"

"Sure, with a positive attitude like that, how can we not win?" Tori pulled over and, with a dollar in hand from each of them, Bev ran in to make the purchase. Afterward Tori drove them past the school where students from kindergarten to eighth grade received their education. "This town's ninth through twelfth grade students attend the regional high school located about fifteen minutes from here. It's where my mom teaches." Tori made a loop of the town pointing out the highlights, drove her past her high school, and headed back toward her house.

"I know you said you came from a small town." Bev laughed and raised her eyebrow. "I had no idea how small. Were you the only gay person in town?"

"I was a late bloomer, so it wasn't really an issue. There were so few of us in my age group that we all just hung out together, kind of like brothers and sisters. I didn't come out till college...only dated a few times before I met Liz my senior year. What about you? You never talk about your childhood or growing up."

"It's best to leave the past in the past. I knew I was different by the time I was in eighth grade. I told you I was an army brat, so my being a lesbian was strictly a 'don't ask, don't tell' sort of existence. I didn't really have anyone to talk to about my feelings, so I just kept to myself. My father wanted me to go into the service following high school and get my education that way. I'd been a computer geek all my life and knew what I wanted to do. Enlisting and following in my father's footsteps didn't even make the list."

"I can understand that." Tori grinned as she pulled to a stop in her parents' driveway. "Here we are all back in the same day, can you imagine? Part two of the inquisition coming up. Ready?"

"Sure. I like your parents and in many ways envy your close relationship with your folks. I never had that."

"Just be patient and give my parents a chance. Once they finish grilling you they'll adopt you, and you'll gain two lifelong supporters." Tori unclipped her seatbelt and opened the car door. "Shall we?"

Tori's parents welcomed the women warmly upon their return. "Did you see anyone, dear?"

"Nope. I never got out of the car, just drove through. Bev ran into Toppers and bought a couple of lottery tickets though."

"Good. I hope you win." Tori's father gave them a quick wink. "I can't wait until the news crew shows up to interview your mother. That will be interesting, don't you think?"

"Oh stop. Dinner is in fifteen minutes. Go wash up while I give my husband what for."

Conversation was relaxed during dinner. Bev kept up a constant barrage of questions, learning details about Mona and Bill's vocations and interests. Following dinner, the group watched two popular game shows on television, engaging in friendly competition to see who knew the answers first, after which they watched two crime dramas.

"What time is the program tomorrow, Mom?"

"The assembly is scheduled for one."

"Oh good. I think I'd like to take the opportunity to sleep in, if that's okay?"

"That'll be fine honey. Your dad is meeting his buddies tomorrow morning and coming over to the school after that, around twelve thirty."

146

"Okay then, we'll see you there." Tori looked over at Bev, "You want to stay up?"

Bev shook her head. "No, I'm ready to turn in as soon as I take a shower."

The two women bid good night to Tori's parents and headed down the hall to Tori's bedroom.

***

Tori opened the door that led from her bedroom to the bath. "Towels are on the shelf there," she said pointing. "You can shower first."

"Thanks." Bev gathered her nightclothes. "I won't be long. I'm sure you're tired. You've only had two naps, a total of four hours of sleep after working last night." Twenty minutes later, she came out of the bathroom dressed in navy blue pajamas consisting of T-shirt and shorts that barely came half way to her knees.

Tori licked her lips and swallowed hard. Her traitorous eyes traveled from Bev's face down her body, and back up.

Bev met Tori's eyes. Unconsciously her hand went to her left breast. "The shower felt good. Your turn." She turned away and busied herself with folding her clothes.

By the time Tori finished up in the shower Bev was in bed, arms folded under her head, staring at the ceiling. Tori slid in next to her. "What are you thinking about?

"You." There was a pause as she shifted to face Tori, their eyes meeting. "I was thinking about how blessed you are to have parents who love you and are close to you. I've never had that. It's not that my dad didn't love me exactly. My father was a hard, cold, and distant man who continually barked orders at my mother and me as if we were lower level recruits. My browbeaten mother died giving birth to a premature child, a sister who didn't survive. Lucky me. I became his sole focus and recipient of my father's abuse until he died in a freak accident on base." Bev gave a sad smile. "In fairness, I guess he did the best he could. I was a disappointment to him in any number of ways. We were more like barracks mates than family."

"I'm sorry."

"No need to be sorry. It's what is...no way to change it. You were twice blessed in having Liz, too. The stories you've told me about her make me wish I knew her before her accident."

"You would have been great friends. She would have liked your pragmatism and your devilish sense of humor. You'd have been drawn to her warmth and caring. She was...I mean is..." Tori sighed and grew silent.

Bev waited patiently for Tori to finish her thought.

"I'm having a hard time lately determining tense when I talk about her. Karolina introduced me to the different stages involved in accepting death. Reading about them, I couldn't believe I'd ever accept that Liz is gone. Now, I think I'm at least starting to accept that the woman in that bed isn't Liz, at least not the Liz I knew. Nor will she ever be that Liz again, even if she were to wake up."

Tori shifted, propping her head on her arm. "I often think that the most convincing proof that we have a soul that we have is at a funeral. I remember the first funeral I went to as a kid. I guess I was twelve going on thirteen the year my grandmother died. I was with my mom when we went into the room where she was laid out. We went in early to see her just before visiting hours. I can still remember the thought striking me, as I looked at her lifeless body, that my grandmother, that unique essence of what defined her, was no longer there. What remained was the shell, the container of her essence. Her soul was gone." Tori's eyes filled. "It's the same feeling I have when I visit Liz now. That warmth, that essential sense of her, it's gone. All that remains is the vessel that housed her soul. My Liz is gone."

Bev reached over, pulling Tori over against her. Tori rested her head on Bev's shoulder and sighed. They were quiet, each alone with her thoughts. "Sleepy?"

"No. Tired, not sleepy. It feels nice to be held. Sometimes I feel selfish. You seem always to be comforting me."

"Right now, I'd say you have a greater need because of life's circumstances. I know there'll be a time I'll need you, and I trust that you'll be there." Bev felt Tori nod.

A few minutes passed before Tori spoke again. "I didn't have a chance to tell you. In preparing for this trip I had to get in touch with Liz's mother. You know we've had a rocky time of it in the past. I guess I don't blame her. I was less than supportive of the idea of them moving Liz at first. In telling her about my visit home and asking her to visit Liz while I was away, I mentioned that I felt comfortable leaving her because I think she's receiving wonderful care. I added that their decision to bring their daughter there has proven to be a good one."

"How did she react?"

"She seemed stunned. Then she said something that sort of shocked me. She told me that she and her husband Frank were surprised by the fact I'd relocated to the shore and that I'd been so steadfast...her word, not mine. She said that she and Frank expected that I'd have given up and moved on by now. She told me she and her husband still disapproved of the 'nature of our relationship' but couldn't deny that I obviously cared for their daughter. Then she dropped the bombshell. She's arranging for me to sit in on any meetings they have with the medical staff regarding Liz's medical condition. She made it clear that the decisions still rest with them. However, I will be able to get information about her condition and ask questions directly."

"Tori, that's wonderful. What did MJ say?"

"You know her. I won't repeat her words exactly to protect your tender ears, but the gist was it's about time."

"I can just imagine her response."

Tori laughed. "Yes, it was pretty colorful. Nothing I didn't think." A comfortable silence grew between them. Tori adjusted her position, turning more to face Bev. "Victor and MJ seem to be really seeing a lot of each other."

"He's head over heels."

"I think she's a goner too."

Bev toyed with the seam on Tori's collar. "Victor told me his parents are coming for a visit this weekend."

"MJ mentioned that on our break the other night. She's nervous about it. She wants to make a good impression."

"He wants them to meet her. I don't think that, since high school, he's ever introduced anyone else to them."

"Really? Wow! That sounds like he's serious. They aren't kids though, so I guess when you find the right person..." Tori moved her leg, repositioning it in preparation for her withdrawal from Bev's embrace. "I don't want to move, but I think it's wise for me to move over there on my side of the bed. I love this, being close to you, sharing our thoughts and feelings."

"I love it too. In some ways this is much more intimate than sex, isn't it? Thank you for letting me in, T."

"I wish there could be more."

Bev felt such longing that she couldn't let Tori go. With her palm against Tori's cheek, she placed a soft kiss on Tori's lips, barely touching her. "Fortunately, we are right down the hall from your parents, so even if we were to put thoughts of Liz aside there's just no way."

The sexual tension broken by humor, Tori chuckled and put her forehead against Bev's. "How are we ever going to sleep tonight?"

"Shh. Think you can just hold me? It'll be enough if you hold me. I'll turn around."

Tori spooned Bev against her. "This feels good. You feel good." She sighed. "Am I just kidding myself that I'm not cheating on Liz? I know we haven't had sex, but you just said that what we share is more intimate than sex."

"I don't know the answer to that. I don't think we can deny that we're involved in a relationship of some definition, nor that we've developed feelings for each other that exceed the boundaries of friendship. There's no sense in either of us denying that we want more. It's just, now that I've spent time with you and Liz together, it just wouldn't feel right to me either, no matter how much I want you. I don't think either of us could get her out of our head, do you?"

"No. I hate this...limbo. Parts of me feel like I've accepted that Liz is gone. I mean, emotionally I've already been unfaithful to her by developing feelings for you. It's just that if I have sex with you, I don't know...it just still feels wrong to me."

"T? Will you be okay tomorrow with being close like this?"

"I think so. You?"

"Yes, I think so, too."

Tori sighed. "It's only going to get harder, you know. We are slowly pushing the boundaries."

Bev thought about that statement. "No. I think it's good we've talked. We're going to be fine. We have a mutual commitment to Liz. We'll be fine. Now go to sleep."

Tori pulled Bev closer and soon they drifted off. During the night each woman had adjusted position several times. Tori awoke on her back. She glanced over to find Bev awake and watching her. Her hand rested lightly on Tori's arm and her calf was on Tori's shin just below her knee.

"Good morning. What time is it?"

Bev checked her watch. "Nearly eleven. You okay?"

"Yes."

"I like watching you sleep. You were smiling a few minutes ago. Pleasant dream?"

"I don't remember. Maybe it was because I could feel you touching me and I didn't feel so alone."

Bev moved closer as Tori pulled Bev's arm around her tucking it around her waist. She rested her head on Tori's shoulder and sighed. "I know it's wrong for me to wish we could have at least this much."

"No. I don't think it's wrong. It's a normal reaction to an abnormal situation. I'm not sure there is a right or wrong to any of what we want or what we're feeling. There's no rule book to follow."

"T, have you ever thought about it from a different perspective? I mean, suppose it were you in a coma, like Liz is. What would you hope she'd do?"

"Interesting question. I'd hope she'd not forget me...that she'd remain involved in my life. However, I'd want her to be happy."

"Would you want her to find someone else, to move on with her life?"

"Early in my counseling, Karolina talked to me about the word should. I've given that word a lot of thought and am still trying to define what I should do, what my shoulds are in this situation. Maybe I'm deluding myself, I don't know. If it were me and my prognosis was as poor as hers, I'd want her to be happy. Whatever that meant for her. As for me, I just don't think Liz would want me to be lonely or unhappy. What about you, Bev. What would you want?"

"I don't know. It really is a hard question. I mean if I were going to wake up and be me again I can imagine how hurt I'd be if my partner had moved on quickly. Of course, then you get into how soon is too soon. It would be a clearer decision to expect my partner to wait if one could be reasonably able to assume the being 'me' again part. If I had no potential to be me, I think I'd want my partner to move on and be happy."

"There's the hard part. Nobody ever knows for sure if you'll wake up 'you' again, or in Liz's case, if she'll ever wake up at all."

Bev hugged Tori, sat up, and swung her legs over the edge of the bed. "Come on, let's get up, I need sustenance. All this thinking about questions with no right or wrong answers is making me hungry. I don't know how you deal with this day after day, year after year. It reminds me of ethics class in college."

Tori stood up and looked across the bed and smiled at Bev. "It's easier now that you're in my life."

Chapter Twenty-four

THE AWARD CEREMONY WAS moving. At the end of the speech given by one of her current students, Mona was shocked as the auditorium curtain parted to reveal a group of former students, one from each year she had taught. As one, they all stood and applauded. As the celebration wound down and she and Tori prepared to leave, Bev felt genuinely sorry to say goodbye to Tori's parents who hugged her as tightly as they did their own daughter.

On the way home, they took turns driving and napping. Before Tori fell asleep, they chatted about their visit and the ceremony, and lamented the fact they hadn't won the lottery. They agreed to start a pool to buy tickets weekly. To kill time on the drive home, they laughed as each listed three frivolous things they'd have purchased if they'd won.

***

Tori was running late and silently thanked the parking gods for the space directly in front of Karolina's office. Getting the spot added to her already upbeat mood. She had a spring in her step as she entered Karolina's office.

"It seems like the weekend at home was a nice break," Karolina said as she settled into her positon opposite Tori. "You seem in good spirits.

"Bev and I had a wonderful time. It was really fun to be home and to see Mom and Dad. Plus I got to show Bev around my hometown. The ceremony was touching, too."

"How did it feel being away from Liz?"

"It was okay. I believe it helped that I know Liz would have wanted me to be there for my mother. Regardless of that, I feel that I've gained some distance from my obsession with always being there at the hospital with Liz. In general I feel less guilty. If I do experience that emotion, it no longer causes the physical response it once did. I'm able to control it by reasoning out what is generating that feeling. Despite the fact that I still spend a lot of time with Liz, I feel my life is more balanced than it was. I've realized that because I'm doing more, I have more to tell her, and that makes my visits with her easier."

"Good. So you feel you've made progress, I always enjoy hearing that." Karolina waited for Tori to share more details about her trip.

"My parents made some changes to the house." Tori described her initial annoyance at the improvements. "The fact they redid my room made it necessary for Bev and me to sleep together."

Karolina studied Tori's expression for clues as to what Tori's exact definition of sleeping together entailed. Tori failed to continue, so Karolina said, "I see. And how did you feel about that?"

"It was nice, and it was hard." Tori stopped, seemingly lost in thought.

After a reasonable amount of time, Karolina asked softly, "What's going on?"

"We'll, as I was saying it was hard, I meant it was hard to just hold her because obviously we both wanted more. We talked though, very openly and honestly, and that helped. What I realized, as I was telling you, is that I don't feel guilty and that surprised me. I mean we both know I've felt guilty about far less serious or intimate situations. Maybe I'm making progress?"

"Yes, I think you've changed your perspective substantially." Karolina smiled.

Tori returned the smile and asserted more strongly. "I am making progress. I feel like I've accepted Liz's condition as one that will not reverse or improve. And although Bev knows I have strong feelings for her, she says she respects my decision to not act on them. It feels good to have all those hidden feelings out in the open."

"I'm sure it does. Secrets are heavy burdens to carry." Karolina glanced down at her notes on the tablet on her desk. "Let's talk a little about what more you want to achieve in counseling. Maybe it's time to review the goals you set when you first came to see me. Maybe you'd like to consider reducing how often you come to every other week or once a month. Give some thought to that and we'll discuss it next time."

***

It was two Saturdays after their return from Tori's folks. Tori and Bev were sitting on the sofa in Tori's condo, side by side, reviewing the photo album Bev had on her lap. Earlier that evening Bev arrived carrying a gift—a framed picture of the gulls surfing in the wind on the bridge. They decided together the best placement for it before they'd hung it on the wall.

"That picture looks nice there." Bev glanced around the room. On the shelf on the far wall, she could see several photos of birds and other wildlife that Tori had taken on their outings, all framed and placed on display. A few older shots of Liz sat alongside of photos of Victor and MJ, Tori's parents, several shots of birds on the boardwalk and a picture of Bev running that Tori had taken from her favorite bench. There was a group shot of the four of them, taken after she and Bev returned from taking the tours of the B & Bs in Cape May. They'd had a great weekend, and their good humor showed on their faces. On the end table was a large vase filled with smooth stones and shells they'd collected during their walks on the beach. Next to that was a small rock, worn into an interesting heart shape by the wind, water, and sand on its trip from places unknown to where they'd found it on the beach. It was a treasured memento of a fun and relaxing day walking the length of the beach. Bev propped her chin on her hand.

"Remember when I first came here? There was nothing about you in this room. Look at it now, filled with almost as many mementos of fun days and pleasant memories as I have in my place."

Tori allowed her eyes to follow a path similar to the one Bev's had taken. She met Bev's eyes. "Yes. Many of them thanks to you. I do feel like I'm living again, not just existing."

Bev smiled. "We've been having some good times." She flipped the page of the photo album, drawing Tori's attention back to the neatly arranged pictures.

Tori poked the last two photos on the page. "I love these photos of the gulls on the lamp post. Those were some of the photos you took on our first bike ride together. Remember? These are taken from an interesting perspective."

"Yes." Bev turned the page and pointed. "These pictures of the gulls surfing the wind currents up on the bridge are some of my favorite shots."

"Is it the same one you had framed for me, Bev?"

"Yup." Bev's eyes were soft as she met Tori's gaze. "I thought it would remind you of me, and some of the fun times we've shared, while I'm in Chicago."

"Mmm...how long will you be there?"

"At the least, a couple of weeks. I'll have to do the initial pitch next week to the two companies who've expressed interest. If I get both jobs it should take, at max, a couple of months or so to do the initial training. There's a programmer there at one of the companies, named Roger, who's pretty good. If I sell the program to the other company that's interested in addition to the one I'm pretty confident will purchase it, I might hire him, give him some intensive training, and let him provide the on-site tech support for me. Anything he can't handle, I can do from here. I can fix the issue and have him explain it. I'll only have to fly out every couple of months just to show my face and do a little hand holding once everything is set up."

"Two months, huh? It's a long time. I'll miss you."

Bev smiled. "I know, I'll miss you, too. It won't be two solid months. I'll have to come back a couple of times to touch base with Victor and make any adjustments to the software that he needs, so it won't be like we'll be separated for two full months."

Tori flipped the page. "Oh, our trip to my hometown." She reached for Bev's hand and gave it a squeeze. "We had a special couple of days, didn't we?"

Bev glanced over to meet Tori's eyes. "Yes."

"Regrets?"

Bev considered her reply carefully. "Some. Although I believe that ultimately we made a good decision. I don't think you'd have forgiven yourself if we'd taken things beyond friendship to a more physical level there or in Cape May. You?"

"Then, and still today, I think it's the right decision. Tomorrow, I don't know. With every day that passes, Liz gets thinner and weaker. I no longer have any hope she'll come back to me. I've finally fully accepted that as a reality."

They fell silent.

"T, before I go to Chicago, I have to go to D.C."

Tori's eyes snapped up. "Oh."

Bev released Tori's hand and turned sideways, enabling her to see Tori's face more easily. "Connie's mother is very sick and we've always enjoyed a close relationship. Connie called and said her mother asked to see me, and I want to see her, so I'm driving down for a couple of days. I'm leaving tomorrow morning. I'd like it if you'd come with me. I'll be home by Friday evening. Then I leave for Chicago on Sunday morning. It'll give us a chance to spend some extra time together that we'll miss if you don't come. Anyway, you can meet my good friends, Kate and Joan."

"Will you have to see Connie too?"

"I'd like not to, yet there's always that possibility."

"How do you feel about that?"

Bev shrugged. "Frankly I'd probably rather have a root canal."

Tori laughed. "A root canal?" She squeezed and released Bev's arm. "I'd love to go with you. I'm sure you'll understand if I say I can't. It's just that I'm afraid of being that far away from Liz that long. She seems so frail lately and has been spiking a fever off and on. Anyway, you don't need me there. You should go strut your stuff and make Connie regret she gave you up."

"She didn't give me up. Face it. She dumped me. It would feel good to have you there to remind me that not everyone thinks of me the way Connie does. I'm finally starting to believe in myself again. I'm worried that seeing her will bring back all those feelings of no longer being worthy of being loved."

"I feel horrible about not going with you. You're always there for me. It's not fair to you that I never put you first. I'm just so afraid of being away right now."

"Really, I understand."

"Bev, you're going to be away in Chicago. Maybe you'll meet someone while you're there. The selfish part of me would hate it if that happened. On the other hand, I mean, just because..." Tori's exasperated sigh revealed her frustration with their situation. "Ah, this sucks. Why do things have to be so complicated?"

"Because you're who you are, a good and loyal person. Because you're the kind of person who honors her commitments, even if it's not easy to do so." Bev grasped Tori's hand and pulled it into her lap where she cradled it in both hands. "What you just said, I'd like to think that you meant it as a very generous thing to say, to tell me to find someone else. Is that what you really want?"

Tori shook her head and glanced away. She quickly brushed at the tears that filled her eyes and turned her still damp face toward Bev. Exhaling a shaky breath, she whispered, "No, not at all. Honestly, it would kill me to see you with someone else."

"So you said this because you think it's what you should say?"

Tori scrubbed her hands over her face. "Yes. That and because you should be free to find someone that doesn't have all the issues I have."

Bev reached for Tori's hand and held it gently in both her hands. "Wasn't it you who told me that everyone has scars...everyone has issues, too...ex-lovers, illness, children, ex-husbands, you name it?" Bev, studied Tori's hand in her own then raised it to her lips for a brief kiss before returning their hands, still joined, to her lap. "You're not getting rid of me that easily. I'm not going anywhere." Bev toyed with Tori's fingers. "I mean, emotionally I'm not going anywhere. Physically, I'm going to be away for a little while."

Pulling away Tori exhaled a long breath. "I'm so sorry that we're in this limbo. I mean, you give me credit for being a loyal and faithful partner, although we both know that I don't deserve that credit because I've obviously developed deep feelings for you. I struggle every day not to act on those feelings, which at the very least makes me emotionally unfaithful to Liz. At times, the only thing stopping me from kissing you senseless is the fact that I know I wouldn't be able to live with myself afterward." Tori looked into Bev's eyes. "You deserve to have better than what I'm able to give you. Although I admit that, at times, I've toyed with the idea that I should send you away, I couldn't bear to hurt you like Connie did. Besides, I don't know what I'd do without you." She looked at Bev, searching her face for her reaction.

Bev slid closer and rested her head on Tori's shoulder. "T, no, please. I couldn't stand it if you didn't want to see me again."

Tori rested her head on top of Bev's "Nor could I. I'm wondering how I'll do without you for the time you'll be in Chicago."

Bev sat up. "We'll have video conversations everyday on the computer. At least the temptation to touch you won't be an issue."

Laughter spilled from Tori. "You really are an optimist. I love that about you." She allowed her eyes to leisurely travel from Bev's eyes, to her lips, downward over her breasts, and back up to her eyes. "Optimism is just one of your many, although decidedly less obvious, assets."

"Tori, you're flirting with me." From her hairline to the collar of her shirt, Bev turned bright pink.

"Maybe, just a little. I don't want you to forget what a beautiful, wonderful woman you are. Especially since you're going back into the lair of that ex-girlfriend of yours. I want you to feel good enough about yourself to tell her off."

"Stop with the mixed messages already. Your lips are saying no, no, while at the same time, I'm seeing come here and kiss me in your eyes."

Tori laughed and put one hand over her eyes and the other over her mouth. Her response was muffled. "There, conversation over."

"Smart ass!" Bev reached over and pulled Tori's hands away from her face, revealing Tori's grin. "If all goes well while I'm down there, I won't even have to see Connie. My intention is to stop and see her mother, Gertie, during the daytime while Connie is at work. She never leaves her office before eight. Figured I could have a leisurely drive down tomorrow morning. I have plans to meet up with two of my closest friends at their restaurant for dinner tomorrow night. Then I'll spend the next day with Gertie. I'll drive home the day after, following another quick visit with Gert."

"Seems simple enough."

"I certainly hope so." Bev closed the album and stood up. "I'd better get to bed. I've got a long day ahead of me tomorrow."

"Yeah, I need to get in to visit Liz, before I go to work." Tori walked Bev to the door where they hugged just a little longer and a little closer than usual. "Drive safely," Tori whispered.

"I will. I'll call you as soon as I get there."

Chapter Twenty-five

A SELECTION OF UPBEAT disco music, to which Bev kept time by tapping her fingers on the steering wheel, pounded from the car speakers. Even though she left late enough to avoid most of the traffic, she ran into a couple of stop and go backups. The first was due to a fender bender garnering drivers' attention and slowing traffic as it passed. Rubbernecking at a police officer ticketing a speeder caused the second delay. The trip that should have taken three hours and forty-five minutes ended up taking nearly four hours and a half.

Tired by the time she pulled into the hotel lot, Bev checked in, took a quick shower, and sent Tori a quick text saying she'd arrived in one piece. Feeling refreshed after a nap, she worked on her presentation for her meetings the following week. She missed Tori already. She glanced at her wristwatch, checking the time. Hoping that Tori would be awake, she picked up her phone and punched in the number from memory. There was no answer so she left a short message saying she'd call later after dinner with her friends. She left a message on Gertie's phone confirming that she'd be there for their visit the next morning, as planned. After a quick check in the mirror, following a light application of blush and mascara, Bev left the hotel to meet her friends.

Kate and Joan waved from their seat at the table near the window of their restaurant and bar. "Hey Bev, over here," Kate called. Bev approached and they greeted her with warm hugs. Once seated, Bev glanced around taking in the pictures decorating the walls. All the photos portrayed famous woman throughout history. Next to each picture was a biography describing her achievements, the name of the woman, her birth date and, if applicable, her date of death. At the end of the room opposite their table the double doors, left open for easy access, led to the bar area and dance floor. Later in the evening it would become filled with lesbians looking to meet Ms. Right and a few couples looking for an evening out where they could eat, drink, dance, and relax in a welcoming environment.

"The place looks great. It's like coming home," Bev said beaming a wide smile at her friends. "You two have built such a wonderful and welcoming place and been so successful."

"Our five year anniversary celebration of buying the place is planned for the third weekend in December." Kate said. "You've sat with us through most every planning session we've had—were often the voice of reason I might add. You helped design and set up our Internet and media presence, and have supported us from the time the place was just a concept. We couldn't possibly have a celebration without you. Please say you'll come."

"If at all possible I will. I promise. I'm pitching to two new companies next week in Chicago. If I get the job, or hopefully the jobs, I may still be out there. I promise though, I'll try to be here."

Joan, always the more direct of the couple added, "Don't forget to bring your main squeeze. I'm assuming after all this time there is a main squeeze."

Kate looked at her watch. "Geez Joan, cut to the chase, why don't you? The poor woman has been in the chair for less than five minutes and you're already digging for personal details."

"I have an inquiring mind."

Kate linked her fingers with her partner's and gave her a love-filled look. "That you do." They smiled at each other before turning in unison to Bev, expectant looks on their faces.

"What?" Bev's innocent expression countered their curiosity. She lost the stare down. "Okay. I don't really have a main squeeze exactly, but there is someone I've grown to care about very much. It's just that, well, it's complicated." Bev found herself recalling her first real conversation with Tori about Liz.

"We have all night, girlfriend," Joan said.

Betsy, their server, interrupted their conversation to take their drink order. She winked at Bev. "Nice to see you again." After a few words of casual greeting, she told them she'd return quickly with their drinks.

"Pardon the pun," Joan said, a broad grin softening her face, "but that was a true example of saved by the belle, spelled b-e-l-l-e.

However, it was only a temporary reprieve. My mind is still inquiring. Complicated, how exactly?"

Bev inhaled a long breath before she began her explanation. "Well, there is someone, I'll admit it. I'm really very attracted to her and have strong feelings for her, but she's in a relationship of sorts already, and very loyal to her partner even though they haven't had a conversation for nearly three years."

"I don't get it. Where is she, in the army, in jail? Even there you're allowed phone calls. Why can't she talk to her?" Kate asked.

Knowing she was being intentionally difficult, Bev transformed the genuine smile she was struggling to contain into a smirk. "Oh I didn't say she couldn't talk to her. She speaks to her every day. I said they hadn't had a conversation."

Kate, the more impatient of the two, recognized that Bev was linguistically toying with them and spoke up. "Look at that face, Joan. We've so quickly forgotten what a smart ass our sweet-faced friend can be. She's been back less than ten minutes and already she's twisting our noses." Kate fixed her steely blue eyes on Bev. "Don't make me come over there and hurt you. Now answer the question."

"Oh, I tremble," Bev said pretending to cower.

Kate grabbed the arms of her chair, pretending to rise, and the three friends dissolved into laughter. Betsy returned with the drink order effectively ending Bev's fun. She left them menus after relating the specials for the evening.

Kate took a sip of her drink as she watched Bev's expression sober. "So, you going to tell us?"

"I guess. There's really nothing humorous about the situation." Bev idly poked at the ice in her drink with the stirrer. "Plain and simple, I've grown to care deeply for a woman involved in a relationship with a partner who's been in a coma for nearly three years."

Kate's brow furrowed with concern for her friend's well being. "What happens if she wakes up and finds out that you've been sleeping with her partner?"

"Wow! That simple question requires so many responses. First, it's extremely unlikely she'll ever wake up, and if she were to wake up, it's even less probable that she'd have any cognitive ability, or even recollection that she was ever involved with Tori." Bev took a deep breath. "Besides, we're not sexually involved."

Though her comment drew blank stares from both of her friends, only Kate responded. "So what kind of relationship is that?"

"A complicated one." Bev explained further why Tori was remaining committed to her partner and how they provided support and companionship for each other.

Joan shook her head in disbelief. "I just don't get it, Bev. I mean you're like her mistress, only without sex. What are you getting from that kind of relationship?"

"I guess, in a way, that's an accurate assessment. I know she'll put her partner's welfare above mine, or her own for that matter. Tori is an extraordinarily loyal and loving woman, and I consider myself blessed to know her. You would both like her and, if you met her, you'd understand. We're so good together." Bev paused, carefully considering if she should say more. "You're my friends. I recognize that my welfare is uppermost on your mind and it's what motivates your concern. I don't want my next statement to be off putting, but I need to say it. I'm not asking for your permission or your blessing for that matter. I only told you because you're my friends and because I want you to know there is someone of significance in my life. I know you'll be tempted to criticize my decision to invest in this relationship because my feelings for her are already go beyond friendship, and I'm risking being hurt again. Please don't. Knowing her has been good for me. She's made me realize that the hurtful things Connie said were not sentiments that everyone would have. I feel stronger than I have in years and I'm confident again."

Joan glanced over Bev's shoulder at the door as it opened. "I'm glad to hear that because Connie just came in."

Chapter Twenty-six

ON HER WAY TO her session with Karolina, Tori wondered what she'd discuss with her counselor now that she seemed to have resolved most of the original issues that brought her to counseling. *I'm clear and on good terms with Bev and have a friendship with her that is enriching and supportive. I'm more at peace, and my life feels more in order, more under control. I'm enjoying the luxury of having a less rigid visitation schedule with Liz and I no longer feel it is a guilty pleasure to sit on the boardwalk and enjoy the sun, or to take a bike ride.*

During her last session, she'd told Karolina that the fact that Bev spent time with Liz pleased her, too. Bev had a whole raft of stories to tell Liz, often sparked by something in one of the novels they read to her. Tori loved the way Bev told a story. They always seemed to have a point, either touching or humorous, and she'd come to know more about Bev's life and character through listening to Bev as she shared them with Liz. She admired how Bev had become comfortable with talking to Liz and getting no feedback, a feat with which she herself sometimes still struggled.

Finding a parking place with ease buoyed her already good mood. Once parked, she made the short walk to Karolina's office where, after a brief wait, Karolina opened the door and invited her in.

Karolina greeted her warmly. As usual, they sat opposite each other across the desk. "So, how was your week?"

"It was good. Really good."

"So what do you want to discuss this week?"

"I'm not sure. You told me last session to rethink my goals. I was thinking on my way here today that my life is pretty settled. I mean, by the time I initially came to see you I was a mess. I was depressed, not sleeping. Now, I'm in a better place, taking time when I need it for my own wellbeing, and doing things I enjoy. Bev and I are in a good place, I think, although I still worry I'm being unfair to her."

"Just remember that you are not responsible for her. She is in control of her life. Because you have been honest with her about everything and she has chosen to remain close to you within the limits you've established, you have no need to feel that you are behaving inappropriately."

"I know. As a worrier, I have to have something that meets that need, don't I?" Tori grinned. "Really, I think it's just more a concern for her that stems from how much she means to me. I don't ever want to see her hurt, and definitely don't want to cause any pain to her."

"I can understand that."

"You know," Tori said, "my anniversary with Liz is coming up very soon, on the eighteenth, actually. I have a tendency to get a little down around that time. I guess I feel sorry for all I lost and all we no longer have."

"Let's talk about that and discuss some techniques to help with that."

At the conclusion of the session they agreed that they would keep their next regularly scheduled appointment on the nineteenth and drop to once a month after that if all continued to be well. Tori felt good as she left the office and ran across the street to her car. Usually, she'd call Bev after her session. Today she didn't want to bother her while she was driving. She ran home and took a quick shower.

Tori missed Bev. She perused the stack of CDs Bev had loaned her from her eclectic collection of music. Before Bev, she'd rarely listened to jazz, classical, or disco music. She passed over the Abba album and picked one of the CDs, popped it into the player, and turned up the volume on the stereo. In the shower, she found herself humming one of Bev's favorite pieces of music, some classical piece by Vivaldi that she played frequently. Bev had very eclectic tastes in music and through Bev Tori had become exposed to artists and styles of music she would previously never have considered listening to. After she dried off, she dressed quickly and went to the kitchen for a snack. As she sat at the counter, she noticed the message bar flashing on the phone. She pushed the button and listened to the message twice. The first time to hear what Bev said, the second time just to hear her voice. She reached for the phone to call her back, but stopped to check her watch. *Oh, damn, too late.* Bev would already be on her way to meet her friends. She was comforted knowing that Bev was safe and had thought about her. Still, it would have been nice to just say hello. She gathered her belongings and left to visit with Liz.

Arriving at the Center, Tori trod the familiar hallway.

MJ called to her as she turned the corner. "Hey, how's it going?"

"Good, really good. Just came from Karolina's. Is everything okay?"

"They started Liz on an antibiotic today. She's got another infection. Nothing is out of the norm other than that. Hopefully we have it early and it won't give us as much trouble as the last time."

"What's the drug regimen this time?

MJ pulled the chart. "Here, take a look."

"Wow! Her doctor is really moving aggressively on this and prescribing the heavy hitters early on."

"Yeah. He's concerned that she's so weak and depleted that her body will have no reserve to help combat the infection if it gets established."

"I'm going in to see her now. We getting together later?"

"Sure. I'll come up to you. Regular time?"

"Yup."

"See you then." As Tori started toward Liz's room, MJ called her back. "Don't be shocked. Claudia and Frank are in with Liz."

"What's up?"

"Not sure. They showed up a couple of hours ago, then left quickly. Forty-five minutes later they returned and they've been in there ever since."

"Hmm. That's odd." *Wonder what in the world would cause them to come here. Both of them, even. MJ had told her that Liz was serious, but stable. She'd pulled through scares like this numerous times before. This time would be just the same, wouldn't it?*

Tori paced thinking that she'd been killing time for at least a half hour. Checking her watch, she was surprised to discover that a mere ten minutes had passed. She sat down in the chair in the waiting area. Her fingers drummed on the table next to her. After a few minutes of that annoyance, MJ shot her a look. Tori stood and resumed her pacing. She checked her watch one more time.

"MJ, there's no sense me wearing a path in your carpet here. I think I'll go up to my office and give them whatever time they need. Will you call me if there's any news?"

"Sure, you know I will."

Giving one final glance down the hallway toward Liz's room, Tori turned away. "I'll see you later."

Chapter Twenty-seven

CONNIE STRODE ACROSS THE room coming to a stop in front of Bev and her friends. "Hello Joan...Kate. I'd hoped I might find you here at our old haunt. Could I speak with you, privately?"

"Could you or may you?"

"Don't be a smart ass, Bev, it's not becoming."

"I'm having dinner with my friends so the answer is no, you may not speak with me in private. I'm busy."

"I can see you are busy. Okay, I'll play your game. I assume you are staying at the hotel on Fifth. I'll meet you in the bar there at ten, if you'd prefer that."

Bev fixed Connie with a glare able to curdle milk. Unfortunately, Connie seemed oblivious to Bev's best efforts to deter her and remained in place. "Connie...why can't you just take no for an answer? I don't want to discuss anything with you in private."

"Fine with me, I don't need to have privacy." Connie reached for the chair at the table next to where they were all sitting. "I'm more than happy to talk in front of them. I'll just join you. It's either that, or you can agree to meet me for drinks later like I suggested."

Already people were starting to stare. "Jesus...You win. I'll see you there, but make it nine thirty. I've had a long day and I plan on being in bed early."

Connie's eyes swept Bev's body. "Works for me." She pushed the chair back under the table. "Ladies..."

Three sets of eyes watched as Connie strode across the restaurant and out the door.

"Well, that was interesting. What do you suppose she wants?" Kate asked.

"I have no idea. I'd been hoping to avoid a confrontation with her." Bev ran her fingers through her hair. "I'm in no mood for her tonight. We finished our relationship and settled our affairs before I moved away. What could she possibly want? Is she seeing anyone that you know of?"

"She's kept a pretty low profile lately. We rarely see her here, maybe once every other month or so. When she comes here, she's always alone, and never leaves with anyone. I don't know where she's hanging out or with whom. Do you want me to ask around? One of the bartenders may know something," Joan offered.

"No. I really don't care. She is yesterday's news. When she dumped me, I'll admit I was crushed. In addition to dealing with the cancer, she dumped all that added baggage on me about the scar turning her off. I'm happy to say I've left all of that behind. I'm confident she can no longer hurt me. I have Tori to thank for that."

"I hope we get to meet this woman. She sounds pretty impressive."

"I'll try to convince her to come with me for the anniversary celebration."

The three friends enjoyed their meal, and caught up on all the news about their mutual friends. They enjoyed coffee and lingered over dessert. At eight thirty, Bev began to gather her belongings. Kate and Joan refused to allow Bev to pay for her meal. She thanked them each and hugged them goodbye. "I'll call you the minute I get back from Chicago. Maybe you can come up for a visit before the weather gets too cold. The shore is gorgeous in the fall. It's my favorite time of the year there."

"We'll think about it. You know how hard it is for us to get away. Owning this place is a twenty-four, seven job. We promise to keep in touch though, don't we, Joan?"

Joan nodded. "Don't forget to call us tomorrow and let us know how tonight went."

Bev promised. She had just enough time to get back to her hotel and freshen up before she met Connie.

***

Connie was waiting at the bar when Bev strolled in at nine thirty-five. She stood as Bev approached and reached out to hug her. Bev stopped her with a hand to the middle of her chest. "I don't think so."

Connie shrugged.

The bartender, who was not busy, took Bev's drink order and quickly served her the white wine she ordered.

"Shall we get a table?"

Bev scanned the room and selected a table off to the side. There were only two other couples sitting at tables on the other side of the bar. Soft jazz played over the sound system at a high enough volume that their conversations were muted. Connie carried both drinks and followed Bev to the table.

Bev fixed her gaze on her former partner. "So. You wanted to speak privately. Get on with it."

"Look, can we start over? I was hoping we could be friends."

"Really? Give me a good reason why I would want to be your friend. You left me at possibly my moment of greatest need. To make an already bad situation worse, you said some terrible things, at a time I was most vulnerable. All of that destroyed my self-esteem and my confidence. I needed you, Connie. Desperately. You hurt me so deeply that it took longer for that hurt to heal than it did for my breast to heal."

"I know. I hope you will believe me. I'm really very sorry." Connie's apology was met with a raised eyebrow. "Really, sweetheart, I'm so, so sorry. I hope you can forgive me." Connie's eyes traveled from Bev's face, down her body, and returned to her eyes. " You're looking hot, baby. I can't believe I gave you up. Definitely hot. What did you do, have reconstructive surgery?"

Bev smiled. "You really missed the proverbial boat, Connie. You thought my scar was, what was the word you used? Oh yeah, hideous. My doctor was so pleased with the results six months later, he arranged for me to have the centerfold spread in the *Mastectomy Monthly* magazine. You'd have appreciated being involved with a centerfold model, wouldn't you? Want to see the picture? It was really quite tasteful, just the one breast showing."

"You were naked in a magazine? Sure. Wow! That's cool. I guess everything..." Connie gestured in the general direction of Bev's breasts. "I guess they came out okay after all." It took her a few seconds to realize that she was being ridiculed. "You're being a bitch and having me on aren't you? I've always hated that snarky sense of humor of yours."

"And I've always hated that you dumped me and said hurtful, hateful things to me when I was down and needed you the most. You are devoid of even one iota of kindness, sensitivity, or caring, and haven't even a modicum of concern for anyone other than yourself. The only thing you have going for you are your looks."

Connie shrugged. "No, there's my money, too."

Bev started to stand up. Connie's hand snapped out and grabbed her by the wrist. "Wait. Please. Don't go. This isn't what I wanted when I asked you to meet me. Maybe now that you've gotten that out of your system we can talk. I really am sorry, Bev. I don't know what came over me. It's just that I was always so turned on by your body. After the surgery, it was like you were someone else. You were no longer perfect...you know like a favorite mug that gets a chip in it."

All the feelings of hurt, need, and abandonment rose up and coalesced into a ball of fire that centered in Bev's chest. She stood and her anger exploded. "I don't know how I didn't realize how shallow you really are, Connie. How could your lovely mother ever have given birth to a heartless creature like you? You're pathetic. If it makes you feel any better I forgive you. I hope you'll forgive me, too." She tossed the glass of wine in Connie's face and strode out of the bar.

Bev took the stairs to her room on the third floor. Still out of breath, she locked the door and leaned against it, hands shaking and her breath coming in gulps. Tears streamed from her eyes—part relief, part anger, and part astonishment at her own actions. *How could I have done that? Who was that woman down there? More importantly, where was she when Connie said those horrible things so long ago? I don't know where she was, but she's here now.* Connie's image, eyes wide, chin and nose dripping wine, flashed into her head. Laughter started slowly, and then built until Bev doubled over, her hands holding her sides.

Bev stripped her clothes off, took a relaxing shower and slid into bed before she placed the call to Tori. Voice mail answered, so she left a brief message, and snapped the cover over her phone. Seconds later, she got a text.

'I'm in my office. Call me when you get in.'

***

"Hey you! I miss you. How was your trip?" Tori hardly waited for Bev to say hello before she started talking.

"I'll tell you in a minute. First, how are you, and how is Liz?"

"We're both okay, I guess." Tori described the scene when she'd come into visit Liz earlier. "I'm waiting to hear how Liz is. Her parents are still in with her. I don't have any more information than that. MJ told me they've been playing with the medication."

"I don't care what time it is, text me if you hear anything else."

"I will. I promise. How is your visit so far? How was dinner with your friends?"

"The whole evening has been...uh...interesting. I'll tell you more once I get home."

No amount of prodding by Tori could get Bev to reveal more, so she changed the subject. "I especially missed you after counseling today. I had big news and I wanted to share it with you."

"Tell me now. My news can wait."

Excitement crept into Tori's voice "I graduated myself, for want of a better term. I told Karolina that I didn't think I needed to see her until a couple of days before Liz's and my anniversary. Usually I have a hard time. This year, I have a different outlook. At least I think I do. Although, you'll be gone, so we'll see."

"I don't know. Three weeks from now. I might be back home. Maybe I won't get the contracts. You might be stuck with me hanging around."

"You know I'd never feel that way. So tell me about your trip."

"Wish you'd come with me. You might have found the trip...what would be the proper word? Shocking? Horrifying? At the very least, I'm sure you'd have been disappointed by my behavior."

Tori had a smile on her face as she responded, "The only way I'd be disappointed is if you got drunk, stripped naked and danced on the bar. Then I'd only be disappointed that I missed it."

"Hmm." Bev chuckled. "I'll have to tuck that bit of information away in my data bank to explore more fully at some later, unspecified time. Actually, my moment of infamy was probably even more dramatic than that. I did something I never in the world thought I'd be capable of. In fact if anyone told me I'd do it, I'd have called them a liar."

"Come on, give it up. Tell me what happened."

Bev related the story of her encounter in the bar. "So, are you ashamed of me?"

"No, quite the opposite. I'm proud of you for standing up to her. Really though, Bev, centerfold of *Mastectomy Monthly*? Where did you come up with that?"

"I have no idea. Nor do I have any idea who threw that drink in her face. Remember that scene in the movie, *Fried Green Tomatoes*, where Kathy Bates' character Towanda emerged and she went ballistic in the

store parking lot? I think this was my Towanda moment. I don't know
what came over me. I'd just had enough of her bull. Boom! It was an out
of body moment. I watched my hand move as everything happened in
slow motion. I saw the wine twisting as it left the glass and sailed
through the air. Her eyes widened, her mouth dropped open, and the
wine made contact. Next thing there are little glistening drops of wine
like fireflies dripping from her eyebrows, her nose, her chin."

"What did she say?"

"No clue." Bev laughed. "Like the coward I am, I beat feet out the
door and took the stairs two at a time up to my room."

"And how about you? How do you feel now?" Tori grinned. "Gee, I
sound like Karolina."

Bev smiled. "Well, doctor, I'm calmer now that I've confessed my
sins to you. Thanks for listening and for not being horrified by my
behavior."

"My pleasure. It was a good laugh. I'm actually quite proud of you."

"Me too, I think. I'd never have stood up to Connie before. It felt
good. At least it will until she sues me."

Tori's brows furrowed. "Why would she sue you?"

"Oh, didn't I mention she's a lawyer? She sues ten people every
morning for breakfast. Suing people is her morning shot of espresso."

"She won't sue you. It would be too embarrassing for her."

"Hope you're right. Will you still be my friend when I'm a convicted
criminal?"

"You're starting to sound like me, worrying about all the things
that'll never happen."

"I know. Geez! I still can't believe I did that." Bev laughed.

"To-wan-da." Tori drew out the syllables and they laughed
together.

Bev was feeling better after speaking with Tori for thirty minutes.
"See you in two days."

"Call me tomorrow night?"

"Try and stop me." With reluctance, Bev disconnected.

Chapter Twenty-eight

BEV AWOKE EARLY THE next morning. She felt homesick and wished she was on her way back to her cozy beachfront condo, and to Tori of course. She got up, showered, and dressed. At eight o'clock she dialed Connie's cell. Connie was laughing as she answered. "I should have bet someone you'd call this morning."

Bev's jaw muscles tightened. She clenched her teeth in annoyance that that Connie still knew her so well.

"So, what is the reason for your call?"

"I called to say I'm sorry I threw the wine in your face. Despite the fact that you deserved it, I'm ashamed of my behavior. I'm sorry."

"It's okay. Apology accepted. I had that coming and more. The whole evening didn't go quite as I wanted it to. I've been a jerk, Bev. In more ways than you are aware of. I had something I planned to tell you last night. Somehow I didn't get the chance." Connie paused waiting for a response. When there was none, she took a chance that there was some degree of equanimity restored between them. "Listen, I'm down in the lobby of your hotel. I was hoping to catch you before you went to Gertie's house. Will you let me buy you breakfast? One condition, though, no throwing of anything allowed. Deal?"

"Give me ten minutes. I'll be right down."

As Bev emerged from the elevator, Connie stood and went to meet her. Once settled in a booth in the cafe, they ordered and received coffee. Bev apologized again.

Connie smiled. "Believe me, I more than had it coming. Last night, I really had pure intentions. I know I was a lousy partner when you were diagnosed. I acted like a fool, said horrible things to you. I have no justifiable excuse other than to tell you my world fell apart, too, when you got sick. I wasn't in my right mind. I wanted to pull you closer, but it was like last night only on a grander scale. Instead of growing closer I somehow managed to push you further away. Things escalated and I said some horrible things to you. You withdrew and things just got worse from there. I'm sorry Bev. I never wanted to hurt you."

"I'm not sure how to respond to your perception of the demise of our relationship. Though, at this point, it really is a moot point isn't it?

"Well, believe it or not, I really do need you to understand, to accept my apology, to forgive me so I can move on. You've steadfastly refused my phone calls, returned my letters unopened. I needed to see you and convince you that I'm so very sorry."

"If it's so important to you, consider yourself absolved. I'm curious though, why now after all these years?"

"I'm not happy, Bev. I want to be happy. I've been going to counseling and part of my therapy is to make peace with my past, with you." Connie moved the coffee cups to the end of the table out of reach. "In order to achieve that goal, to get to speak to you, I've done something that I know is going to really piss you off, and maybe undo the peace we've managed to achieve. I may have misled you a bit to get you here so we could talk. Bev, Gertie isn't home. She's on a cruise down some river in Europe...she's fine."

Incredulity, shock, and anger sped through Bev's mind, each showing on her face as she processed the information. Bev drew herself into a standing position. "Trust me, you need more than forgiveness from me. I hope you find what you're seeking. My advice to you is to search for your humanity first. You've always been very Machiavellian, but this is beyond what I'd ever expect from you. Goodbye Connie. Don't ever contact me again."

Bev walked to the elevator, entered it, and when it stopped, she calmly walked to her room and packed her suitcase. Twenty minutes later she'd completed checkout, retrieved her car, and was headed home. Her mind raced with emotion and disbelief. *How could I have ever loved that person? She's simply unbelievable, so arrogant, so selfish, so self-centered, and so different from Tori. Tori, I can't wait to get home to you.*

Three hours and seven minutes later Bev pulled into her parking lot and parked. She hurried across the street, through the condo lobby, and up the stairs to Tori's apartment. Pushing the doorbell repeatedly, she finally stopped when she heard Tori say, "Okay, okay, hold your horses, I'm coming."

The door opened and she threw her arms around Tori. "I need you." She buried her face in Tori's neck and felt like she was coming home as Tori's arms went around her and pulled her inside. No words were spoken and none seemed necessary. Tori simply pulled her to the sofa and embraced her, cradling Bev against her chest.

After allowing herself to be comforted Bev finally felt more stable and in control. She pulled back and looked at Tori. She reached up and touched her face. "Thank you. Wait until you hear what happened." She told Tori about her encounter with Connie.

"My God, she's beyond belief."

"I couldn't wait to get home to you, I needed you so much. Thank you for being here for me." She reached for a tissue and wiped her eyes. "How could I have ever thought I loved someone like that? How could I have let her words hurt me, damage me for so many years? Now I see who she really is, and what she's really capable of doing to get what she wants." Bev wiped her hand across her brow. She turned around and snuggled against Tori who wrapped her in her arms. "I'd better get out of here before I ask you for what I need from you right now. Although I respect your dedication to Liz, right now I'm feeling selfish." She kissed Tori tenderly on the cheek.

Bev pulled away and when Tori reached for her, Bev said, "No." She stood up and backed away.

Tori stood and walked Bev to the door. "You don't have to go."

Bev smiled a sad smile. "Yes. Yes I do, for both our sakes. I'm not strong enough to stay any longer tonight. I'm okay. I'll get it back together again and I'll call you later." She gave Tori a quick hug and left for home.

Chapter Twenty-nine

SUNDAY MORNING, THE DAY of her departure for Chicago, Bev's phone rang. "You all packed?" Tori asked.

"Yes. Are we having lunch before you drop me at the airport?"

"I'll pick you up in fifteen minutes, okay?"

"Yes. That's perfect."

Lunch was at their favorite Italian restaurant. Once settled, they chatted briefly. Bev asked, "How's Liz?

"I saw her this morning. Her temperature is elevated again. They suspect they may need to try a stronger last-ditch type of antibiotic. She's already getting two powerful ones."

"What does MJ say?"

"She's off today. I'll talk to her tomorrow. There's a staffing to discuss Liz's condition. Her mother called me this morning to tell me about it. At least I'll be able to hear what's happening first hand this time."

Bev sought Tori's eyes. "Maybe I should stay here with you until we're sure Liz will be okay."

"No. I'm sure she'll be fine"

"T, if this gets serious, call me and I'll come home."

"Thank you. She's had some pretty serious infections in the past and her doctors managed to get them under control. Before, though, she was stronger. I'll admit I'm worried, but I'm sure everything will be okay."

"Please, promise you'll call me if she gets worse. I'll catch the next flight back."

"I will. I swear." Tori began to gather her belongings. "Come on, we'd better get going."

The ride to the airport was quiet, each woman deep in thought. Tori pulled into short-term parking and helped Bev remove her bag from the trunk.

Bev pulled out the handle to the suitcase. "I wish you were coming with me."

"I know. Me too. You know I can't."

"I know. The fact that I understand why you can't doesn't make me wish it any less. I'll call you the minute my flight lands and we can talk on the computer later, once I'm settled in my hotel." Bev pulled Tori into a close embrace.

"I wish you didn't have to go." Tori pulled back to search Bev's face one more time, committing her features to memory. Their eyes met. They were so close she could feel Bev's breath on her face as she exhaled. Tori's heart pounded as Bev leaned in to kiss her. The kiss was soft and slow, and filled with longing.

Bev pulled away removing her lips and replacing them with her finger. "Shh, don't say anything. It's just a little kiss goodbye. I'm leaving now and I just couldn't go without doing that."

Tori nodded. They both had tears in their eyes as Bev picked up her bag and turned to walk away. She watched until Bev disappeared into the terminal before she started her car and drove straight to the hospital.

***

Tori's heart warmed as she watched the computer screen, waiting for the dimple to appear in Bev's cheek as her broad smile and twinkling eyes greeted her.

"Hey there you are!" Bev's standard cheery greeting as she answered Tori's call never failed to garner a warm smile of her own in return.

Tori gave a little wave. "Hi there, yourself. Busy day?"

"Yes. Very." Bev propped her chin on her palm. "A good busy, though, especially now that I'm working with both these companies."

"I'm so proud that you were able to sell both of them your program. I know from experience what a wizard you are. I thank you every time I do my reports that, by the way, take me half the time they used to." Tori stopped and licked her lips. "Um, change of topic here. How much longer will you need to be there?"

"If I can finish up gathering the data I need, I should be home next week."

Tori sighed. "Oh good. I miss you. I've come to expect to be able to share with you nearly every thought, feeling, and event that occurs during my day."

"I know." Bev's dimple reappeared. "I miss you too. This working during regular daytime hours sucks! I never realized how much working similar hours makes communication easier."

Tori laughed. "How true, how true."

"How is Liz doing?"

"No improvement yet. She seems to be holding her own. She's struggling though, Bev. Her breathing is so ragged. They have adjusted her meds again. If they're going to be effective, the new antibiotics will have to kick in soon and there should be a positive change in her condition in the next couple of days. She just seems so weak and still. Her breathing is so shallow. If this keeps up they'll intubate her again."

"I'll get home as soon as I can, T. If she turns worse, call me and I'll come right away."

"Thanks, Bev. I appreciate you offering that. She'll be okay though. We've been through this several times, and she always pulls through."

"I know. Still I want to be there with you if she gets worse."

"I promise I'll call you if there's a change either way."

Bev reached out and adjusted her computer screen to get a better view. "How was your session with Karolina today?"

"Good. I seemed to manage to get through the anniversary without my usual depression. During my session we actually discussed my missing you more than anything else."

"Oh? I'm glad Karolina has helped you so much."

Tori smiled. "Taking a piece of my life back, and sharing it with you, doing things with you, Victor, and MJ, also helped. I was lost."

"And I'm so glad I found you right there in the fruit section of the market."

Tori chuckled. "Where better to find a lesbian?" They laughed together.

Bev checked her watch. "As much as I don't want to, I'd better let you go. I'll get home as soon as I can. I'm talking to that programmer tonight. You remember the one I'd mentioned to you before, Roger? He's very sharp. I floated the idea to him about working for me, and he seemed interested. If we can agree on a package, I plan to hire him part time, initially, and full time later as we get going on the project. If he proves as good as I think he is, it'll give options for expansion and growth of my program."

"That's great. I can't wait to see you." After a few more minutes, they disconnected.

***

The next week was doubly difficult for Tori due to a combination of factors, foremost Liz's delicate condition. Although she sat nearly motionless at Liz's bedside watching her lover struggle to breathe, Tori's mind raced. *Normally, Bev would have shared my fears and worries about Liz. Bev would have been nearly as concerned as me. Instead of sitting here alone at Liz's bedside watching her struggle to breathe, Bev would have been here with me to share this burden of watching Liz inhale each agonizing breath. God I wish she were here.*

MJ came in and stood behind her resting her hands on Tori's shoulder. Tori reached up and patted her hand. There were no words exchanged, but knowing MJ was there helped. MJ gave Tori's shoulder a squeeze before she went to check Liz's vitals.

"Any change?"

MJ shook her head. "No...she's about the same. She's a fighter."

Tori's eyes filled, but she'd vowed not to cry in front of Liz. She blinked back her tears and resumed her silent vigil. When she couldn't tolerate sitting there watching Liz's struggle any longer, she'd leave for a short break and go sit on her favorite bench on the boardwalk to take solace from the ocean. It was in those quiet moments she thought about how many times she missed Bev, but also of how often they usually interacted on a daily basis. *I can't speak to her the numerous times every day I reach for my cell phone to tell her something, or to get her support and reassurance, but thank God we do have the capability of talking, and even seeing each other on the computer at least once everyday. I can't imagine how I'd get through this if I couldn't share my thoughts with Bev.*

Tori closed her eyes and allowed her thoughts to return to Liz. Tears filled her eyes and tracked down her cheeks as she reviewed the less than promising reports the doctors had been providing about her condition.

I need to stop now. I'm just feeling a little sorry for myself. Liz's breathing is so ragged. It sounds like each breath she takes might be the last. Then after a pause, she exhales and does it all over again. It's torture to watch. Tori propped her elbows on her knees and her chin on her fists and recalled the confession she'd made to Bev during their chat the night before.

"I have these awful thoughts, Bev. Sometimes I wish Liz would just let go. She's suffering, and it's so horrible to watch. Then I feel so bad about my thoughts, because she's fighting so hard."

"I should be there with you. I want to be with you Tori."

"No. I'm okay, really, and the doctors are still holding out some hope they can come up with something to help her. I'm just feeling sorry about the whole situation. I'll be better now that we've talked."

"I miss you too. Call me if you need me and I can come right away if you change your mind."

"No. You need to be there and the situation here is stable so far."

Tori checked her watch. She really needed to get back. But she needed a shower and decided to do that and then head back to sit with Liz before work. Tori took solace from her conversation with Bev, the previous night. Just knowing she had Bev gave the strength she needed to go back to Liz's bedside.

Tori left home on her way in to see Liz. She stopped for gas after she picked up a sandwich at the deli. Her phone buzzed indicating she had a text message. Resisting the urge to check it while driving she reasoned, *I'll be at work in less than ten minutes and I'll check it then.* Her sandwich and purse tucked under one arm she used her free hand to dial MJ's number. The call went straight to voice mail indicating MJ was on the phone. Rounding the corner, she glanced at the nurse's station before going to Liz's room, and was surprised to see MJ there in street clothes.

"Hey, MJ," she called. "You're in early. Working a double?" Seeing the concern on her friend's face, she waved a greeting to the other two nurses at the desk as well, and scrapped her plan to go directly to Liz's room when she saw the concern on her friend's face.

"No, I came in to sit with you and Liz."

"What's wrong, MJ?"

Pointing to Sue, the nurse on duty, MJ said, "She couldn't reach you, so she called me to let me know that Liz's condition had worsened. She thought maybe I could get in touch with you. I couldn't get you either"

"I was probably in the shower or in the car on my way in. What's up?"

"Liz's doctor checked her early this afternoon, shortly after you left. He was concerned enough to call Liz's parents. They've agreed to hospitalize her. I wanted to be with you. Victor too. He's off getting us something to drink. The Parkers are still here, they're in with her now."

Tori blinked, trying to take in and process all the information MJ had just shared. "I'm surprised her condition worsened so quickly. I was with her this morning. What changed?"

"Her breathing got worse. They're transferring her to the hospital soon. They expect the transfer team any minute now."

"Yes, I was concerned before I left. Her breathing seemed worse than it had been." Tori grew silent as she processed the new information. "Why didn't anyone call me?"

"You know that Liz's parents are the contacts of record. Sue asked them for permission to contact you as soon as they got here. Sue called your home the minute they gave permission. She couldn't reach you, and thinking we might be together, she called me. Victor and I came right over. We got here about five minutes before you did."

The Parkers came down the hallway from Liz's room. Liz's father went to the desk to speak to Sue, while Claudia approached Tori. "Hello. I'm glad to see they were able to contact you."

Tori smiled. "I was already on my way in and missed the call. Claudia, I'm sure you must know MJ, my friend and colleague, and one of Liz's nurses. She usually works nights with me."

"Yes, MJ. How are you?" Claudia didn't wait for a response. "The transfer team just arrived. Will you be coming to the hospital?"

Tori bit her tongue and gave a quieting glance at MJ who looked ready to pinch Claudia's head right off. Instead of uttering the response that immediately shot into her head, she smiled sweetly and replied in the affirmative. "We'll see you there."

Claudia nodded and left to join her husband.

Victor returned with coffee and after handing it to MJ, he pulled Tori into his embrace. She snuggled into his massive chest. "Thanks for being here, Victor. You and MJ are the best."

"Did you call Bev?"

"No, I didn't have time. Would you mind doing it for me? Tell her I'll call her as soon as I get to the hospital and find out any new information. I have to arrange for coverage for tonight and tomorrow night for work. Fortunately, I have the next couple of days off after that."

MJ spoke up. "I have a better idea. How about Victor drives you so you can call Bev. I'll make arrangements to get coverage for both of us. You go. Don't worry. I'll take care of everything here."

"Perfect! Great idea. Thank you." Tori hugged her friend. "Ready, Victor?"

"Sure." He gave MJ a quick kiss goodbye. "We'll see you there, sweetheart."

Chapter Thirty

AS VICTOR DROVE, TORI dialed Bev's number. The call transferred to voicemail. Tori took comfort from the sound of Bev's voice even though it was only her recorded greeting.

"Hi Bev, it's me. I'm in the car on the way to the hospital. Liz's breathing took an abrupt turn for the worse this afternoon. Victor and MJ are with me, so I'm okay. I don't have much information right now. You're probably meeting with Roger. Call me when you get this message, please."

A little over two hours later, the phone rang causing Tori to jump. She snatched it up and eagerly checked the caller ID. Following a flurry of greetings, Bev apologized. "I'm sorry, I just got your call. I turned off the phone while I met with Roger. What's happening? How's Liz, and how are you?"

"We're here at the hospital, taking turns visiting. Liz is in intensive care, so visitation is limited. Gowns, gloves, and booties are required for visits. The infection now appears to be an antibiotic resistant one and isn't responding to the medication she was on. There should have been improvement by now if the med she was on was going to work. Her doctor just adjusted her medication again. We should know if the new drug regimen is working within the next forty-eight hours. Until then, it's a waiting game."

"I'll call for plane reservations as soon as we hang up."

"I appreciate that, and as much as I want you here with me, there's nothing you can really do. We're all just sitting around holding each other's hands. You are almost finished with your work there. If she improves, you'd have wasted a trip."

"First of all, no trip to be with you is wasted. I want to be there to hold your hand, too. Like it or not I'm coming."

"I'd like it very much. I just..."

"Shh. I know. Tori, did you call your folks yet?"

"Not yet. I'll call them, in the morning. You know them, if I called them tonight, they'd leap in the car and I don't want them making that trip in the dark."

"Okay, let me go so I can get a flight. I'll call you with my arrival time later. Maybe Victor can pick me up?"

"I'm sure he'll do that for us." After a brief pause, Tori said, "Thanks for coming. I feel better knowing you're on your way."

"I don't want to hang up, but unless we do, I can't get the reservation. I'll call you later. Don't forget."

"Don't forget what?"

"That I'm coming to be with you. And that I care."

"I won't. You too."

***

It was a long night. Victor had left earlier to go to work, promising to return in the morning. MJ sat with Tori as they waited their turn to see Liz. Frank and Claudia decided to go home to catch a few hours of sleep and take a shower before returning. Victor returned at eight thirty and stayed with Tori until MJ returned freshly showered with a change of clothing for Tori. MJ had a friend who arranged for Tori to use one of the hospital on-call rooms so she could shower and change her clothes. She returned to join her friends. Victor got them breakfast, and they sat in the lounge drinking the huge cups of coffee and consuming the breakfast sandwiches he'd gotten in the hospital cafeteria.

"I spoke with Bev this morning just before she boarded her flight. I'll go collect her around ten thirty."

"Bless her, she was able to get the early flight out...I've talked with her a couple of times."

"You look surprisingly awake." Victor said, as he squeezed MJ's hand.

Gesturing to the four recliners on the other side of the room, away from the television, Tori said, "Those are surprisingly comfortable. We took turns, and each of us got about three hours of sleep."

At nine, Liz's mother returned. Claudia's eyes widened when she found the group in the waiting room. "You're all early birds. We thought we'd beat you here this morning."

"Oh, we never left."

Her face registered surprise. "Really?" She glanced at her husband as he entered the room. "Were you able to arrange the conference?"

"The doctor will meet with us after rounds this afternoon. Tori, we'd like to speak with you privately before we see the doctor this afternoon."

"We'll leave so you can use this space," MJ said standing up. She reached for Victor's hand. "We'll be just outside, Tori."

The sound of the door closing seemed inordinately loud in the quiet room. Tori waited for one of Liz's parents to reveal the purpose of their meeting. Finally, Frank spoke. "Claudia and I did a lot of soul searching last night and think we've arrived at a difficult decision that we wanted to share with you before we meet with the doctors this afternoon." Frank looked to his wife who nodded for him to continue. "When Liz first had her accident, we hoped for a different outcome, I'm sure you did as well. You know we didn't approve of the nature of your relationship with our daughter." He paused and Tori nodded. "I guess we still don't. However, credit where it is due. You've been steadfast in your caring for Liz. Both of us figured you'd move on. You surprised us by moving here and your devotion to her on a daily basis has, frankly, been nothing short of astonishing to us."

Tori looked at Claudia whose eyes were filled with tears. Frank inhaled a deep breath. "Unless you can convince us otherwise, we plan to sign a DNR today. The doctors tell us her chances of surviving this time are...well, they're not good. If Liz arrests, or succumbs to the pneumonia, we have decided it's time to let her go and don't want them to resuscitate. We think she's had enough. We've had enough. We can no longer stand to watch her..." He choked up and fought back his own tears.

Tori sat trying to process the meaning of Frank's words. On some level she knew this time was different. Still, she wasn't prepared for Frank's admission.

"Tori?" Claudia's brief touch on her arm caused her to jump. She shifted her eyes to meet Claudia's. "This hasn't been easy for any of us and we know you haven't always agreed with our decisions. We've never enjoyed a close relationship, although we do want you to know that we respect your commitment to Liz. You've earned the right to be here, to be involved, and we hope you will concur with us in this decision."

Tori closed her eyes, her mind racing. A hundred thoughts sprinted through her head as a tear slid down her cheek. Claudia pressed a tissue into her palm causing Tori to open her eyes. "Thank you." She dried her eyes and wiped her nose gathering her strength to speak those two difficult words. "I agree. Liz would hate living like this. If she goes, we should respect her body's wish to surrender."

"Do you think your friend MJ can advise us of how we go about arranging this so everything is in order when we speak to the doctor later?" Frank asked.

"I'll go speak to her." After a few words with MJ, Tori invited her into the room. She provided the advice they needed and Frank and Claudia went to arrange for signing the DNR.

Alone with Tori in the lounge, MJ said, "Victor went to meet Bev's plane."

"Oh good. Thank God you're thinking efficiently."

"How do you feel about all this?" MJ asked.

"I don't know exactly. It's a shock. I mean for so long they were so oppositional to our relationship, kept me isolated from any decisions related to Liz's care. Why are they involving me now?"

"What did they say to you?"

Tori related the details of her conversation with the Parkers.

"From what you say, and what I've seen, it seems they do want your agreement about their decision. It is a change in thinking for them."

"I can't help feeling that the last nearly three years have gone by so slowly, watching her day by day as she lay there in the coma, all the close calls Liz had. And now, doesn't it seem sudden to you that just like that," Tori snapped her fingers, "they've decided to let her go?"

"Don't do what you usually do and worry this to death. Think about it. They've been mellowing for a while now. It's been a recent development that they've let you get information from the doctors and ask questions of them. And when you went to visit your parents, Claudia came to see Liz while you were gone. Whatever the reason, I think it was important that you agreed with them. They seemed relieved that you supported their decision."

"Hey you two." Bev stood at the doorway.

"I'll leave you two alone. Victor and I will be outside." MJ pulled the door closed behind her.

190

"I'm so glad you're here." Tori stood to welcome Bev's embrace.

"Me too. I've missed you so much." They held the embrace, each reluctant to let go. Finally, Bev pulled back and asked, "How's Liz?"

"No change in her condition. I just had an interesting conversation with her parents though." Tori told Bev about the decision to not resuscitate.

"Are you really okay with that?"

Tori nodded. "Liz would have hated this existence. She was so full of life. I nibble at life, she was someone who grabbed off chunks full and gobbled them down. It always amazed me that she chose me to be her partner. I'm a plodder...she was an explorer. No, more than that, she soared. We couldn't have been more different."

"They say that opposites attract."

"I guess. I did ground her, I think."

MJ knocked at the door. "It's your turn to go in to visit Liz. Let Bev go with you this time. Victor and I are going to go get some lunch for everyone."

"Thank you." Tori gave both Victor and MJ a hug. "You guys are the best." She and Bev followed behind till they all arrived at the nurses' station where MJ and Victor turned to head for the front door. Tori and Bev approached the Parkers. "Frank, Claudia, this is my very close friend, Beverly McMannis. Bev, I'd like you to meet Liz's parents, the Parkers." Turning toward her in-laws, Tori added, "Bev flew in from Chicago this morning."

"You are the woman who sometimes reads to our daughter, aren't you? One of the nurses mentioned that to me."

"Yes. Victor and I work the night shift. That leaves me with a lot of free time during the day. I offered, and Tori agreed, that the added stimulation would be good for Liz. I've grown very fond of her."

"Thank you for your kindness."

"Bev, we'd better go so we don't miss our visit."

"Oh, Tori, we are meeting with the doctor at three thirty this afternoon in conference room two on this floor."

"Okay, thank you."

Chapter Thirty-one

DR. JACOBSEN SAT AT the head of the table and greeted Frank, Claudia, and Tori in turn. "I guess we should begin with a summary of Liz's current condition. As you know, we changed your daughter's medication yesterday when she was admitted, hoping we would see some improvement in her condition within twenty-four to forty-eight hours. So far, that has not happened. In fact, I was just in to check her prior to our meeting, and her breathing has deteriorated to a point where we are concerned..." Doctor Jacobsen's phone beeped interrupting him. At the same time, several tones sounded over the intercom. "Excuse me. It's Liz." He shoved his chair back and jogged from the room leaving the group staring at each other.

"I guess we should go see what happened." Frank stood and took his wife's hand, leading her from the room. They hurried down the hall. Tori followed close behind. Arriving at the waiting room, they joined Bev, MJ, and Victor. Six sets of eyes were glued to the double glass doors where they watched Dr. Jacobsen rip off his protective gown, cap, and gloves before disposing of them in the hazardous waste bin. He scrubbed his hands at the sink and dried them carefully. The doors swished open and the tall, scholarly appearing doctor strode across the hallway, a serious expression on his face. "Please, if you'd like me to speak privately, we can return to the conference room."

Frank glanced around. "These are all Liz's friends. What happened?"

"I'm very sorry to have to tell you that your daughter just passed away. She has fought long and hard. In the end, she couldn't beat the infection. I'm very sorry. We did everything we could medically. In keeping with your request we did not attempt to resuscitate her. You may go in if you'd like."

Everyone was so numb they simply sat staring at the floor deep in his or her own thoughts. Dr. Jacobsen looked to Liz's parents. "If there are no questions, the nurse will have some forms for you to sign and will provide you with a packet of information that gives you an idea of any additional papers you need to file related to legalities and the rest. If you have any questions, please don't hesitate to call."

"Thank you doctor." Frank extended his hand. "We know you tried your best."

"Thank you. Again, please accept my sincere condolences." He nodded to Liz's parents and in the general direction of the group of friends before he strode down the hallway.

They took turns going in to say goodbye. Mr. and Mrs. Parker went to sign the papers. Before they left they told Tori they would inform her of the arrangements as soon as they made them. After they left, MJ, Victor, and Bev went in for a few minutes. They came out, and Tori went in. She sat in the chair next to the bed where her partner's body lay.

Tori studied Liz's features looking for subtle changes to indicate she was really gone. She reached out and took Liz's hand, drew it to her lips, and touched it to her cheek before returning it to her side. She remained seated there, her mind blank. Realizing there was nothing more she could do, she knew she should leave so the nurses could take care of whatever it was they were waiting to do. She waited for the tears to come, but none did. *Maybe I'm just too tired to cry.* The realization that her life had just changed dramatically began to sink in. *Where will I go tomorrow morning?* Regret that Liz would never know the end of the book they were reading flooded through her. She looked up when Bev came in to stand next to her, putting her hand on Tori's shoulder.

"T, it's time to go."

"I know. Somehow I just can't bring myself to leave. I don't know what to do."

"You need to say goodbye. MJ, Victor, and I are going to take you out to get something to eat, and then I'll take you home. You'll feel better able to cope with all this after you get some food in you and are able to rest."

"Okay. Give me one minute more. I'll be right there."

Bev nodded. "I'll be outside."

Tori stood, carefully replacing the chair and taking comfort from restoring order before she left. She tidied the sheet and brushed Liz's hair back from her forehead. Heaving a shuddering sigh she whispered, "Well, safe journey, my love." She turned away, and with one final glance backward, she pushed the door open and left Liz behind.

***

The group went to a diner near the hospital. As they ate, conversation centered quite naturally on Liz. Tori looked at her group of friends. "I just can't believe she's gone. I guess I just never thought it would really happen...you know, because she'd beaten all the other infections. I guess I just never expected it to be so sudden. I expected I'd be better prepared."

Everyone was silent as they mulled their private thoughts. MJ reached over and touched Tori's hand. "Victor and I will stop over and let the staff at the Center know. Is there anything there that's yours?"

Tori shook her head.

"The staff will box everything up and give it to her parents then. Bev will take you home, okay?"

"Yes. Thank you all for staying with me." Tori sighed, exhaustion finally catching up with her. She'd obviously been running on adrenalin.

MJ grasped Victor's hand. "Do you want us to come over after we've taken care of things?"

"No, thanks. Although I appreciate the offer, I'm exhausted, and I'm sure you and Victor are, too. I'm going to go home, have a shower, and go to bed."

"I'll be at Victor's if you need me or us."

"Thanks." Tori stood up and started to reach for the check.

"I'll get it, and then I'll take you home." Bev picked up the check and went to pay the bill. In the parking lot, the friends hugged each other before parting ways. Bev opened the passenger door of Tori's car and Tori got in. Bev slid behind the driver's seat and headed across the bridge toward their home. "My place or yours?" Bev asked.

"I don't care. You decide."

"Let's go to mine." Bev put the car into gear.

***

"You want some tea?" Bev asked Tori. They were sitting in Bev's living room.

"No, I think I just want a shower and a good night's sleep."

"I'll turn on the lights and turn down the bed in the guest room. I'll leave some pajamas on the bed for you."

"Thanks. Bev, can I have a hug?"

"Of course." Bev crossed the room sat on the sofa and pulled Tori into her arms.

"Why can't I cry? I mean my lover just died and I haven't shed a tear."

"I don't know. Maybe it just hasn't sunk in yet."

"Maybe." Tori sat up, pulling away from Bev's embrace. "Thanks, for everything. For flying home and being here. I appreciate everyone for being there for me, especially you for coming back at such a critical time for your business, you know with new contracts and all." Tori settled into Bev again and rested her head on Bev's shoulder. Bev encircled her within her arms and kissed the top of Tori's head.

Tori's mind raced with different things she needed to do. "I'd better call my folks and let them know about Liz. They didn't even make it here in time to say good-bye. Frank and Claudia told me they were having a private funeral service. I don't even know if I'll be able to go. I'll call Claudia tomorrow. I'm sure my parents will want to come, too, if we're allowed."

"It's awful that you have to ask permission to go to her funeral. What's wrong with this country? It's just not right."

"When do you have to go back to Chicago?"

"I'll stay through the funeral."

The thought of Bev leaving brought a sheen of tears to Tori's eyes. "I'll miss you."

"I have to go back for a couple of weeks. I'll try to finish up everything so I can be back here by the end of October. After that, I can work on the program here and, when I'm done, I'll go back out to deliver it, train the staff and provide initial support and troubleshooting. By the way, Roger agreed to work with me, part-time initially, with the potential for full-time in a few months. So, like I told you before, I won't have to be gone often. I just wish I didn't have to leave you right now."

"Oh, Bev, it's what you'd hoped for and what I'd hoped for you. Congratulations. Now, I just wish it had happened sooner or later...you know, just not now. I don't know what I'm going to do with myself."

"Come with me to Chicago. Although I'll have to work, at least we'd be together. Besides you must have weeks of vacation time coming. Did you ever take a vacation day other than to go see your folks a couple of weeks ago?"

Tori smiled. "No, not that I recall." Tori pulled away and stood up. "I'd better go call my folks before they go to bed and tell them about Liz. Oh, can you help me tomorrow? Somewhere in my storage bin is a box where Liz kept all her important papers. Some may be documents they might need. I have a copy of her birth certificate, insurance policy, and maybe her passport. Do they need to turn that in?"

"I don't think so, though these days you never know."

Tori reached out, touched Bev's cheek, and said good night. Following her shower, she dressed in the borrowed pajamas Bev left for her, called her parents, and settled into the bed in the guest room. Feeling suddenly alone, she surprised herself with the realization that it was not Liz she missed. She missed Bev. "This is just stupid."

Bev called, "Come in," in response to Tori's soft knock on her partially closed bedroom door.

Tori pushed the door open but remained in the doorway. "I don't want to be alone...actually that's only partially true. I don't want to be alone. I want to be with you."

Bev smiled. "I'm glad, I want that, too."

Tori crossed the room and slid into bed. Bev wrapped her arm around Tori and brushed the hair from her face before placing a chaste kiss on her temple. "Okay?"

"Perfect. Are you okay with just this much for a while?"

Bev nodded. "I think we should date."

"Date?"

"Um hmm. We've had a relationship that was a strange blend of attraction and friendship. Maybe we should be sure that the attraction isn't just because you were unavailable. You know, like a forbidden treat."

Tori sat up. "Are you serious? That's the way you feel for real?"

Bev pulled a slightly resisting Tori down against her. "Honestly, no. I was trying to be respectful. I just didn't want you to think...well, that I expected you to want a more intimate relationship right away, and I didn't know how to say it. I don't know what you need from me right now."

"Tonight, I need to be with you, close to you. That's enough for now. We'll know when the time is right to move forward. I know you understand that because you put me in the guest room. Our feelings are deeper than friendship and we both know that. I'm the one who came to you. I just need a little more time, okay?"

"That feels right to me, too. Now go to sleep. I'm glad you're here with me. It feels good to be close."

Chapter Thirty-two

"WHERE THE HELL IS that box? It's got to be in here somewhere." Tori's voice came from deep within her storage unit where she'd stored the remains of her home she'd shared with Liz. Artwork, boxes of books, extra furniture she didn't need in her smaller condo, had all been placed there when she'd sold their house and moved to the shore. "Well here's a job that can keep me busy for a while. I can get rid of most of this stuff, especially all of these old boxes of books. They were all Liz's from college and from the summer workshop she took six or so years ago." She shifted things around, looking for the box she recalled Liz labeling 'WILL/LEGAL PAPERS' years ago. After the accident, Tori had moved it from its home in the back of the closet straight to the storage bin, where it had remained untouched. "Ah ha! Here it is. Whatever possessed me to put it in the back? Can you get this?" Tori struggled to hand the box to Bev who was helping her.

"Sure. Hand it out. Can you get out of there? You've got yourself boxed in."

Tori began shifting boxes to clear a pathway to the door. "I've got to drop off these legal papers to Liz's parents later this morning. Let's take this to my place first. I'll go through it and pull out the stuff they need."

At her condo, Tori put the box on the coffee table and went to the kitchen for a knife to cut the tape holding the lid in place. "I spoke with her parents this morning. They told me they'd arranged for cremation. There will be no service other than at the graveside when they bury her ashes. They aren't religious, so they said it would be very informal. Anyone who wishes to speak may. The service will be Monday. My parents are coming in Sunday."

"Why not let them stay at my place? You won't have to sleep on the sofa bed that way. You take my room and I'll stay at your place."

"Thanks for the offer. We'll see." Tori slit the tape holding the lid of the box in place. "Gee whiz, she really wanted this stuff secure. She used a half a roll of packing tape on it." Tori removed the lid. "Okay, get that manila envelope for me that I put on the table, please. I'll put the stuff for her parents in it. Let's see what all she has in here." Tori lifted the stack of papers from the box and started to sort through them. "What's this doing in here?" She handed Bev a small book of poetry. "I think this is everything her parents might need right here. While I look through this stuff, can you look through and see if there's anything in that book they might need?"

"Sure." Bev picked up the book and opened it to the page that was marked with a photo of a gorgeous woman with dark hair, magnetic eyes, and a dazzling smile, holding Liz in her arms. They were dancing in a very formal and fancy restaurant. Bev turned the photo over. "Who's Bernie Maxwell?"

"Who?"

"There's a photo from July 2008, of Liz with a woman named Bernie Maxwell."

"Let me see. I don't know anyone by that name." Tori examined the photo. "The picture looks like it was taken while she was in California for that two month course she took. Must be a friend from class. Wonder why Liz didn't mention this fancy dinner and why this stuff is in here? I have to admit, I'm jealous. She'd never dance with me."

There are two letters in the book as well. Bev examined the letters. "This one is from that woman, Bernie, and addressed to Liz. The other is from Liz to her, stamped 'Return To Sender'. Here." Bev handed the letters to Tori.

"I guess there's no harm in opening them now." Tori withdrew the letter from the unsealed envelope addressed to Liz and began to read. "Oh, my God! I can't believe this. Damn her!" Face flushed, she held her head in both hands, the letter crushed against her head. "My God! All these years I've devoted to her. I thought she loved me. I waited for her to come back to me. All those hours I sat at her bedside. For what? For a lie? For a cheater," she wailed as tears streamed from her eyes. "Listen to this." She read from the letter. "I can't live without you, Liz. Come to me...share my life and my bed. Blah, blah, blah. I can't live without you.

The week we spent together was amazing." Tori tossed the letter across the table and stood up.

Bev jumped to her feet and went to Tori trying to appease her. Tori pulled Bev to her. Tori felt a mixture of emotions, at first seething and then crying in anguish. She pulled Bev to her and the kiss she gave her exuded anger more than passion.

Bev pulled away, pushing against Tori's shoulders. "T, no. Not this way. Come to me in love, not out of anger or need for revenge."

Tori sagged against Bev. "I'm so sorry. You're right. That was an awful thing to do. I went crazy for a minute." She pulled away. "How could I have not known? I thought we were happy. Why? Why would she want someone else? How could she have done that and then come home to me and pretended to love me? That woman talks of their 'wanting more of their hot sexual encounters'—encounters, plural. That means it wasn't just a mistake, a one-time lapse. She had an affair with that woman while she was away."

Bev led Tori back to the sofa and retrieved the letter. "May I read this?"

Tori wiped her eyes and nodded, sitting silently while Bev read. "Wow! This woman is something else. She sounds like a real player. Did you read to the end?"

Tori nodded her head. "I did. She refers to finding herself suddenly single. She must have been in a relationship, too."

"The other one might be a response from Liz, to this letter. It was returned unopened. Maybe there's an explanation of some sort that will make you feel better. Think it's okay if I open it?"

"Yes, please. Read it with me."

Bev opened the letter and they began to read.

Bernie,

I've told you before that I won't see you again. I must have lost my mind. I love my partner, and regret my betrayal of our commitment to each other. Yes, no doubt, as you boast, you are a skilled lover and sex with you was hot, but it pales in comparison to the sweet and tender caring my partner shows me. I don't know what I was thinking. Your pursuit of me was flattering, I was lonely and I was bored. I can list a million reasons for falling under your spell. I call it a spell because you are mesmerizing. Still, the fault was mine. I was weak. I knew what I was doing was wrong, and I did it anyway. I haven't told Tori of my transgression yet. I'm not sure I will, as I doubt she'd forgive me. So I live with my guilt every day although I do, selfishly, want to confess and know she forgives me. I love her with all my heart. Please don't contact me again as I won't respond.

> *Liz*

Tori exhaled the breath she'd been holding as Bev put her arm around her shoulders. "Feel a little better? At least you know she was sorry and that she did love you."

Tori put her hand to her head to quell the pounding headache. "I just can't believe it."

"I know. It's a real shock, even to me and I wasn't her partner. I wonder why this Bernie person didn't open the letter, why she sent it back. Let's look her up."

Together they went to the computer and did a search. "Here's another picture of her. She is stunning. Oh, T, look. Look at the date. She died. The letter must have been returned because she died between the time she sent her letter to Liz, and a few weeks later when Liz's letter arrived."

Tori retrieved a tissue and blotted her eyes and blew her nose. With a final sniff she said, "I thought I knew her. So many years together and I didn't even know who she was. I wonder why she put this in here with her will and other legal papers."

"It was probably a safe place, a box you'd never open while she was living."

"Why keep them? Why did she want me to know after she died?"

Bev shrugged. "Conscience? Or, to make you let her go and move on? Sadly, there's no way to know now."

***

Tori's parents arrived Sunday morning. Tori finally agreed to Bev's suggestion, and as she and Bev had discussed, they put her parents in Bev's guest room. After lunch, Tori pulled her mother aside and showed her the photo and the letters Liz had left behind. "I don't understand why she didn't just destroy these things, Victoria. Obviously her intention was to remain with you. Why didn't she just dispose of the evidence of her indiscretion and leave it at that? Obviously she expected you'd find these, since she left them with her will. It's puzzling."

"I have chosen to believe she meant me to know so I would find it easier to move on with my life. I'd prefer to think kind thoughts about her rather than some of the others that I've had to struggle to push aside."

"And have you moved on? You and Bev seem pretty comfortable with each other."

Tori paused to consider her feelings for Bev. "I do have feelings for Bev...care deeply for her, and she cares for me. It's just that we've held those feelings in check for months, and we want to be sure all my past, uh...for want of a better word, baggage is out of the way before we move forward. The past couple of days, since Liz died, I haven't wanted to be alone. I've stayed here with her and she's held me at night. That's all. She's leaving after the funeral, for a couple of weeks. We plan to date, to start fresh, when she returns. I know it sounds strange, but we agree that it feels right for us."

"Your father and I like Bev. I think, given the chance, you and she will have a good relationship. She's a positive person, and you laugh when you're with her. Your father commented about that during your visit home, you know, that it's good to hear you laugh again. It seems so long ago since we heard that."

"Thanks Mom. I love you."

"I love you too, sweetheart."

Chapter Thirty-three

THE FUNERAL WAS A very brief, less than twenty minute affair attended by Liz's parents, Tori and her friends and family, and two of the nurses who had taken care of Liz for the past three years. Following the funeral, unlike most families and friends who congregate together to enjoy a meal, tell stories, and share remembrances, the Parkers made no arrangements for such an event. Instead they formally thanked everyone for supporting their daughter and declined the invitation Bill and Mona extended to join them at the restaurant.

"I really never understood those people...never have, never will." Bill said after everyone had settled into their seats and ordered something to eat.

Mona, sitting on his left patted his hand, leaned over and using a low voice replied, "Well, you'll never have to interact with them again."

While the group chattered on, Bill turned to his right and in a quiet voice said to Bev, "So when are you coming to see us again?"

"That depends on your daughter," Bev said.

"She tells me you're leaving for a while."

Bev smiled. "Yes. Work. It pays the bills. I tried to convince Tori to come with me and she turned me down."

Tori's dad glanced over at his daughter. "Be patient and give her some time. She's had a rough couple of years. Besides, you don't have to wait for her to invite you, I'm telling you that you can come visit us at any time."

"Thank you, that means a lot to me."

The group finished eating around two and bid each other goodbye. A smaller group comprised of Tori, her parents, Bev, MJ, and Victor moved the gathering to Bev's house where they sat around talking. Stories about Liz were shared until attention shifted to MJ's boyfriend. Bill and Mona did their tag team inquisition routine on Victor, who parried each question thrust upon him with candor and, upon more than one occasion, humor. Victor and MJ left around five, hoping for some sleep since both of them had to work later. At seven, Tori ordered some pizza and soon after eating it, Bill and Mona retired because they wanted to get a good night's sleep in preparation for their ride home.

"And then there were two...dun dun duh." Bev grinned.

"Oh stop. You know perfectly well we're going to bed alone. You in my place and me here in your bed, just like last night. Anyway, you have to be at the airport by ten thirty, but my folks want to leave here by seven. You can get a couple of extra hours of sleep if you stay there."

"I know you're right. Still, I loved holding you the other night. It wasn't even about sex, which we've agreed is too soon...just being close was nice. Although there are any number of things I might rather be doing with you, I love lying in bed holding and talking with you."

Tori pulled Bev up from her chair and wrapped her arms around her neck. "Okay, here's the deal. You go home, get into bed and call my cell. By then I'll be in bed and we can talk until you're sleepy."

"I like that you are an extremely reasonable woman." As they walked to the door hand in hand Bev asked, "All joking aside, how are you doing?"

Tori paused to form her disorganized emotions into words able to convey her thoughts and feelings. "I think I'm going to be fine. I'm having a harder time getting over the fact that Liz cheated on me than I am accepting the fact she's gone. I've been saying good-bye to her, letting her go, for a long time, especially since I began counseling. So I'm good...really."

"Are you feeling good enough about things to kiss me goodnight?"

"I hug and kiss you hello and good-bye all the time."

"I don't mean a friend kiss, I mean a more than friend kiss—a real kiss. I'm sorry, I know it's wrong for me to want you so soon after...I just can't help myself. I'm sorry...I'll leave before I make an even bigger ass of myself." Bev pulled away and reached for the door handle.

As Bev turned, Tori grabbed her arm and pulled her back. She ran her hands up Bev's arms to her shoulders and pressed her back against the wall pinning Bev to the door with her body. Linking their fingers, she raised them above shoulder height, leaned forward, and paused just centimeters from making contact with Bev's slightly parted lips. Tori could feel Bev's breath quicken in anticipation of contact. She watched her pupils dilate and felt her body strain to make contact.

"If it's wrong for you to want, I'm sure it's doubly wrong for me to want too, but I do." Crossing the last fraction of an inch Tori took Bev's mouth with her own, gently at first. As the kiss deepened, Bev's lips parted, welcoming Tori's entrance. Neither was sure who groaned first as their tongues met. Maybe it was both of them. The kiss continued until Tori gained control and pulled back.

It took several seconds for Bev to open her eyes. She licked her lips before she breathed out, exhaling a sigh. A slow smile curled her mouth, exposing her dimple. "Well that was everything I'd imagined it would be and more. When do we get to do that again?"

"Maybe tonight in your dreams. I'm sure I'll be dreaming about it." Tori leaned in again, this time just brushing her lips lightly against Bev's. "Now go. I'll see you tomorrow morning after my parents leave."

"It's not what I want..."

"I know what you want. I'm sorry, I'm not quite there yet. On a positive note, I doubted I'd be here, at this point, this soon, so..." Tori arched her eyebrow.

"Okay, I'm going. See you tomorrow. Expect a high water bill. I plan on taking a long, very chilly shower when I get to your place."

"Don't forget to call me." Tori gently cupped Bev's face with her hand.

"Hope I make it to your place. My knees are actually wobbly." Bev emphasized her condition by wobbling her legs as she walked away, making Tori laugh.

***

Tori stood and waved good-bye to her parents at seven forty-five the next morning. She and Bev had talked on the phone the night before until after eleven. She smiled as she recalled answering the phone, Bev started the conversation by saying, in her sexiest voice, "What are you wearing?"

"Nothing but a smile," was Tori's reply, in an equally sexy tone that caused both of them to laugh.

"I'm so relieved to hear you laugh."

"You know, you're the second person who said that to me today. My mom said the same thing, in so many words. She and my dad like that you make me laugh. They noticed it during our visit with them."

"I like to make you laugh"

"I like to see you smile. I can't tell you how many times I've wanted to kiss that dimple. It's like an invitation to play."

"Hmm. I'll have to remember that." Bev waited a few seconds. "Can I ask you a serious question?"

"Sure." Tori burrowed deeper into the pillow getting comfortable.

"How are you feeling about all that's happened over the last few days?"

"You mean about Liz's death, about finding out about Bernie, or about kissing you?"

"Let's take them in order."

Tori sighed. "Okay...Liz's death. If I'm honest, I have mixed feelings. No doubt I'm sad. It's a loss. I'm not sure it's proper, but I also have a sense of relief. I don't have to worry about her any more. No more concerns about her health, her infections. And no more guilt. After you leave tomorrow, I'll have no playmate, and about seven or eight extra hours on my hands a day. She filled up my life...or at least filled the hours of the day. That's gone and it concerns me. I'm going to have so much free time."

"Give yourself a chance. Go walk the boards, bike, read, sleep, relax. Start taking pictures again, or take a class. I'll be back as soon as I can. If you're really feeling at sea, come visit me, or go visit your folks. Your mom and dad would love to have you."

"I know. I might go for a few days. Okay, what was the next question? Ah, yes, about Liz cheating. I'm still really pissed. I mean, who wouldn't be? She took this course one summer, a two-month trip to California to learn about deaf babies. She debated about going because she didn't want to leave me for that long. We were happy, I thought. I mean we rarely disagreed, enjoyed being together...even had a satisfying sex life. At least I thought we did. Obviously, I was delusional." Tori paused. Self-doubt shot through her like a knife. "Maybe I wasn't a good enough lover. I just don't understand. I could maybe understand and forgive her a one-time fling. Maybe. From the letters it was more than that. We'd made promises to each other. I don't understand how she could do what she did then come back to me and never mention it."

"I'm sure it's hurtful knowing that those questions will never have answers. And what about the kiss? How did that feel? How does it feel? Are you okay?"

"It was just a kiss, Bev. It wasn't even our first. You kissed me at the airport when you left, remember?"

"I do. No comparison. I kissed you. You barely kissed me back. It was...um...chaste. Tonight was...geez, T! It was amazing. If we make love half as good as we kiss..."

Tori snapped back to the present and looked at the clock—almost eight o'clock. She'd been lost in thought nearly fifteen minutes. *If I want to see her, I'd better get a move on or we won't have any time together.* As she walked to her condo she thought about the kiss they'd shared the night before and felt her body respond just at the memory of it. *Was she over her relationship with Liz so quickly and ready to deepen her involvement with Bev so soon after Liz's death?* Her conscience stuck in its two cents. *'Be honest, you're already very involved with Bev. You've been a couple in every way but one for quite a while, now. Liz has been dead to you nearly three years. Emotionally, you've been linked to Bev practically since you saw her the first time, a bond that's only grown deeper as you've come to know her. You're already in love with her. That's part of why you've been feeling so guilty even though you haven't acted on those feelings in a physical way.'*

Tori stopped walking as the thought settled in. *I am in love with her. Maybe I'll just keep that thought to myself for a little while longer.*

Tori took the stairs to her condo instead of the elevator. It was faster. She unlocked her door and stepped inside listening for sounds of activity. The shower wasn't running, no smell of coffee...*tell me she's still asleep.* The bedroom door was open. Tori stood in the doorway and heard the soft sound of Bev's regular breathing. She called Bev's name as she settled on the bed causing some movement. "Hey sleepy head."

An arm reached out to pull Tori closer. "What time is it?"

"A little after eight. You need to get up."

"I know. I'm packed already. I just need to shower. How are you this morning?"

"I'm okay. You?"

"I missed you last night. I will admit I had a wonderful dream." Bev slid over making room in the bed. "Want to get in and cuddle?"

Noticing Bev's exposed arm and shoulder she asked, "What are you wearing?"

"Besides cologne?" Her dimple appeared.

"Maybe that's not such a good idea. You've got a plane to catch and I've got to go make you some breakfast."

Bev stuck out her lower lip in an over exaggerated pout.

Laughing, Tori turned around and stretched out on top of the covers next to Bev who pulled her close and exhaled a contented sigh. "Now isn't that better?"

"Incredibly so."

"I like being together like this. I'd like it even better if you'd get under the covers with me." She tugged Tori's shirt. "It would be even more better if you didn't have all these clothes on."

"More better?"

"Betterer?" They laughed, enjoying the banter. Bev began to slowly stroke Tori's back. "You know we talk like lovers. I'm looking forward to sharing moments like this with you when you're ready to be under the covers with me. I want to feel your skin on mine, to touch and taste you, to find all those special areas that raise goose bumps on you...to find the ticklish spots, and the intimate places that make you moan."

Tori groaned and rose up, seeking Bev's lips. Finally pulling away, Tori whispered, "Soon, I promise. If you keep talking like that, you'll make me come. That wouldn't be fair to you because we don't have time for me to make love to you the way you deserve." She kissed the exposed skin on Bev's shoulder, inhaling her warm and sleepy fragrance, committing it to memory. "What will it take to get you out of this bed?"

Bev murmured as Tori nibbled her neck. "Ummmm...oh, you are the cruel one. Certainly not what you're doing is going to roust me from bed. Don't ask me any questions for which you're not ready to hear the answer." She grasped Tori's face and kissed Tori on the nose. "Today, my love, I'll settle for some tea and some toast. Next time, you won't get off so easy."

With one last quick kiss, Tori pulled away. "I'm off to do your bidding. Holler when you're five minutes from being ready and I'll start the toast. You sure that's all you want?"

"We'll, before I go I intend to collect another kiss like the one you gave me last night. It'll keep me warm all the way to Chicago."

Tori left for the kitchen and Bev showered and dressed. The aroma of her now familiar perfume drifted through the open bedroom door. She came down the hallway, carrying her suitcase and jacket.

Bev sat at the counter after thanking Tori for the breakfast that awaited her. Patting the seat next to her she said, "Come sit next to me while I eat." As Tori slid onto the stool, Bev reached for her hand, drawing it to her lips. "I'm going to miss you."

"And I you. I've been thinking over your suggestions. I think I could use a break. I have a few things to do at work. You said you'd be back around the end of the month. I think I'll finish up what I need to do at the office this next week and arrange to take off a couple of weeks. That'll give me a week to rest up at my folks' home and, after you get back, another whole week to spend with you. I know you'll have work to do. I can putter around, fix you lavish dinners, and see what I can think up to distract you from your labor."

"Maybe," Bev countered, "I'll work harder while I'm in Chicago so maybe I can make it back a bit early."

All too soon it was time for Bev to leave for the airport. Bev stopped at the door, set down her bag and turned to face Tori, a smile on her face. "Now's your chance to prove last night's kiss wasn't a fluke because I hadn't been kissed for so long."

Tori moved into Bev's arms and kissed her dimple before taking possession of Bev's mouth with her own. Tori slowly released her and backed away, Bev's flushed face, dilated pupils, and rapid breathing answered the question. She steadied herself against the door and Tori placed her hand on the wall for support. "I never fully appreciated the phrase 'weak in the knees' until you kissed me."

"No more kissing, or we'll never make it to the airport in time. Give me a hug and let's get out of here before I lose my resolve. You are way too kissable." Bev pulled Tori tight against her. "This will be the longest two weeks of my life. So let's get going. The sooner we get underway, the sooner I'll get home to you."

A quick kiss, a hug goodbye, and Bev's promise to call as soon as she arrived in Chicago were all they exchanged in the parking lot of the condo before Bev got into her car and they waved good-bye before heading their separate ways. It was a last minute decision for Bev to drive herself to the airport, since they were unsure of where Tori would be when Bev got back home.

Tori reported for work, although it was not really her scheduled time to be there. She typed up and submitted her request for two weeks of vacation. She went straight to her office because she wanted to get ahead on her paperwork so she would be ready to leave as soon as her vacation was approved.

A few hours later Tori received a phone call from Bev. "I just arrived in Chicago. I am waiting for my bag now. Then I have to go to the hotel."

"Thanks for letting me know you arrived okay. Will you call me later, or will you be too tired?"

"No, never. I'll call you later, before I go to sleep."

With a smile on her face, Tori held the phone to her chest after she hung up, hoping to sustain their connection just a little longer.

Chapter Thirty-four

THE TRIP BACK TO her family's house had been uneventful. The long drive home gave her an opportunity to review her last meeting with Karolina. They started their discussion by examining Tori's feelings after learning of Liz's affair. Karolina asked, "How are you feeling about the affair?"

"I'm not sure. Sometimes I'm pissed off, and other times I'm just numb. I do know that the feelings of guilt I've dealt with, for the past six months or more, are no longer taunting me."

Karolina nodded. "Eventually you'll figure it all out. You have time. If you feel you need some help, come see me."

"I will."

"Would you like to talk about the status of your friendship with Bev?"

"I think we're ready to move forward. We've waited a long time to be happy about our feelings. I'm not sure if the comfort level I'm feeling has anything to do with the fact that Liz cheated on me during our relationship or not. Regardless of the reason, I'm just decidedly happy that I feel free to pursue a relationship with Bev. I'm looking forward to getting together with her. We'll have a week of no work to interrupt us as soon as she finishes up in Chicago."

Parting from Karolina was bittersweet. Although Tori felt proud of how far she'd come, she knew the relationship she'd developed with her counselor would be something she'd miss.

***

It was the first official day of Tori's vacation. While sitting at the breakfast bar eating her morning meal, Tori flipped on the TV to see the weather forecast and to catch up on the status of the presidential election. The critical third debate was scheduled for Monday, October twenty-third in Boca Raton. Pundits from both parties were projecting a potential victory for their favorite candidate, and the race was down to the wire. "I'm looking forward to watching the debate. How about you Dad?"

"Yes, me too. I'm looking forward to hearing each of them promising me everything none of them can deliver."

Tori knew her father would be swearing at the television at some point in the evening. She loved his passion about, and involvement in, the upcoming election. Her mother was equally passionate about her opinions, but far less vocal. "How about you, Mom? Going to watch with us?"

"You know I will. For once, I agree with your father."

As was the tradition of Tori's youth, the family watched the news and weather every evening. The weather forecasters were beginning to sound the drumbeat about a tropical storm forming in the Caribbean. The tropical depression was scheduled to become a hurricane in the next couple of days and was projected to track up the East Coast of the United States. With each passing day projections about the potentially devastating damage from the storm they'd dubbed Sandy increased.

Tori and Bev spoke several times a day. It was during one of these conversations that the topic of the storm came up. Tori admitted, "I'm relieved that neither of us is on the island. With the storm projected to hit on Sunday and into Monday, I'm concerned about your return trip."

Bev calmly responded, "Look, it's only Thursday night. Things can still change. Maybe it'll hang a right and head out to sea. The computer models aren't even sure yet what the track will be."

"Just promise me," Tori stressed to Bev, "that you'll use your head. It's more important that you remain safe than to make it back home on your projected timeline. If there's any doubt, just stay there until the storm is over."

"I will use my head. I promise. What about MJ and Victor? Will they be okay?"

"They will be safe," Tori assured her. "Victor and MJ taped our windows and checked our places to make sure the water was turned off, so we don't have to worry about that. No matter when you get here, I'll be waiting...so be safe."

On Saturday evening Tori was at home watching television with her parents. The channel they had on was running storm updates in the crawl line with dire predictions for the shore area. She really wasn't interested in the program, and she allowed her mind to wander to Bev. She couldn't wait to see her and hold her. Just before the show they were watching ended at ten, there was a knock at the door. Bill looked at Mona and Tori.

"Are you expecting anyone?" Both women shook their head. "I'll see who it is," Bill stood and headed off toward the front door. A short time later Bill returned down the hallway with a surprise visitor in tow. "Look who I found standing out there on the porch."

"Bev!" Tori jumped up and wrapped her arms around Bev. "I thought you weren't coming until next week." Tori breathed in Bev's scent and her eyes slowly closed. She sighed as a feeling of relief and warmth overcame her. She blushed as she turned around and saw her parents watching.

Bev gave Tori another brief squeeze before releasing her. She smiled at Bill and Mona. "With all the projections about the storm, I was afraid I wouldn't be able to fly in. So I put in extra hours and finished up early." Bev turned to Bill. "I took you at your word that I have an open invitation. I hope you were serious when you said it, because you're stuck with me now. I'm sorry it's so late, my plane was delayed and then I stopped home to get some information that I need so I can work on my program. By the time I finally got underway it was already much later than I expected."

"I meant every word of it and I'm glad to see someone finally paid attention to me." Bill gestured toward Tori and his wife. "The rest of the women in this family certainly don't."

"Oh Bill, stop! You're going to give this young woman the wrong impression." Mona stood up and went to Bev to welcome her with a warm hug. "Bev have you had something to eat?"

"Thanks Mona, I grabbed something about an hour ago."

"How about at least something to drink?"

"Just some water would be great, thank you." Tori helped Bev shrug out of her jacket and hung it on the peg by the door.

Tori pulled Bev by the hand over to the sofa. They sat next to each other their legs touching. "I can't believe you're here. I'm thankful you made it before the storm."

Mona returned with a glass of water for Bev. "What time did you leave Chicago?"

"I've been up since four this morning...left Chicago at six thirty." Bev smiled. "It's been a very long day."

"Tori, why don't you help Bev with her things and take her down to your bedroom. We can visit with her in the morning."

"Thank you, Mona," Bev said. "I think what I really need is a hot shower. I feel like I've collected every bit of dust that there was between Chicago and here."

Tori picked up Bev's travel bag and Bev grabbed her computer and carry on. "I'll see you both in the morning. Thank you." Tori led them down the hallway.

"I'll get you some fresh towels." Tori went to the closet and selected a large bath sheet and washcloth for Bev. "Oops! Almost forgot the hand towel."

Bev, her movements slow because of her exhaustion, shuffled across the room and took the bundle from Tori's hand. "Do you have a kiss for this weary traveler?"

"I'll not only have a kiss for you when you come out from your shower, I'll have a back rub waiting."

"Well then, I guess that's your idea of motivation."

"Precisely. Did it work?"

"Like a charm. I'll be out in a few minutes." Towel in hand, Bev turned toward the bathroom.

"My turn after you, then the backrub."

"No, no." Bev turned toward Tori. "That wasn't the plan. You forgot the kiss part."

"Okay, how's this?" Tori wrapped her arms around Bev's neck. "A quick kiss now, you shower, another quick kiss, I shower, then back rub."

"Hmm. How quick?" Bev cocked one eyebrow.

Tori pulled Bev to her and delivered the promised kiss, which was sufficient to prove how happy she was to see Bev, but not ardent enough to get them in trouble.

Tori kissed Bev on the nose. "Now into the shower with you. You get another like that if you hurry."

Bev chuckled and her eyes sparkled. "You are definitely a skilled negotiator. Okay, I'm on my way."

Twelve minutes later, Bev emerged from the shower dressed in dark green pajamas, a towel wrapped around her wet hair. She went to Tori to collect her kiss. "Your turn. Don't dally, or I'm liable to be asleep by the time you get out of there."

Tori finished her shower and emerged wearing knee length navy PJ bottoms with a white, waist length short-sleeved top. She saw Bev sitting on the edge of the bed blotting her eye with a tissue. "Are you okay?"

"What? Oh this. Yes...I think I have an eyelash or something in my eye. I tried flushing it out with eye drops and it feels a bit better, although still irritated. I'm not sure if I got it out or not."

"Let me take a look." Tori approached, straddled Bev's legs with her own, and tilted Bev's face up using both hands. Bending slightly at the waist, she gently lifted Bev's eyelid and moved her face closer to peer into the injured eye.

Bev's hands came up to rest on Tori's hips.

Tori's mouth was only inches from Bev's. "I don't see anything. You must have gotten it out." Her eyes locked with Bev's. "Ready for your back rub?"

"Maybe. Eventually. I have something a little more welcoming in mind. After all, I did travel several states today to see you." Bev slipped her thumbs under the edge of Tori's PJ top, making contact with the sensitive skin there.

Tori's eyes slammed closed, and her breathing increased. She began to stand upright, but Bev leaned back, gave a tug and pulled Tori with her. They landed with Tori's thigh snugly settled between Bev's legs. Bev slid her hands under Tori's shirt and up her back, pulling her closer. In a move that would have made any professional wrestler envious, Bev smoothly rolled Tori onto her back sliding her thigh between Tori's legs. "I've wanted you for months. Please don't say no." Without waiting for a response, Bev sought Tori's mouth with her own. The kiss, tentative at first, bloomed into passion. Tori moaned as Bev's tongue entered and searched. As their tongues met, they both moaned.

"Shh," Tori whispered. "My parents will hear us. This is just wrong here in my old room with my parents right across the hall."

Bev pulled back and started to pull away, her ardor cooled by Tori's words.

Tori stopped her. "Don't, please. It's not that I don't want you, I do. It's just that I envisioned our first time somewhere romantic. My childhood room in my parents' house doesn't even come close to fitting the definition of romantic."

"I love you, sweetheart. I need you. For the first time we're free and still you don't want me." Bev stood up and started toward the bathroom, her anger evident in her sudden withdrawal.

Tori followed, grabbed Bev's hand pulling her back into her embrace, kissing each cheek before placing a soft kiss on her mouth. With each kiss, Tori said a word. "You. Love. Me?" Bev nodded. Slowly, Bev began to respond to Tori's kisses. Tori lifted her shirt and Bev closed her eyes but didn't resist. "Look at me Bev."

Bev opened her eyes, the love she saw on Tori's face causing her to relax.

Tori turned Bev around and moved behind her, putting her chin on Bev's shoulder. She slid her arms around her waist, stripping Bev's clothing, and then quickly removing her own. They watched their reflections in the mirror as Tori's hands traveled slowly upward to cup gently before smoothing across Bev's breasts. As her hands traveled downward, Bev's head fell back onto Tori's shoulder as her eyes closed in pleasure. Tori watched Bev's breathing increase as she made love to her, her own desire growing. The blended aroma of their mutual arousal filled the air.

Tori kissed her way down Bev's neck and murmured into Bev's ear. "You're beautiful. I love your body. How quiet can you be?"

Bev met Tori's eyes in the mirror. "As quiet as a mouse. As quiet as a feather falling on cotton...as quiet as a smile."

"Come into bed and prove it."

They moved into bed and began to explore each other's bodies with their hands and mouths. Tori spent a long time concentrating on making love to Bev's breasts before exploring other parts of her body, always returning to lavish attention on both breasts equally. She brushed Bev's nipples with her own giving them both pleasure.

"Oh God, I've waited so long for you. I need you now, inside me." Bev whispered, eyes closed, her voice hoarse with emotion and need.

"Look at me, Bev. I want to see you come. I want you to watch me and know it's you that I'm making love to. Come inside me, we'll do this together." Tori supported herself on her forearm to give Bev room to slide her hand between them. They slipped inside each other's slick openings and began to move.

"Oh God, that feels so good," Tori whispered.

"Umm," Bev exhaled softly as she arched against Tori's hand.

Tori picked up the pace of her thrusts. She pushed her final thought of Liz aside knowing she loved the woman beneath her, and gave in to the sheer physical pleasure of Bev moving inside her. She could feel Bev close down on her fingers and knew she was close. Tori gave herself over to the sensations and when Bev came she let herself climax, collapsing against Bev.

Bev sighed in contentment as she wrapped her arms around Tori snuggling close. "That was nice. It's been so long, I'm glad we didn't forget how."

"Umm."

"Are you okay?" Bev raised her head to seek Tori's eyes.

"Yes. A little disappointed perhaps. I wanted to make you scream."

Bev laughed. "You told me to be quiet. Remember? I was screaming inwardly." Bev's dimple made an appearance.

Tori traced her finger down Bev's chest between her breasts, to her navel then reversed the path up to the scar. Using the most tender of touches she traced it with her finger then leaned over to place a kiss first on the scar, and then on the nipple."

"Is this okay, I mean is this hard for you?"

"Not with you." Bev touched the appendix scar then trailed her hand up Tori's belly, over her breast, stopping to rest her palm on Tori's heart. "What about you? Was it hard for you?"

Tori exhaled a long sigh. "You mean because of Liz? No. Not hard. It feels right." She rolled over pulling Bev on top of her. "You feel so good. I love you Bev."

"I love you, too. I want you again," she whispered trailing her hand up Tori's side. "That time was too urgent. I want to explore your body, touch you, taste you." She began her journey finally settling between Tori's legs where she used her mouth and tongue until Tori was begging her for release. Just before she came, Tori pulled the pillow over her face to muffle the sounds of her pleasure.

Bev slid up Tori's body and pulled the pillow away. "Hey there, you didn't suffocate yourself, did you?" Bev grinned. "That was fun. I loved making you beg."

"I hope you're the only one who heard it. This is so weird, making love here in my parents' house."

"You'd better get used to it. I like your parents, and I think they're fun. I hope we'll spend a lot of time with them over the years, because I intend to grow old with you, if you'll have me."

"Oh, I'm going to have you...starting right now." Tori chuckled. "You'd better get the pillow ready, you're going to need it."

Bev laughed but when Tori turned serious, Bev reached for it.

Too tired to make love again, they cuddled, arms and legs entwined. Tori murmured, fighting sleep, "Let me turn off the light. Do you want your clothes?"

"Will you feel more comfortable with your clothes on?"

"Probably." Tori smiled and brushed Bev's hair back, tucking it behind her ear. "Only because we're here. Don't get used to sleeping with your clothes on though."

"T? Do you wish we'd waited, you know, hadn't made love?"

"How can you even think that? I feel so many things. Blessedly, regret isn't one of them. At least not in the way I think you mean. My only regret is that tomorrow we have to be up at the crack of dawn to spend time with my parents instead of making wild and passionate love all day. We only have a few hours to sleep before we have to get up and be bright eyed and bushy tailed."

"Are you always so sensible?"

"Bev, think about that question a minute."

Bev's laughter filled the air. "Yes, you are."

"Will that aspect of my personality eventually make you crazy?"

"Only when I want to make love to you."

Chapter Thirty-five

BEV AWOKE TO FIND Tori staring at her. Bev smiled and reached for her lover, pulling her close. "Good morning, sweetheart."

"Hey there."

"Do you always wake up with a smile on your face?" Bev traced Tori's lips with her finger.

"What's not to smile about? I'm with the woman I love, I had mind blowing sex, even if it was the silent version of what would be described in those cheesy novels as a screaming orgasm, and I'm about to be ravaged by someone who can nearly make me come with her kisses. Aren't I?"

"It's a distinct possibility, because we're alone. We've got about an hour and a half. This is looking like it's going to be a bad storm, so my folks went out for breakfast. They plan to stop at the hardware store to buy lanterns and batteries and at the food store for some things we can eat without electric. We're stockpiling ice in case the electric goes out, so we can keep the food cold. Our job is to haul in some wood for the stove. But I mentioned to them how tired you were."

Bev stretched and grinned at Tori. "I hope you didn't tell them why I'm so tired this morning. Why aren't you tired?"

"I'm used to minimal sleep. Last night, was certainly a much more satisfying justification than my usual reason for my lack of sleep."

"I need another shower." Bev reached for Tori's shirt, tugging it loose. "Hey you did say we're alone didn't you?"

"Yes, and I did mention that I wanted to make you moan." Tori kissed Bev. "I suspect the shower has great acoustics for that activity."

"Hmm, and if we might lose power, we should probably be clean, don't you think? Come on, let's test out that theory."

AJ Adaire

***

They were in the kitchen just finishing breakfast. Tori's parents returned. Her mother set her purchases on the counter and went to the sink to wash her hands. "Hmph. That's funny, there's no hot water." She turned to her daughter, whose bright red face gave her away.

"Uh, yeah," Tori stammered. "We had really long showers."

"Showers, eh?" Mona cocked her head and looked at her bright red daughter before turning her gaze on Bev who tried to hide her grin. "I see. Well, I'm glad there's nothing wrong with the hot water heater. You know your father and I were thinking that if you and your *friend* Bev might be visiting more often, we might change that queen-sized bed in your room to two twins so you'd be more comfortable. I see that won't be necessary."

"Oh God, please take me now," Tori groaned as she covered her face with her hands that caused Bev to burst into laughter.

Mona patted Bev's hand. "Welcome to the family, honey. Now, the two of you need to get out there and start lugging in some wood. Dress warmly. The temps are dropping and the wind is kicking up."

"Thank you, Mona, for the welcome. We're going right now."

Mona came around the counter and hugged Bev first. "I hope you'll be a regular visitor, honey." After embracing her daughter, she said, "Good. Now I have to go tell your dad the happy news." She hurried away.

"Gotta love your mother." Bev gave Tori a quick kiss. "Come on, I don't want to piss off my new in-laws. Get a move on."

"I'm so tired. You wore me out. And look," she said holding up her hands. "My fingers are still wrinkled like prunes."

"Is that a complaint?"

Tori's expression softened as her grin appeared. She stuck her index finger in her mouth then very slowly withdrew it. "You can wrinkle me any time."

"Victoria. You two going to do that today?" Mona called from the other room.

The two women stifled their laughter. "Yes Mom, we are, just as soon as we possibly can."

***

222

On Sunday afternoon, Tori called Victor and MJ. The island was under mandatory evacuation. Victor was planning to go into work with MJ to help in whatever way he could. The center, just over the bridge on the mainland, was in less danger than structures on the island and was well prepared with ample supplies, adequate staff, and generators. Patients who were able enough to leave or be transferred to a different facility had been moved earlier in the week. Those too ill to move had been moved to interior parts of the building.

Tori was relaxing on the sofa in the living room, the book she'd been reading rested in her lap as she recalled her conversation with MJ. "I'm so sorry, MJ, that I'm not there to help. It sounds like a nightmare."

"Not really. So many patients left, we only have the most fragile ones here, those we felt wouldn't have survived a transfer, and more than enough staff. Victor came, as did several other spouses and significant others."

"I should have been there to help."

"Why? We're all okay here. You took vacation. Enjoy it. You are enjoying it, aren't you?"

"I am, very much. Bev got here Friday night and we've had a wonderful couple of days just hanging out with each other and my parents."

"Good. Have fun. Don't worry about us. We're fine. I'll talk to you after the storm ends. They're projecting it will come right over us. A lot of the businesses spent all day today moving their stock either to the second floor of their shops, or to their warehouses over here on the mainland. They expect serious flooding on the island and a lot of damage from the wind.

"Well, stay safe. I'll talk to you after the storm."

Bev came in from the kitchen, carrying two cups, and placed one in front of Tori drawing her attention back to the present. "What'cha doing?"

"Just thinking about MJ and Victor. Hope they'll be okay. I just watched the weather. It's enough to scare any sane person to death."

***

The President declared a state of emergency for the District of Columbia, Maryland, Massachusetts, Connecticut, Rhode Island, Pennsylvania, New Jersey, and New York. By Sunday night, the wind was steady. The weather channels were talking about Sandy being a 'perfect storm.' On Monday, shortly after noon, the storm made the turn that had been predicted. Two days of high winds and rain battered the shore area with untold numbers of fallen trees causing widespread electrical outages. The storm was still inflicting damage on the Atlantic coast north of New Jersey.

Despite losing power on Monday morning, the storm had no serious impact on their daily life other than the drone of the generator Tori's father had purchased after hurricane Irene. On Wednesday night, they decided that they would make their way home the next day.

The trip home was plagued by numerous detours caused by downed power lines and trees. Tori led the way and Bev followed. Exhausted, they were relieved as they made their way over the bridge and down the streets to their condos. Sand and debris were everywhere. They were surprised to find more damage on the bay side of the island than the ocean side. They spoke with a policeman who told them the south side had sustained more damage than in their area. "We were lucky here. The storm made landfall a bit farther north than projected, so the shore areas north of here were really walloped."

"Your place or mine? Bev asked as she pulled in behind Tori as they parked on the street.

"Let's check my place first. You can help me carry in my stuff then we'll head over and check yours. Yours has a better view than mine, too." They looked around. "Wow! Look at all this sand in the condo's lot. Half the beach is here."

They found Tori's place undamaged. "Isn't it amazing, after all the destruction we saw on the way home, that this place thirty feet from the boardwalk is still in one piece? Even my folks are still without power, and our power is fine."

"Yes. I mean, there's obviously a lot of destruction and damage, but from the news reports, I expected much worse. The bay side caught the brunt this time. We got off lucky here."

"I'm glad Mom sent us home with some food. I'm starving."

"Me too," agreed Bev. "We need to call them and let them know we're safe. I'm sure they're worried."

Call made and chores attended to they settled in at Bev's condo where they watched the news and reports about the storm as they ate their dinner. "It's horrible, isn't it?" Tori punched the off button on the remote.

"I know. So many people homeless." They grew quiet. "Are you as tired as I am?"

"Now that you mention it, I realize I am. Hey, how big is your hot water tank?"

"I don't know, probably forty gallons or so, why?"

"Want to see if we can use up all your hot water together? We had fun doing that at my folks' house, remember?"

"I thought you were tired."

"You need to know something about me. I'll never be too tired to make love to you."

Bev took Tori's hand. "Prove it."

It was a luxury to be alone. Although they had managed to make love at Tori's parents' house, this was their first time they didn't have to worry about being heard or, like their first time in the shower, having to hurry. They undressed each other, adjusted the water temperature and stepped under the spray. "I like your shower. You know what my favorite part of it is? Being in here with you." They soaped each other, took turns washing each other's hair, and explored each other's bodies. "I love your tattoo. Why did you get it?"

"Let's dry off and get into bed. I'll tell you, and then I want to make love to you without a pillow over your face. I want to see you as you come. No one will hear you here."

They settled naked in bed. Tori held Bev who trailed her fingers over Tori's stomach and breasts causing her nipples to harden. She placed a soft kiss on her lover's lips. "I think you planned to tell me a story about your tattoo."

"You may have to stop doing that so I can keep my mind on what I'm saying."

Bev moved her hand a little lower playing with the soft curls she found there. "Your hair here is so soft and silky. It tickles when I'm kissing you there."

"You're not helping my concentration."

"Tell me the story and I'll make you happy."

"I'm already happy."

"Okay then, I'll make you happier. Start talking." Bev sucked Tori's nipple into her mouth, tonguing it until Tori moaned. She released the nipple and began to kiss her way downward. Teasing Tori's navel with her tongue, she paused long enough to ask, "Why did you choose the phrase, *'Someday I'll understand'* for your tattoo?"

Tori gasped, as Bev's mouth possessed her. Her hands clasped the sheet and she clenched her teeth as Bev's tongue entered her. Bev pulled away. "Talk."

"It's not easy to keep my mind on the story with you doing that," Bev stroked upward with her tongue. "I can stop."

"Oh please don't."

"I love to make you beg." Bev made another pass over Tori's clit with her tongue. "Talk or I stop."

"The saying is no big deal." Tori exhaled the words through clenched teeth. "Oh, God, don't stop."

"Keep talking." Bev went back to work making Tori gasp again.

"When I first figured out I was a lesbian...ummm." She shifted her legs wider. "I didn't understand why I wasn't like everyone else." Her heart was pounding and her breathing irregular. "I hoped someday I'd fig...oh God. Yes. Right there."

Bev added a little more pressure and Tori slid over the top. Tori calmed and Bev kissed her and rubbed her nose across her pubic hair. "You smell so sweet."

"Come up here. I need your kisses."

"You didn't finish," Bev admonished.

"I did."

Bev laughed at Tori's misunderstanding. "You didn't finish your story."

"Oh that." Tori pulled Bev to her and settled her against her shoulder. Her fingers found Bev's nipple and began to tease it. "Liz and I were out with some friends in P-town and we had a few too many beers, I think. Someone got the bright idea to get tattoos. We found a place. At first I didn't know what to get, then I recalled hoping someday I'd figure out why I was gay. So I got the question tattooed on my back."

"What did Liz get?"

"A heart with an infinity symbol woven into the design and the word always beneath it...a bit odd, now that I think of it. She told me it would always be me. Ironic, huh?"

"And have you figured out the answer to your question...'someday I'll understand?'"

Tori rolled over and kissed Bev. Her kiss conveyed the overwhelming love she felt for her lover. "I did. If I weren't a lesbian, I wouldn't have you." She touched Bev's face with her palm and kissed her again. "I love you." Tori poured her emotion into her lovemaking, showing Bev through her touch just how much she cared.

Later, sated, they lay entwined. Bev lifted Tori's fingers to her lips. "That was beautiful. I love you, too." She shifted so she could see Tori's reaction. "I know this isn't the most romantic way to do it, and maybe it's a little too soon."

Tori cuddled up next to her lover. "What's too soon?"

"Is it too soon to ask you to move in? Maybe we could rent out your place to someone who lost theirs."

"I'd love to. Not only does it make perfect sense, but we've waited to long to delay any longer."

Epilogue - Two Months Later

"YOU LOOK NICE, SWEETHEART." Bev slipped into her shoes. "Heels. I haven't been this dressed up in a long time. Life here is so casual most of the time. At least MJ and Victor have a nice day for their wedding."

"Umm, you look delectable." Tori put her arms around Bev's neck and hugged her. "I can't wait for our ceremony next month."

"Me either. Your mom and dad are almost as excited as we are."

"They're happy just seeing me happy, and they adore you." Tori gave Bev a quick kiss.

"We're really blessed. We have good friends, your family to love us, jobs that we both like. What more could we ask for?"

"Just forever."

The End

AJ Adaire

About AJ Adaire

Let me tell you a little about myself. Twenty years ago, I wrote my first book just to see if I could do it. The novel occupied space on my bookshelf, unread for nearly twenty years until one day, while in a cleaning frenzy, I considered disposing of the neatly stacked but now age-yellowed pages. As I began to read the long forgotten work, I was surprised to discover that the story was enjoyable!

Editing and retyping the first book provided a new sense of accomplishment and additional tales followed. Completion of *This is Fitting* encouraged me to write five more romance novel all of which have been published. *Sunset Island*, first book of the Friends Series was released in September 2013. *Sunset Island* was quickly followed by the remaining books in the Friends Series: *The Interim (a novelette), ,Awaiting My Assignment,* and *Anything Your Heart Desires* and a stand-alone novel *One Day Longer Than Forever.* Now I am back looking at *I Love My Life* and doing a massive rewrite for release in the spring of 2015.

Now retired, there is all the time in the world to write. I live on the east coast with my partner of thirty years. Because we love a challenge, we provide a loving home for two spoiled cats instead of a dog. In addition to writing, any spare time is devoted to reading, mastering new computer programs, and socializing with friends.

Contact Information
E-mail: aj@ajadaire.com
Website: http://www.ajadaire.com
Facebook: http://www.facebook.com/ajadaire
Desert Palm Press: www.desertpalmpress.com

Other books by AJ Adaire

Available at Amazon, Smashwords, and CreateSpace

Friend Series

Sunset Island
ISBN: 9781301136629

Ren Madison is certain her life couldn't be more perfect. She owns a private island with an Inn off the coast of Maine. She treasures her loving relationship with her older brother Jack, his wife, Marie, and dotes on her niece Laura. She has a passionate and supportive relationship with her partner, Brooke, and a successful business that doesn't require her undivided attention allowing her ample time to pursue her true passion, painting.

Ren's idyllic world crumbles when Brooke dies. Friends and family worry that Ren may never fully recover from her loss.

Dr. Lindy Caprini, a multi-lingual professor, is looking for an artist to illustrate the book she is writing comparing fairy tales from around the world. To make working together on the book easier, Lindy takes a year sabbatical and leaves friends, home, and boyfriend in Pennsylvania and moves to Ren's island. Ren soon discovers that the beautiful and mischievous Lindy is a talented author and a witty conversationalist. Their collaboration on the book leads to a close, light hearted, and flirtatious friendship. Will their collaboration end there?

The Interim (a novelette)
ISBN: 9781311099051

Devastated that her partner cheated, Melanie flees to a new job in Maine, where she meets Ren Madison. Ren is dealing with issues of her own after losing her partner Brooke in a plane crash

What happens in the interim after one relationship ends and you're really ready to love again? For Ren Madison, Melanie was what happened.

The Interim fills in the details of Ren Madison's life on Sunset Island after Brooke but before Lindy.

Awaiting My Assignment
ISBN: 9781310825248

Bernie was a liar. Amanda learned that much when she caught her lover cheating the first time. Upon discovering a second indiscretion, Amanda vows there will never be another. She leaves the relationship, fleeing to her friend Dana in New York State. While staying at Dana's home, Amanda meets and falls in love with a wonderful woman named Mallory.

Amanda is ready to move on. However, the consistently surprising Bernie isn't finished yet. Amanda learns of Bernie's rudest betrayal yet when she receives a package from her recently deceased ex-lover. A very surprising revelation and one final request are contained therein. The favor comes with a gift that delivers dramatic and life-altering changes, not only to Amanda's life, but to the lives of her closest friends and new partner as well.

Anything Your Heart Desires
ISBN: 978131163912

"Whoa—lesbians!" That was Stacy Alexander's first thought as she observes the group of women in the new shop across the street kiss each other in greeting. Stacy had been staring out her apartment window trying to think of a motive for the death of the character she'd killed off in her mystery novel. Ah ha—extortion! What could be a better reason for the murder of my heroine than being blackmailed because she's a lesbian? Now all I need is a lesbian to teach me about the 'lesbian lifestyle.'

That's where policewoman Jo Martin enters the picture. Jo has two rules by which she religiously lives her life: never get involved with someone already in a relationship and never, ever date a straight woman.

As Jo and Stacy collaborate on the novel, will Stacy want to gain a more intimate knowledge of the topic, and will Jo hold steadfastly to her rules?

Desert Palm Press

One Day Longer Than Forever
ISBN: 9781310847738

Dr. Kate Martin needs a vacation after a failed romance with her business partner nearly ruins her.

Lee Foster is recovering from her first lesbian relationship that self-destructed when her partner moved several states away, leaving her behind.

Two failed romances, a double booked vacation cabin, and a blizzard—will fate intervene again and turn a passionate affair with a stranger, into something more?

7970445R00144

Printed in Great Britain
by Amazon.co.uk, Ltd.,
Marston Gate.